COPY BOY

COPY BOY

A Novel

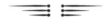

SHELLEY
BLANTON-STROUD

SHE WRITES PRESS

Published 2020
Printed in the United States of America
ISBN: 978-1-63152-697-8
ISBN: 978-1-63152-698-5
Library of Congress Control Number: 2020900063

For information, address:
She Writes Press
1569 Solano Ave #546
Berkeley, CA 94707

She Writes Press is a division of SparkPoint Studio, LLC.

Book design by Stacey Aaronson

This is a work of fiction. Names, characters, places, and incidents either are the product of the author's imagination or are used fictitiously. Any resemblance to actual persons, living or dead, is entirely coincidental.

First chapter previously published in *This Side of the Divide: Stories of the American West* (Baobab Press, 2019).

For Nonny and Poppy

"What a brave man she was, and what a good woman."

— IVAN TURGENEV

CHAPTER ONE

DEBT

You think you're a body, but you're not. That's just the container you collect in. Your body's a light bulb. If it burns out or breaks, the electricity's still there—you're still there, still you.

Benjamin Franklin Hopper was born into a shattered bulb, shards buried under the loose, gray silt of a ravaged Texas plain, but his energy never diffused. For seventeen years, he hovered in particles over the heads of his family as they plowed their soil too fine, dodging tightfisted bankers, riding the Okie trail, Route 66, sleeping under railroad bridges, in lean-tos made of potato sacks, flattened tin cans, and orange crates. He hovered as they built a canvas-and-cardboard home just off the levee at the confluence of two rivers—the clear American and the muddy Sacramento.

No, he didn't stay underground back in the gray Texas dirt. He rose in a silty cloud and floated over their heads for seventeen years, waiting for a shape to fill.

Finally, under pressure, his sister cracked. Though she didn't shatter—not yet—that hairline fracture created a vacuum in her, a charged emptiness that siphoned his particles to her, causing a surge to her filament, making her glow.

That's how she would explain it to herself.

JANE walked home on the levee that night, no breeze coming off the delta. After a long day picking, her arms were sticky yellow, the tomato-leaf smell of piney, bitter sunlight under her fingernails. The river was finally slowing after months of running fast and clean with melted Sierra snow. In Indian summer, with the grass bleached white and the blue burnt out of the sky, she looked down as she walked home from the field, even at night, in case a rattler stretched fat across the path in the heat. That may be why she didn't see at first what was happening in front of her as she approached the campsite.

Uno Jeffers's headlights shone on the dirt between his Ford and her family's tent, the Cotton Bollers loud on his radio—"Lace up them boots, let leather meet tar." His car was loaded with their things: shovel, mattress, blankets, pots, crowbar, washtub, Jane's hope chest of books and awards, everything they'd carted from Amarillo to Sacramento in the great caravan of Okies. Everything they'd collected since.

Daddy's banjo and hat were on the dirt, not in the tent, not in the car.

Momma stepped out of the tent, full belly first, squinting into the headlights, her black hair frizzing like ideas shooting out of her scalp.

"Where's Daddy?" Jane asked.

Momma spit out a toothpick. "In town. With Elthea."

ELTHEA was married to dumpy Leroy Lathrop, editor of a skid row newspaper, the *Swale*. She herself owned Do or Donut Shop, a base from which she was able to meet up weekly with Daddy, who seemed to like her feminine smell of maple.

Just the Sunday before, for what seemed like the hundredth time, Jane had walked for donuts with Daddy and witnessed it.

Elthea came out to the counter from the back room when the front doorbell jangled.

"Abraham Lincoln Hopper."

Daddy smiled, putting off heat. Neither of them said anything for a good minute while Jane focused her eyes on the display case, thinking, Order the damn donut.

But instead of that, he started singing as if Elthea were the only person on earth who might understand just how misunderstood he was—"Big man stoopin' so low, gotta stand up some day." He sang it hoarse, hitting some notes off-key, lingering a beat long on words you might not expect. He made the air quiver around him like heat waves that distract you from your blisters while you walk.

He delivered this particular performance in a sulfur-yellow donut shop for a chubby waitress on a Sunday morning with no less style than he conjured every Saturday night for paying customers—scab-armed pickers, sitting on dirt, tilting beer, tithing a dime each to Abraham.

When he finished singing, Elthea clapped real slow and rocked her curls back and forth in appreciation, the moist flesh around her collar turning pink.

Momma didn't react that way to his talents anymore.

Daddy smiled, his teeth white under a scruffy mustache.

"Do you need some help with the boxes, Elthea?"

"I always need help with the boxes, Abraham."

"I'm gonna help Elthea with the boxes, Jujee."

He followed her to the back room, his eyes on her wide hips in a tight white uniform.

Jane moved without a donut to the front booth under the window and watched people pass on their way to the market. She licked her finger and pressed it on each donut crumb left behind on the table, one at a time, bringing it to the tip of her tongue.

Just the week before, she'd dropped a fat envelope of her *Daily Dragon* clippings on the corner of Leroy's desk. She'd told Daddy about her plan to get on at that newspaper. He *knew* about her plan. It would ruin things for her if Leroy showed up wanting to see his wife and found her in back with Daddy.

She wandered up to the counter and cocked her head at the coffee mugs jiggling on the back wall shelves, at the back room breathing, like a pierced heart and lung, that burbling release of liquid and steam. Her eyebrows lowered.

She went to the front door and locked it, flipping the OPEN sign to CLOSED.

She sat at the counter and wrote on a napkin to the beat of the jiggling mugs and the flow of their breath. When she finished, she went behind the counter and used a wax paper square to pick up a maple old-fashioned, took one bite, and set it back on the shelf. She also took a bite of a sprinkle and a bear claw and a cinnamon roll, carefully turning the bite marks back to the wall when she was done. Then she returned to her seat at the front table.

A few minutes later, Daddy came back, flushed and messy.

Elthea waved goodbye, her dimpled fingers close up to her eyes, waggling like lashes.

It must have done something for Daddy to leave her alone at that table while he went off to rut with Elthea every week and then came back to find her waiting there. It may have been a test of her loyalty or taste or of Daddy's appeal. It may even have been his idea that it was a gift to include her in his life this way. Or maybe he was teaching her something about the way of things between women and men, about the necessary differences between them.

For some months, it looked like a donut would pay for it—

she was, after all, a hungry girl—but not anymore. Didn't he care what she was trying to do? He was putting something big at risk for her now. She didn't like this feeling, when two things she wanted conflicted. It made her want to choose one fast and forget the other, to make the confusion go away.

Back at the tent, she wrote the napkin story in her notebook and called it "Donut Ass." That didn't change anything, but it made her feel better to write it, scratching an itch.

MOMMA had always said Jane was gonna do something. Not that she *was* something, but that she was gonna *do* something. Momma never said what that something might be, but still it shone in the distance, like Jane's North Star.

Growing up, whenever she'd brought home a B-plus in English or a science fair ribbon, her raised eyebrows would ask, Is this it? Is this the thing I'm gonna do? Momma's silence was the answer—That ain't it—so Jane would fold up her achievement and file it in her hope chest, one more artifact in the historical record of Not Quite Yet. Though Jane didn't know what she was going to do, she did know why she had to keep trying.

Jane owed Momma.

Her supposedly ten-pound, twenty-two-inch body had ripped Momma open at birth, taking so long in the push out before her brother Benjamin that she'd blocked him from pushing out at all. Daddy wasn't there when this happened.

Momma said Granny had to pull Benjamin out, rough, with tongs.

"Selfish from the outset," Momma said.

She said Benjamin had been born blue and never cried once before they buried him behind Granny's place and he became spirit, a stream of particles, charged like light. Jane would often think about the magic or physics of that, and it worried her, though the story made them special, and she did like that.

From her birthday tear, Momma developed an infection that almost killed her, and when she was out of her mind with pain and grief, passing in and out of consciousness, she suckled Jane the offender, too big for her womb, as if it were her greatest calling, passing that virulent secretion into her daughter, so that the incident and what it seemed to mean became a part of her.

The two of them surprised everybody by living.

That's why Jane owed Momma.

Now, at seventeen, she still hadn't cleared the account, though she'd tried in a thousand off-target ways. No matter what mile time or exemplary attendance record she brought home, Momma found fault—"Who got first?" "Perfect record of bootlicking!"

Momma kicked her ass and waited for thank you.

Daddy seemed to like her better but not enough so to counteract the Momma effect. He was insufficient for that. His strengths lay elsewhere.

Momma used to tell Jane stories about it in their tent.

"Your uncle Arthur drove us from Bonham over to Paris—Paris, Texas—to watch baseball. We was sitting in the stands, all those folks hollering and cheering and drinking beer. But the only thing I could see was your daddy. Such a handsome man. Slick and strong, like a new truck . . ."

She put a piece of watermelon in her mouth and licked a red bit off her finger. Even in the dark, you could see she was beautiful, her heart-shaped face, her heavy arched brows.

"Watching him out there?" She sighed, shook her head. "And then his voice. After the game, he come on over to us in the stands and picked up another fella's guitar and started to sing. You remember this one?—'Will you miss me? Miss me when I'm gone?'"

She sang it high and thin, a complaint, making Jane's eyes water.

"I could see he was doin' it just for me." She smiled. "Charged straight through me." She kneaded the skin over her heart. "Your daddy had a certain kind of power."

Still has it, Jane thought.

"Wasn't no stopping it. We made you and your brother. God's greatest blessings, no matter I was just the age you are now."

Momma had delivered two babies, buried one, when she was just fifteen.

"But you know what, Jane? Your daddy don't have that power over me no more. Power I need now? Electricity. I want a man who can turn on the lights."

That wasn't Daddy.

IN spite of Momma's prophesying, by seventeen, Jane didn't look like the kind of person who was gonna do something. Though she was tall, coming up on six feet, she only weighed 125 pounds—"All vine, no taters," Momma said. She couldn't consume enough eggs and biscuits to stop her collarbones from sticking out further than her bosom. She wore her thick brown hair in a single braid wrapped in a coil at the nape of her neck to hide her irregular schedule of washing, which was hard to do well with a bucket of river water. The hairdo called attention to her wide mouth and dark lips just covering an abundance of teeth. If she'd had a big mirror in the tent to examine the effect of the hairstyle, she might have rethought it. But she had eyes the color of spring peas, and you could see how her features might be improved with a skillful hand and money for makeup.

Momma would grimace when she caught sight of Jane, no doubt wishing she had the time and tools to fix her appear-

ance, cogs turning in her pretty-woman mind, probably calculating how she might divert the tragedy of Jane's ugliness,
making her more useful, if she didn't have to work so hard
appeasing creditors or corralling Daddy, advancing their circumstances in a world that required constant vigilance.

That may make her sound mean, but people who didn't
know Momma almost always seemed to like her, the way in-
nocents sometimes like a shrewd woman. She'd always been
smart about earning at cotton, timing their picking and the
weighing of the bags according to the dew, and she'd share her
tactics with some of them who were new to the fields, city
transplants who'd joined the exodus to California, where
everybody said money grew on orange trees.

Even if a person knew Momma well enough to fear her,
that person would often move closer to her spot at the side of
a field, offering to share a sip of water out of a lidded mayon-
naise jar, mimicking the way she stretched her back and arms,
the way she laughed loud at a joke. Though she was only five
foot one, she was powerful and real and completely herself,
not a fake. And when a person stood near enough to her, he
had a good chance of hearing the truth about his life—"Baby
oughta be crawling by now." "Stop howling and get off the
porch." "Don't like the shape of that mole."

Jane heard a lot of her honest talk. Heard she was too slow,
too careless, too noisy, too sloppy, too selfish. If it was Momma's goal to improve Jane, then it worked, because Jane always
tried to fix what Momma criticized. She'd had a lot of practice
trying to win her approval. It got to where she wouldn't enter
a contest she didn't think she could win—spelling bees, high
jump, *Daily Dragon* features editor—winning them all in spite
of being a white trash Okie, freckled with pollen and tent dirt.

Nothing much came of her successes. She hadn't pleased
Momma yet, and she wouldn't have money for college, so she
quit school after her junior year and went to work full-time in

a Natomas tomato field instead of just-before and right-after school, thinking maybe earning a good amount of money was what she was supposed to do. After a couple months working harder in the 106-degree heat than any boy, woman, or man, she'd begun to understand no farmer would promote a girl picker to foreman. There would be no payoff in tomatoes.

She'd been wondering if there was going to be any payoff at all for her, living in a tent between the river and the tracks, no matter how hard she worked. That's what she was thinking the night she came home to find Momma packing their belongings into Uno's Ford.

UNO lifted the tent's sheet flap with his good left arm and sneered. "Evening, beauty queen."

She scowled. "What're you doing with our stuff?"

"Don't be rude to Mister Jeffers."

"*Mister* Jeffers?"

Momma stepped out of the headlights' glare, closer to Jane. "Our names were drawn for a cabin. We're back in."

Uno was manager of Tumbleweed, the federal labor camp. The wait list was long, and the Hoppers had a black mark next to their name.

"You musta bent some rules," Jane said. "Does Daddy know?"

"Well, he should know," Uno said, "but he probably don't."

Momma pointed her melon belly in his direction, looking up through her lashes.

Jane said, "He knows plenty."

Momma pinched the skin on Jane's arm. "Don't sass."

Jane pulled her arm away, rubbing the red spot. "Daddy won't like it."

There'd be a blowup, everybody talking—white trash Hoppers, all that, and the thing with Leroy.

Uno set the basket and jar in his Ford's front seat, and he

and Momma went back in the tent, so Jane started unloading what they'd packed, even the mattress, almost everything but the hope chest, making a pile on the dirt.

It was her job to keep the family together, stealing money from Momma's bean can when Daddy asked her to, though never as much as he wanted. She bought him whiskey from the Watkins tent down the levee with the bean-can money, topping off a three-quarter jug with water. She lied for him about how he lost the Studebaker, keeping the card game a secret. And the personal stuff with Elthea and the others before her.

She protected herself and Daddy from Momma's knowing the details of his behavior. Any kind of family was better than none. Her parents required a lot of managing so as not to botch up her life entirely, beyond what was already messed up by nature, economics, and ruinous government policy, but Jane was optimistic and liked to control what she could, believing her effort would make a difference.

When Momma and Uno came out of the tent again, carrying stools, Momma's eyes bugged at her daughter's boldness. She threw her stool down, crossing the space between them, gripped both sides of Jane's jaw with one hand and squeezed hard. She was small but bulldog sturdy.

She let go, and Jane rubbed her second red spot. "We can find some place better."

Daddy wouldn't move back to a camp Uno'd kicked them out of for no good reason. Not even for hot showers and an outhouse.

"Give us a minute, Uno." Momma tilted her head toward the levee, and he put down two stools and walked off in the dark, lighting a cigarette. She waited until the glowing tip was a distance off. "I won't drop this baby on dirt. Daddy'll risk it, but I won't."

Jane looked toward a rustling in the bushes. Must have been the collie dog.

"You owe me," Momma said, for the millionth time, rolling both fists into her lower back. "We're moving to Tumbleweed, the doctor'll come, and he'll get this baby out of me, live. Uno —Mister Jeffers—fixed it."

Maybe this would make up for her brother Benjamin. Maybe this was *something*. But still, people would talk if this happened. And Jane was too low around here already to get the things she wanted. And Uno. They couldn't go through all this for the prize of Uno.

Momma wiped the palms of both hands against the feed-sack dress stretched over her middle. "Moving back to Tumbleweed'll put us ahead."

"Won't put Daddy ahead." She didn't mention herself.

"He won't be around forever, Jane."

This was something she said when it would further her argument, when it was more useful to be alone than leashed to Daddy, who did lurch after every fresh scent. It was true he wandered in and out, but he'd never crossed the line to hurt Jane in a way she wouldn't forgive. She was a practical girl, knew what mattered and what didn't. He wasn't good, but he was good enough.

The bushes parted on the other side of the car, and Daddy came around it into the light—thatch of blond hair, tiny-lined, sunburnt face with a scar on his left upper cheek matching the curve of another guy's shovel. The air buzzed when he stepped into their circle, the smell of beer steaming all around him.

"Don't act like I wouldn't give you no license. You never wanted it. Not from day one. Day one! It'd interfere with your plans."

Momma's face brightened. "You wanna be tied down? Ha!" Her belly jutted between them. "If you won't provide, I'll find a way." Her eyes sparkled.

"What way is that?"

"I got us another cabin."

"How'd you get it? What'd you have to sell?" His mouth twisted up, contemptuous.

Jane's hands opened and closed, blood flooding her extremities.

"Well, it wasn't the car. I believe you sold that cheap for town tail."

"Got yourself a scheme? Working with Uno?"

"Least he works. Like a man."

"You ain't too big to slap."

Jane's head rattled, thoughts boiling. She'd heard this talk before but never heard it escalate so quickly. She scanned the campsite for options.

Momma laughed, like she didn't know how he'd react, or like she was ignoring that knowledge. Or counting on it.

"You're a disrespectful woman."

"Man's got to earn respect."

Earn money is what she means, Jane thought.

Uno stepped back from the dark, into the headlights, next to Momma.

"Get back to town, Abraham." Time slowed, Uno's words drawn out— *towwwwwn, Abrahaaaaaam.* He inched up taller. "I'm driving their things to Tumbleweed."

She couldn't believe he'd step up against Daddy. Stupid. Momma didn't need him.

Daddy pointed his long arm at her. "You think I'll let you steal from me? My woman? My girl?"

"They don't belong to you—you ain't got the papers. Kate wants someone who can provide. I'll give her the papers." He said it like papers were cash.

"You?"

Uno puffed up, a barrel-chested Chihuahua. "You think you're a musician? Haw! Show me two dimes you ever earned by music!"

That did it.

Both Daddy's clenched fists exploded, punching right, straight at Uno's head, left and right again, knocking him to the ground, silent, bleeding, like a dog dead in the road, though he wasn't dead—his chest shivered up and down.

Later, some people would claim about this night that Jane hadn't any heart. But that wasn't true. At the sight of a man her daddy felled, even though it was Uno Jeffers, her heart rose in her throat, blocking her breath, threatening to jump out her mouth before she swallowed it back down again. She thought, It's okay. We'll get him to a doctor. I can fix this.

But that wasn't how it would go.

Momma, in her eighth month, came at Daddy with a stool —lifted it up and cracked it on his back, like in the movies, brought it down hard enough to burst it into tinder all around him.

Daddy turned, roaring, and shoved Momma to the ground with two hands.

Everything stopped, Jane's feet, hands, and head still. She'd worked hard for so long to keep something like this from happening, but now she couldn't see a path.

"Come on then! Finish us off! Don't starve us to death. Do it fast, like a man!"

"Momma, stop!" She had to pull things back.

"Shut up, Kate! Have you got to always push?"

"Do it! Such a man! If you're such a man, do it!"

He unbuckled his belt, removed it.

"Daddy, no!" Jane yelled, but he didn't seem to hear her.

Momma was still on the ground, propped up on her hands, her knees wide, yelling.

Jane cried, "Momma! Why?"

He flicked his belt back and forth, walking circles around her.

Jane reached in the Ford's open door and grabbed the crowbar.

Then he did it. He swung that belt at Momma, so it made a

wide, whooshing arc, slowed-down, like he was pitching side-armed, slapping her skin with a crack, releasing her scream.

His face was lit up, his arm muscles popping like a cartoon bully.

She knew he wasn't finished.

Momma looked straight at Jane and yelled, "Come on!"

"Come on" wasn't enough to make her do what she did next. It was something new inside her own head that did it. Not a voice exactly, but a force, a great surge, a sparking, an ignition—a loud, crackling static—shocking her to action.

She swung the crowbar the way Daddy taught her to swing a bat, loose in her hands, stepping into it, aiming for his shoulder, connecting, maybe with his shoulder, maybe higher.

He fell in stages to his knees, his bloody hands and then his face to the dirt.

She felt a horrible amazement, like she'd chopped down a tree.

She dropped the crowbar and looked at Momma, thinking, Oh my God.

The inside of her head was quiet again.

Then she thought, Is this it? Is this the *something*?

She was washed with shame at thinking that now.

"We ain't got much time," Momma said. "Let's get rid of him."

Not get him to a doctor to fix him up, when his breath was so ragged Jane was sure it would stop. Momma'd moved to next steps.

"Take him up Jiboom, to I Street, down 99." She waved her arm toward the Golden State Highway, half the north–south double barrier, along with the Southern Pacific tracks, separating them from the nice people. "Go south of Galt. Leave him on the shoulder. We'll say he's gone for a gig."

Her idea was so complete.

"Let's go, before the sheriff gets here."

He'd be coming for Jane and Daddy, the criminals in this situation.

Momma got a rope from the car and tied his hands in back. She was good at knots. She grabbed a quilt from the pile and spread it next to Daddy—"C'mon!"

Uno lay behind them, his chest rising irregularly, each breath a plea—Save me.

Jane had to choose right then, so she did. She chose Momma.

She bent with her to roll Daddy onto the quilt, grabbing its short end so they could drag him to the car. She knew the system. They'd done this before, getting Daddy, passed out, from where he shouldn't be to where he was supposed to be. Still, he was heavy and Momma was huge and they struggled. They had to stop and rest repeatedly, laying the blanket down in the dirt, watching it rise and fall with his breath, and then picking it up again.

When they got to the Ford, Momma unwrapped him and told Jane to sit him up, reach under his armpits, and grab his wrists, which she did. Momma crossed his ankles and put both legs over her shoulder, dangling over her belly. "One, two, three," she said, and they stood and lifted him at once into the back seat, their joined breath making the car's air thick. They draped him over Jane's hope chest, an Arkie Boys chorus loud on the radio—"This game, ain't for losin', I'm fixin' to win the next hand."

Momma got out and pointed at the wheel, panting.

"You're coming with me, right?" Jane asked.

Momma rolled her fist on the side of her belly, "I'll handle things here. You go on."

SHE'D only ever driven a car for an hour, two years before, when she was fifteen, when they still had the Studebaker,

Daddy narrating instructions the whole way. He didn't repeat that driving lesson after she ran off the road into a tree stump outside Marysville, requiring a week's labor to fix the front end. He said she drove like a girl, like he forgot what she was. She could kill him this night just by putting him in the back seat of a car she was driving. But she got into the driver's seat and laid her hands on the wheel.

Momma came around to her window and passed her the bloody crowbar.

"In case he wakes up," she said.

Jane dropped it on the floorboard. She wasn't going to use it again.

She closed her eyes and then opened them before doing what Daddy said back then—"Pull back on the emergency brake, Jujee. Now push the spark control all the way up, all the way. Pull the hand throttle halfway down. That's it. Now turn the gas valve open. Turn the choke control valve full clockwise, wait! Now back off a quarter turn. Okay, turn the ignition switch on. Push in the clutch and put the transmission in neutral. Now pull the choke control out. Almost there. Turn the engine over three revolutions—choke in on the third."

The engine started.

"Push the throttle lever up and the left lever all the way down. Push the accelerator pedal. Now turn the choke control."

A hot breeze blew through the window, sprinkling ragweed pollen on the front seat, making Jane cough.

She backed up in a jerk, stalling.

She started over, did it all again, finally turning Uno's car around, off the levee, onto Jiboom, to I Street, to the two-lane highway, gripping hard when a truck passed, headlights shining on roadside trees, branches reaching overhead to grab at each other, Daddy's gargly breath behind her.

"Thirty miles. Pull him out of the car. Untie his hands. Drive home." She whispered it over and over as she drove past vinegar-smelling canneries, tomato fields, ripe, tangy cattle, orchard stumps like headstones. "Thirty miles. Pull him out of the car. Untie his hands. Drive home."

When they were nearly to Galt, his face rose up into the rearview mirror like a ghost, causing her to jump. The car swerved off the road onto gravel before she could straighten it out again, back onto the asphalt. Her ribs ached with fear.

"Stop the car. I gotta throw up." His voice was rough and slurry, the ends of his words chopped off.

Should she? No. She couldn't stop.

"Go ahead, Daddy. It's okay."

He doubled over, gagging onto the floorboard.

"Stop the car," he repeated, craning to wipe his mouth on the seat back. "I'll drive."

"I'll stop soon."

"Come on! I don't blame you, what happened back there."

Was that true? Did he blame her?

In the rearview she saw the blood all over his neck and face and shoulders. Under the blood, his skin was chalk white. Looked like he was missing a tooth on the bottom.

She felt something strong but didn't know what to call it.

"You was acting on instinct. I know. But we gotta get back there now. 'Fore Uno steals everythin'."

His eyes looked loose, like each one saw something different.

"I don't think we'd better."

"Girl, I got this. I'm in my right mind now. I can fix things up. Your momma shouldn'ta put this on your shoulders."

Everything was always on her shoulders.

"Let's get back, fix it up."

His whole face looked wrong, his flexing jaw muscles, his flaring nostrils. A melted mask of a face.

The skin near Jane's ear pulsed. "I don't think so."

"Whassat?"

"I don't think it's a good idea."

He waited before answering. "You talking like that to your daddy?"

He wasn't acting like a daddy. What kind of family would they be if she took him back? She couldn't fake that hard now.

"If you're my girl, you bes' untie me now."

His girl.

"I ain't going back," she said, "and neither are you."

He was quiet for a minute.

"You ain't goin' back to Momma?"

When she didn't say anything, he went on. "She thinks she got us under her thumb, makin' out like money's everything."

"This ain't about money."

"It's always about money! No appreciation. She don' understand what I do, though I've stayed with her all those years . . . all those fields and tents."

"This is about a cabin."

But she knew he was right. It *was* about money. A cabin was about money. Momma always talked about climbing up off the bottom rung, where they'd been stuck for years, living in that tent, cordoned off by river, tomato fields, train tracks, and highway. Momma told everybody how she got them out from under a Texas bank's bootheel, all the way to Sacramento. If Momma wanted power over her fate, she needed money for leverage. She'd do what it took.

"You think this is 'bout us? You think that baby's mine?"

She didn't answer, wondering if it mattered who the daddy was. In her experience, it was the momma that mattered.

"Okay, then. You're right," he said. "We'll head down to San Luis. Get us some pea work. There's some nice little bars there that like a good singer. You untie me, and I'll drive us there."

She understood he was trying to trick her.

"I'm not going with you."

Her eyes blurred. Her cheeks were wet.

"What are you sayin'?"

"Momma's moving to Tumbleweed, you can go to San Luis, and I'll . . ."

What would she do?

She thought of a poster at the theater downtown, for the movie *San Francisco*. It reminded her of Uno's daughter Sweetie, who'd run off to the city some time ago. The name of that movie rose up before her now, as a place you run off to.

"I'll go to San Francisco."

He was quiet at first. Then he exploded in laughter, a mean look on his face. "Sounds like you got a bona fide plan. Yes, ma'am! Whole lot of pickin' work in Frisco, acres and acres of tomatoes. Yes, ma'am. Who'm I to interfere with a girl's bona fide plan?"

He thought she was stupid. She hadn't known that.

She slowed for the Galt stop sign—dark Texaco station, butcher, feed store, depot. A spotted dog ran across the road. Daddy looked left and right. She shifted and pushed her foot on the pedal, and the car lurched forward.

Galt was in the rearview now, nothing but road and sky and the SP tracks and Tokay grapes near harvest, glowing on the vine.

"You can't leave a person on the side of the road," he said, a jagged edge to his voice.

She thought of Uno, wondering at the limits of that code.

"I'll untie you. You can catch a ride to Stockton."

She pulled the car over, crunching onto gravel, its front wheels stopping just at the shoulder before it dropped into an irrigation ditch. She got out and opened the back door.

He stood, five inches taller than her.

She saw his black blood, and the skin on her face felt cold.

He turned his back so she could untie him. It took a while, as her hands were shaking and Momma's knot was good.

The rope dropped and he turned back around.

They stood there a minute, his face scrambled. Was one eye higher than the other? Had it always been? He wasn't right.

Water rushed in the ditch behind him.

He grabbed her right wrist, twisting it, making her drop to her knees.

"Wrong choice, girl."

Her face contorted in pain from his twisting, but she didn't drop the key on its chain. He wouldn't go any further. He couldn't do that to her. He didn't have any other people— Granny was buried next to Benjamin back in Amarillo. He wasn't going to cut the last real connection he had.

This is what Jane thought.

He twisted harder.

"Disloyal," he said. "You ain't so good's I thought. You turned out a disappointment. Not so special after all."

Her head burst into noise again, like an out-of-tune, full-volume radio show in her head, music and static and a screaming voice, too, and her skull nearly split, like something new had entered her, or something old wanted out. Then a husky radio voice yelled, *Hit him!*

So she did.

She punched Daddy in his groin with her left fist, felling him for the second time. She'd always been good with both hands, like he was.

He lay there moaning and clutching himself.

Scrambling up to get away, she dropped the key.

Though he was doubled over, he rolled and grabbed it.

She snatched the blood-sticky crowbar off the floorboard—"I'll do it again!"

He threw the key in the dark, and she could see it flipping through the air. It took so long before she heard the clank, metal on metal, up near the car's front end.

Why'd he do that? Throwing that key seemed like the

worst thing he did that night, the worst thing any of them did that night.

Cain't trust neither of 'em! the radio voice in her head yelled. *They ain't for you!*

She saw it was true.

Better off on your own!

Hearing those thoughts as that river of anger rushed through her, she brought the crowbar down on his hip, this time like a pick, not a bat, releasing some essential Jane that had never gotten out before, almost like this had nothing to do with him or with her.

He bellowed and grabbed her feet, knocking her down, and she fell into the ditch. Her face hit cold water, and she sputtered and rose up, coughing. She struggled to stand, the water waist high. She stepped on something sharp—a branch? —tearing right through her shoe into her foot. She pulled it out, screaming. The pain moved in a wave through her body, into her head, pounding to get out. But still she crawled up the edge to the muddy bank.

He was standing over her now. "I thought you were different!"

You are different! raged the voice in her head.

"I am!" she yelled.

Different than he thought, different than she was a few hours before.

She thought he was going to throw her back in the water, drown her. She knew it. This was how she would end. Momma was wrong. She wasn't going to do something. She was going to end right there, in the muddy water. Not in the papers, on the radio. Just a dirty, ugly girl, white trash, dead in a ditch, alone, if she didn't do something now.

Her fingers sank in the mud, inches from moonlit metal, the crowbar. She reached and gripped it again, rose up and swung a third time, hitting him hard on his knees.

He cried out, tumbling into the ditch himself, splashing, yelling.

Her whole leg throbbed. Her skull was brittle, like it might explode from pressure.

She climbed up, sobbing, her face muddy, streaked red, brown, white.

Finally she stopped crying. The only sound left was the rushing ditch water. Still she waited, her heart pounding, but nothing happened—something should happen! She waited longer. Still nothing. No one. An empty space between then and now.

She breathed—one, two, three, four, one, two, three, four, one, two, three, four. When her breath no longer rasped, she thought, Maybe he swam off, climbed out of the ditch down the road. He's hitching a ride to Stockton. He won't come back.

She waited some more, but still nothing happened.

Her ears filled with that sizzling static.

He cain't come back. He's dead.

She waited on the dirt until her thoughts had gone to ash.

She got up and threw the crowbar in the ditch. She limped to the car and opened the glove box, finding what she wanted, a matchbook. She struck one match, pushing too hard, breaking it. She struck another but couldn't make it light, scratching it over and over before tossing it. Then one smoked and lit right up, but by the time she held it out in front of her it burned her fingers, and she flung it away. Next one she got a little light from. Finally she struck one that shone onto the key, lying against the front tire.

She got back into the driver's seat and started the ignition, without Daddy's voice in her ear, and turned the car around, toward home.

When she got to camp, the tent was gone, Momma and Uno too. Even Daddy's banjo. Just trash, empty cans, a broken plate, spilled nails.

You paid your debt, said the voice.

"That ain't it. That ain't what I'm gonna do."

She kicked the dirt, looking for any small thing that belonged to her—a book, a bag of marbles, a comb—but found none of it. Near where Daddy hit Uno, she found seven pennies and a hand-printed card—"Sweetie, 3528 Clay Street, San Francisco."

She felt a knot of pain in her forehead and fingered an almond-sized lump there, which worried her. She knew deadly wounds were often bullet small.

But she wasn't dead yet.

She put the pennies and the card in her pocket, got back in Uno's Ford, her hope chest filling half the back seat, and started the car, heading west.

CHAPTER TWO

CLAY

L et me in," Jane said to a sliver of face visible through the chain-locked door.

Sweetie's left blue eye traveled the length of Jane, over her bloody overalls, her cut-up forehead, her bare left foot—she'd removed her shoe as her foot swelled over the five hours it took her to find her way to this Clay Street doorstep. She'd rolled down her window a dozen times on the drive, desperate enough to talk to all manner of people who were not like her, asking Orientals, Coloreds, Italians, Irish, prostitutes, police, and swells how to get to this porch of the only person she knew who lived in San Francisco—Sweetie Jeffers, daughter of Uno.

"Janie? What happened?"

"A fight."

"Here?"

"Home."

"How'd you get here?"

"Let me in, Sweetie, please."

"Why are you here?"

"You said I could come if I ever needed anything."

"When did I? I . . . I couldn't have. I left without . . ." Her voice quavered.

In fact, Sweetie hadn't said it to Jane but had said something like it to a crying, jilted, eighth-grade girl, years before.

Jane had been so touched by Sweetie's salve-like tone in that overheard conversation that she'd filed the moment in her memory, retrieving it for practical use tonight. She hadn't seen Sweetie since she'd disappeared from Tumbleweed right after Jane and Daddy and Momma first moved in, but Jane thought Sweetie would be on her side, having already escaped Uno herself.

"Please," Jane said. "I need your help."

Sweetie's one visible eye grew bigger, softening what Jane could see of her face. "Help" looked like the magic word.

"I can't have you stay here. It's not my place."

"You're the only one I can go to," Jane said.

Sweetie closed the door, unchained the lock, and opened it all the way. "Come in," she said. "But be quiet."

She led Jane, limping, upstairs into a front parlor, settling her on a brown velvet sofa facing a piano the size of a truck bed, sheet music papering its top.

Looking down at Jane's foot, she said, "Looks like a ham hock," which it did.

Sweetie's nose crinkled up at that. She had a sprinkle of freckles across its ridge and the rise of her cheeks. Jane had never known a redhead with so few freckles. Uno never put her in the field with the other kids, Jane recalled, keeping her inside their Tumbleweed cabin instead, cleaning up, cooking, sewing, ever since her mother had died of tuberculosis. She'd always looked like a little lady, no matter how patchy her wardrobe.

Now, grown up, she had the same small peach mouth over a pointy chin. Her pearl earrings matched the buttons of her navy shirtdress, tailored to her curves, belted at her waist just so. She was still in her day clothes, not her sleep clothes, at two in the morning. Her navy leather heels were waxed over scuffs. She'd always been so pretty in a clever way, the kind of girl who knew how to make herself look good, even if she hadn't looked good by nature. Jane remembered watching her sew a cheerleader outfit and spot-bleach it at night by the fire all season, captivating the younger camp girls. The way she let them into that intimate work by the fire showed a real generosity, a willingness to share her success, to say they were worthy of it, to let them—who were so low—connect with her —so far above. That was the memory that had risen up when Jane found her address left behind like a charm in the dirt.

"Do your momma and daddy know you're here?"

Jane leaned back on the velvet and waited, mute, for a steep hill of pain to flatten. Then she said, "No." She'd told Daddy about San Francisco, but he was dead now.

The phonograph breathed a moaning kind of music from an instrument Jane didn't know, sounding like it was coming through the room's thin plaster skin, from its lungs.

Sweetie blew a puff of air that raised the fringe of hair on her forehead. "Don't go anywhere." She headed out the door, down the hall, leaving Jane alone.

Jane took in her surroundings. Bookshelves anchored the lower two-thirds of the parlor walls. Three books were stacked next to her on the sofa, scraps of paper sticking out the sides, strange words on the books' spines: *Tchaikovsky's Impossible Concerto*, *Great Thinkers on Ligeti's Etudes* and *Hearing the Macabre: Ravel's Gaspard de la Nuit*. Double doors on the nearest wall were pulled closed.

Pencil drawings of people with tall white hair and hats like ships, canes of vining flowers and swords of fire, were strung all around with twine. Over the fireplace hung a gold-framed painting of a John Deere tractor up close, its grill huge, parked on black soil under an orange sky with pink clouds, signed "SJ" in the corner. The room smelled toasty, acidic, lingering proof of cigarettes, all of it chaotically impossible to decipher.

Though the music stopped, the record kept spinning, scratching.

She heard a conversation down the hall.

"She is not my problem. I do not need another project."

"I won't ask anything of you. It'll just be a short time."

"Right. You won't ask anything. Nothing at all."

"What, do you want me to call the cops or something? Silly, Rivka, think about it."

This was a mistake, better to sleep in the car, near the hobos, by the water. Jane pushed off the sofa, stepped once—*unh!*—and dropped back again.

Settle down. There was no static around the voice this time. It was coming in clearer.

"Break that foot and we'll have to shoot you," Sweetie said from the doorway, laughing in a tinkly, nickels-dropping way. "Sorry. Joking, joking." She crossed the room and turned off the phonograph.

Another girl, dark-haired, stood with her hands on her hips, assessing Jane. Her lips twisted to the side, like she was having a private joke.

"Jane, Rivka. Rivka, Jane," Sweetie said.

Rivka looked like a Cherokee girl Jane remembered from a corn stand in Oklahoma. Her lids covered the top third of her eyes, making her look almost sleepy, though below the lids her brown eyes were focused, critical. Her nose bone rose in a bump and then veered to the left on the way down. She wore pajamas, top and bottoms, buttoned all the way up to her throat, and a bracelet of oddly shaped pearls, each wrapped in silver strands, spinning around her ankle. On her *ankle*, Jane thought. Her feet were bare, toenails buffed and shiny but unpainted. Jane remembered how everybody treated the Cherokees bad in Texas and Oklahoma, needing to feel somebody was below them. Rivka didn't look like she'd had that sort of treatment.

"Pills and bath," Rivka said, and walked out again.

When she'd gone down the hall, Sweetie said, "I recall

your momma and daddy had a habit of fighting." Her voice rose up at the end, inviting Jane to talk.

She's gossiping about me, to me, Jane thought. "Your papa ain't no Jesus."

Sweetie sat up straighter and patted the skirt of her dress. "He's a good enough man. He isn't violent. I know that."

"He's a good number cruncher. Ain't a good man."

In spite of how she felt about Momma and Daddy and how badly she needed help, she wasn't going to lose a parent contest to Uno's girl. Judging by a little slump in Sweetie's shoulders, it didn't look like she planned to argue the point anyway.

Rivka returned with water and a small bottle, shaking three pills into her hand, passing them and the glass to Jane, looking her straight in the eye, like she saw who Jane was, knew she didn't measure up, was a waste of her medicine.

"Go on," Sweetie said, nodding, and Jane swallowed the pills.

Rivka left, and moments later Jane heard water running.

"Come on! Before it gets cold!" Rivka yelled.

Sweetie put her arm around Jane's waist and helped her to the bathroom, the two of them at the end of a rope pulled by Rivka.

Sweetie removed Jane's clothes and undergarments and settled her into a clawfoot tub of hot, foamy water, all the way to her chin. Jane winced at the heat at first, and then it felt better, numbing her body. She began to disappear that way in her head, too, and was grateful for the pills and the heat, in spite of the vulnerability they created.

Rivka returned, grumbling as she used Jane's ruined clothes to mop blood and clay off the tile, and then she carried the clothes out of the bathroom by her thumb and pointer finger, away from her body—"Would that we had incinerator."

Even fuzzy-headed, Jane thought there were words missing in that sentence.

Sweetie sat on a towel on the floor, pushed up her sleeves, unbraided Jane's hair, and used a measuring cup to pour bathwater over her head, lathering it up with a thick, orange-smelling soap that foamed into a crown. Jane sank below the water and considered staying there but rose up anyway when she had to breathe.

Sweetie scrubbed the mud from Jane's hairline and the creases around her nose and the cleft in her chin. Then she scrubbed in and around Jane's ears and the dirty necklaces of skin around her throat. She scrubbed her hands, not just the red stains in her calluses, but also all the way round and under her rough fingernails, until they looked pink and clean as a schoolgirl's. She brushed Jane's knotted hair until it lay flat and plaited it, right there in the tub.

Then Sweetie reached into the water and picked up Jane's foot, holding it in the light.

Jane didn't like her touching that.

Sweetie shook her head. "I'm sorry, hon."

Something wedged in Jane's throat.

Sweetie put the foot carefully down and took Jane's hand to help her out of the water. With her own free hand Jane covered her bosom. When she was standing, balanced on one foot, she covered her other private parts. She'd not stood this way in front of another person in years, and even so medicated, she was ashamed to be stared at.

Rivka held out a nightgown, looking at Jane's skinny frame, and whistled.

"How old are you?"

"Eighteen," she lied.

"Apparently you need more than pills and bath."

Sweetie giggled. "You make such a nice nurse, so empathetic."

Then she handed Jane the towel and the gown, which she pulled over her head before she was dry.

With Sweetie's support, Jane limped down the shotgun hallway after Rivka, through a black-and-white kitchen, and out a glass door to a white wood room with uncovered windows on three walls and a second glass door to the landing out back. A narrow bed was laid with chenille blankets in a space scarcely bigger than the Ford.

Sweetie turned down the covers.

Jane lay down, and Sweetie sat on the side of the bed, lifting Jane's foot. Rivka came back and handed Sweetie a small tool, which she used to pick splinters and grit from the wounds. Tears wet Jane's face. She was defenseless, prone to Sweetie's small surgery.

Rivka returned again with a pile of extra blankets, dropping them on the end of the bed with a grieved exhalation.

Everything here was different than home—the mineral smell was different, no irrigation-on-dirt smell. Here it was brisk, even inside, but also spicy—garlicky aromas floating in from the neighborhood.

When Rivka walked out again, Jane took her chance. "Can't I please stay for a while?"

The skin under Sweetie's eyes pinked. "She won't like it. She'll say no."

"Can't you just tell her?"

"That's not how it works. I tend things for her. She rescued me when I showed up." Sweetie dimpled, like she was proud to be chosen for rescue or proud to be needed, maybe both.

"Rescued how?"

Sweetie frowned. "Got me together." She looked down at her dress. "She's something," she said, shifting. "Plays piano in the symphony on KGO. She knows everybody, all the musicians, of course, but also the celebrities who come to the radio. She knows Dorothy Lamour!" Sweetie beamed at this. "She opened me up to so much." Sweetie looked around the bare little room, appreciative.

At home, Jane had pinned a picture of Dorothy Lamour in a sequined aqua gown up on the wall of her tent over her pallet as some kind of ideal. Rivka knew the real Dorothy, and Sweetie knew Rivka. Jane understood how she must feel about that.

"Do you work at the radio too? Did you meet her there?"

Sweetie's eyes rounded. "Oh no! We met sitting next to each other at the Castro Theater to see *San Francisco*. I had hardly any money, but that didn't stop me going to the movies. We both got the hysterics at this one part—have you seen it? —Clark Gable tells Jeannette MacDonald to show him her legs. She says, 'I said I'm a singer.'" Sweetie recited this in a loud, offended voice with her hands on her hips, her laughter trilling.

Jane hadn't seen the movie, just the poster, but the poster was what had gotten her here.

"We were a team from the start. I moved in, and Rivka fixed me up—got me a starter job at the opera. Now I'm head assistant to the costume designer! So I guess I'm redeemed for spending food money on a movie."

This new Sweetie was nothing like the girls back at the river, or even the farmers' kids who lived in houses. She was already special back then, pretty, well liked, clean. But now, her voice and mannerisms, her expectations, they were all different. She was like a girl in the movies, Janet Gaynor, the funny heroine. There wasn't an ounce of Okie left in her. She could go anywhere, Jane thought.

Sweetie floated two more blankets over her, settling them in a warm cloud.

Jane liked her gestures, how much gentler she was than Rivka, who'd helped her on this night but with such a dark attitude that it scarcely felt like kindness. Sweetie made you feel you were being helped.

She straightened Jane's covers at the edges of the bed and

rose to go, clicking off the lamp. "We'll find a place for you in the morning."

Her mind eased from the pills and the bath and the bed, Jane thought, This is the place I want. This place—these blankets, this bed, this room, these crackers, that music, these pills.

She could bond Sweetie to her, remind her that though they weren't blood, they were from the same clay. She sensed what Sweetie might want to hear and gave it to her.

"My daddy did this."

Sweetie stood still and then sat back down on the foot of Jane's bed, waiting without visible breath.

"He fought me."

Sweetie's body gave off a hum, like it was doing great work to stay so still, listen so well. Jane could hardly see her face, just sensed a blurry glow of energy. Jane closed her eyes, thinking how it might feel to tell Sweetie what happened, to trust someone. The muscles from the base of her skull to the edge of her shoulders relaxed imagining that.

But, even drugged, she knew she couldn't tell the truth.

What she'd done to Daddy, what he'd done to her, would sound too bad. She didn't know if Sweetie could understand how so many strands had wound together to create a rope Jane had to cut—had to!—just exactly as she did. Only a certain kind of person, someone like Jane, could understand that. A lie would be better for now.

Besides, there was something about the tension wafting off Sweetie when Jane said Daddy fought her, that he'd caused these injuries. It bothered Jane. She didn't want to reward her morbid eagerness. She could blame Daddy, but she didn't want Sweetie to do it. So she changed her story right there.

"Then your papa fought him over my momma," she said. "He killed my daddy."

Sweetie gasped, and the glow of her face shrunk to a pencil point of light Jane could hardly see. The air in the room flowed into that dot, after that shrinking face, altering the room's pressure, tightening Jane's lungs.

Would Sweetie believe her? Uno was a fearful man, but scared dogs bite. Somebody like that can do damage. He was cruel in the way a coward can be. This was his fault, she thought, though she knew that was a lie. She could feel the crowbar in her fingers even now.

Sweetie's hand, which had been resting on Jane's knee, now gripped it hard as she looked over her shoulder to the door and then back.

"Quiet! Don't ever say that again. To anybody!"

She'd gone too far, but she could fix it.

"I won't. Never."

She put her own hand on Sweetie's, but Sweetie threw it off.

"Rivka's an important person. I can't bring that into this place! It would ruin her, that mess! You want me to help you? Then don't bring that in here, get it? I don't need you throwing mud all over things. Nobody can know anything—especially that—about Papa. Nothing about Sacramento, the camp. Not your momma, your daddy, none of it!"

Jane's throat burned, wanting to backtrack, make a new story, but instead she answered simply, "It didn't happen. None of it."

"Promise?"

"Promise. I'm gonna start over, like you. You'll help me, won't you?"

Sweetie groaned. "I'll talk to Rivka."

She understood how it would be.

Sweetie rose to leave the sunporch, and, when she did, Jane's bones melted into the bed, the smell of ocean seeping through gaps in the windows like ether.

LIGHT speckled through salty windows onto her bed. For the first time in three days, when her eyes opened, she wasn't thinking about pain.

On the first night she dreamed about what she'd done, a dream like a memory, a precise retelling of horrible facts, and woke to her foot throbbing, her whole body vibrating to it, especially her head. On the second night she dreamed about Momma, what she'd made her do, things she'd said, traps she'd laid, and in the morning her foot pain was more in the skin, less inside. On the third night she dreamed of Uno, and in that dream she got it the way it needed to be. His power—his cabin, his paycheck—had tempted Momma, causing her to push Jane and Daddy into the things that happened. In that dream Uno was nothing compared to the three of them, but still, it was his fault. They didn't feel like her own dreams, not like the kind she'd ever had before, but like somebody else was dreaming them.

Through her windows were the backsides of several tall buildings, porches, and stairwells leading down to a patch of grass where a terrier and dozens of cats went to do their business. She pushed off the covers, examining her foot, sore but normal sized, swallowed another of Rivka's pills, just in case, put on a housedress and pink slippers Sweetie had left for her, got Uno's key, and opened the back sunporch door, walking downstairs to the square patch. She exited the back gate onto Clay Street. She hadn't been outside since her arrival. The air was a salve, though people stared at her, like she'd escaped the county hospital.

She walked two blocks to Uno's Ford, unlocked it, and got into the back seat, keeping her feet off the part of the floorboard where Daddy had vomited. She opened the hope chest and picked a notebook off the top of a pile nineteen-deep, a pile surrounded by real books stolen from libraries in Tucumcari, Albuquerque, Holbrook, Flagstaff, Kingman, Needles, Barstow, Bakersfield, and Fresno.

When they'd been packing up the Studebaker to move to California four years ago, Jane had told Daddy she needed help finding paper because she was going to write up their trip.

He'd seemed to like this idea because it put a nice polish on it—an adventure, not a failure. So he had gathered wrinkled, pocket-stuffed, left-on-the-sidewalk handbills—MEN WANTED! GOOD PAY! LAND OF MILK AND HONEY! NO CHINESE!—printed in capital letters, underlined, bolded, always exclamation marked, stapled on road signs, tree trunks, and fence posts.

He'd stuck the point of his pocketknife under each staple to pry them off without tearing the edges. He'd tucked the sheets, folded once on the vertical, into the car's glove box, so by the time he'd gathered enough, they all smelled of tobacco and motor oil. He'd gathered enough of those sheets for nineteen books.

While Momma made dinner, Daddy and Jane would heat a cast iron presser at the edge of the campfire, lay one piece of paper at a time on a flat rock, place a cotton picking bag on top, sprinkle it with a few drops of water, and then press the paper until the steam laid it flat, embossing a pattern of fine scars on the underside in the contours of the stone, so you could almost see the fish and ferns embedded there between *No Chinese!* and *Men wanted!*

Daddy had hammered holes through the pages and the covers she'd made from cardboard boxes left behind at gas stations, after she'd stained them with beet juice and egg paint. She'd coiled a piece of wire through the holes. It all stayed together if she flipped her pages carefully while she wrote. In her tiniest print, she had filled those notebooks with the details of their migration.

She flipped through this one now, reading about ripped upholstery, stuck windows, the smell of mites and sweat, gritty blowing clouds, inside-the-tent moans and laughter, hard paved gray dirt, red clay, and fine brown silt. The musky smell of beer in the morning, fingertip calluses, a gasoline station Coke's cool condensation drops on a hot, puffy hand, and the bitter, fatty taste of red-eye gravy—coffee grounds, lard, and water poured over fried bread and butter.

Then she returned her notebook to the hope chest, latching it. She locked the car and walked back to her sunporch.

BACK at the flat, everything was still quiet, just the occasional sound of one of the girls turning in bed. Jane decided to make breakfast for them the way she'd watched Sweetie do it for her.

She filled the percolator, got the metal basket out of the drying rack next to the sink, scooped in ground Folgers, settled the metal post into its hole and capped it. She plugged the tines into the wall socket and the machinery *thunked* itself awake, its yellow light blinking. Easy electricity, shiny machines.

She got a loaf of Wonder Bread out of the breadbox, opened the cellophane, and smelled the sweet white dough before putting two slices in the toaster. Listening to it click, she took Welch's grape jelly out of the icebox.

Cooking here, eating here was much better than doing it on dirt by the river.

"Getting winky."

She heard Rivka say this through the vent into the girls' room, where they slept in matching pine beds with matching dressers and nightstands. How'd they pay for all the matching furniture?

"That's a new one. You'll have to get me a glossary."

Jane tilted her head up, toward the vent.

"She is better now."

"It's just been three days."

"She is throwing everything off."

Jane leaned into the tile counter's rounded edge.

"What's off? We do the same things."

Jane held her breath, trying to make no noise.

"It is not same," Rivka said in her strange way—no *the* or *a* or *an.*

"What's *winky?*"

"So distracting, with all your mothering. I cannot practice with constant flow of mercy."

Jane looked down and pointed the toes of her injured foot, back to its natural size. How much mothering had it taken? She hadn't asked for much.

"We don't want her just wandering town."

"It has been week."

"Three days. What can it hurt for me to help her get a start?"

"Oh. So you have time to help her?" Rivka asked. "You have nothing else to do?"

Jane looked around at the neat kitchen, at its stocked cupboards. Sweetie was the one keeping things nice, before and after work, but Jane figured it was Rivka who paid for the things Sweetie kept nice.

Sweetie said something garbled. Jane's heart raced, anxious to hear. She lifted up one knee and then the other, climbing onto the counter, standing on clean tile, and pressed her ear against the vent next to the dish cabinet.

Rivka said, "We had arrangement."

This was a nice place to live at the height of the Depression, a clean, well-fitted floor of a fancy building in a fancy neighborhood of a fancy city. They had an *arrangement.*

"Simmer down." There was a soft thud and a scrape. "She's almost healed."

"What then? Toss her out? What do you see as finale? Shall we send her home?"

Jane gasped and kicked the hot percolator, rattling it, spilling coffee on the counter, down the cabinet, to pool in a black puddle on the white tile, white grout. Her hand rose to her mouth.

"What was that?" Rivka asked.

Jane's breath came shallow and fast.

"She'll get a job."

"There is depression on. She will not."

Jane squatted on the counter and climbed down, grabbed a cloth, started wiping up the spill, then wet the cloth, scrubbing furiously at the grout.

She didn't want to go back, couldn't after what she'd done. There was no home to go to. She tossed the cloth in the trash, leaving no evidence.

She was going to stay on Clay Street, her bed piled with blankets, windows all around, this kitchen with these appliances, this food—soft bread and jelly, the smell of yeasty warmth. She couldn't lose this. She'd established things with Sweetie. They hadn't said a specific word yet about her staying, but they had a kind of pact—she could tell—the kind you silently make. Rivka just didn't understand Jane yet, didn't know what she could do. Jane would learn how to become someone here, so neither of the girls would think of kicking her out. She had to get a job and make both of them her friends. That's what survival meant now.

She buttered and sliced toast, putting paired triangles on matching plates next to a dollop each of purple jelly, and then put the plates and mugs of black coffee on a handled tray.

Carrying breakfast to their room, she composed a list in her head of the work a tomato-picking Okie girl was qualified to do in San Francisco, California. She didn't need a pencil or paper as it was a very short list.

≡ ⊫

SUNUP, Monday, Sweetie brushed Jane's hair until it shone. Working with lotion, she finger-waved it so it moved in an S near her cheek before she pinned it up in a bun, the whole thing softening her face, making her look almost good, like a handsome woman.

Sweetie dressed her in a body-hugging girdle that stretched from her shoulders to her thighs, snaps attaching to dark hose, seams down the back, which made her legs itch. Next came a beige silk slip, which Jane couldn't enjoy the feel of because of the interfering girdle. She'd never worn such things before. Momma'd sewn her baggy panties out of feed sacks with a twine drawstring. When they came untied, her drawers sometimes dropped below the hem of her skirt.

On top she wore a lined, jade gabardine suit Sweetie had brought home from the opera discard bin and altered over the weekend, a wide-shouldered, three-button jacket nipping in at Jane's waist and flouncing out all the way around her hips, just where she needed it, implying flesh that didn't exist. The high lapels covered her collarbones, softening her edges. She'd never worn anything that complimented her before. She scarcely knew herself. She looked like a McCall's pattern figure. She could be somebody, a city girl, this way. Even so, she felt a prickly dread in this costume. She wasn't quite herself.

Sweetie had jumped into the project, sewing and styling cheerfully late into the weekend nights, chattering as she worked. Though she wanted to see this as proof of Sweetie's genuine attachment to her, some of her comments were overly flattering, tissue-like. Jane did enjoy a compliment but had an ear for insincerity and thought she heard it in Sweetie's "You're so pretty!" and "Just like a model!" But she put that aside as unnecessary distraction.

JANE sat on a hard mahogany chair in the reception area of the NBC Blue Network radio station where Rivka worked. Thirty other girls sat on other hard chairs in a circle around the room, with so much perfume in the air—orange blossom, jasmine, lemon, narcissus, lilac, hyacinth, cloves, rose, sandalwood, musk, violet—that she felt nauseous. They were all waiting for their turn to land a receptionist job, which Rivka described as "looking pretty while answering telephones."

She sat for two and a half hours in the radio lobby, twisting her handkerchief and trying to picture herself at the desk in the middle of this room. She'd ripped the hose on her right shin and had to remember to tuck that leg behind. Her girdle twisted, tugging her waist. No other girl in the reception room was squirming like she was. The others were delicate, right sized. Jane took up too much space, her head rising inches higher on the wall than theirs.

When her name was called, she hobbled, unsteady on her tender foot in a heel, into a room with a massive wood table, gold shaded lamps at every seat. At the end of the table was a pink box of pastries, its lid open. Her mouth watered for flaky sugar. She'd been too nervous for breakfast.

"Good morning, Miss Hopper. Aren't you a striking one?" said a tiny woman with a powdered face and ruffly eyelashes, her hair still and geometric as shellacked brown concrete. "Nice to meet you."

Jane was so focused on slumping to get her head in the same range that she didn't see until too late that she should reach out to shake the lady's hand, and, by the time she did, the lady had already pulled hers back.

"I'm Mrs. Fazio. I'm helping Mr. Simpson, our president, choose our new receptionist." Everything dimpled, little parentheses on both sides of her mouth, on the outside of her eyes, in the middle of her cheeks, precise, delicate. "Have you worked as a receptionist before?"

"I've picked tomatoes. Cotton. Walnuts." She almost belched these wrong things.

"My." Mrs. Fazio frowned and smiled at once. "Well. As a receptionist, you answer telephones. Sit at the front desk and greet people. Get them to the right other people. You're the first line of defense for the busy staff inside the building. You use your charm to manage the expectations of people who come to see someone or do something." She closed her mouth, turning its edges up into a pretty smile that ended at her nostrils.

Jane had no idea what she meant by all this, and her lip chewing must have telegraphed that. Did she have charm? This job didn't sound like her, though she did wonder what the busy people inside the building did. Something in her didn't want to play along with this.

Mrs. Fazio blew air through pursed lips. A little more pressure and it might've been a whistle.

"Why don't we go on to the next step?" Mrs. Fazio looked at the clock over the door and dragged a big black telephone in front of Jane. "Sit. I'll leave you here. When the telephone rings, pick it up and talk to the person on the other line. Any questions?"

Her head was full of doubt, but she couldn't form a question.

Mrs. Fazio clicked her way out of the room and pulled the glass door shut behind her.

She thought Mrs. Fazio was probably having a cigarette or going to the bathroom, relieved for some privacy. Jane wished she could escape too. She didn't fit here.

The telephone jangled six times before she picked it up. She'd never used a telephone before, though she'd seen it in the movies. The handset felt cool and heavy against her face.

41

"Hello?"

There was silence, and then a whiny male voice asked, "Who is this?"

"Jane."

"What place of business?"

"Don't you work here?"

"I've got an idea. Why don't you pretend you work here too?"

Piss-ant, said the voice in her head.

The contempt she heard in the phone would run through this place. People would make fun of her here. She couldn't take that. This was a poor use of her effort.

"This how folks prove their worth in Frisco?"

A moment of silence passed.

"Mrs. Fazio!" the man yelled.

Jane's receptionist interview was finished two minutes later but not before she'd stashed a cinnamon roll in her purse.

Showing her back to the reception area, Mrs. Fazio advised, "Don't call it Frisco."

THE next morning, Jane struggled to keep pace with Sweetie, weaving in and out of the bodies flowing down Van Ness, heading to the opera costume shop where Sweetie'd gotten Jane an interview for a junior workroom assistant job, the very one Sweetie had held at the beginning of her climb to head assistant to the designer.

Sweetie said she liked to walk to work rather than take the bus, liked the cold morning wind, up Clay to Van Ness. Jane didn't see how she did it so fast in heels.

"Forget the radio. That wasn't for you. All show, no go. Just practice."

Jane was grateful for Sweetie's not acting like the radio interview was a failure.

"This won't be so fakey-fake. You'll be doing actual stuff, in a hurry, for people who are making actual stuff. Much better."

She tried to see herself in a hustle-bustle place, comforted by the idea there would be a ladder to climb. She liked a ladder.

Sweetie waved to the guys on a horse-drawn Sunset Scavenger wagon, stomping garbage.

"*Buongiorno!*" A mustached guy at the top of the pile waved at Sweetie.

"Abyssinia, Mr. Cirelli!" she answered, without slowing.

The gaunt guys in his crew stared as the girls passed.

"You'll get a kick out of this. So, I'm in charge of our costume bible. I record everything used to costume a production. The amount of fabric, how much it cost, where we got it, how we dyed it." Sweetie swung her arms, taking up all the air around her on the sidewalk. "And, of course, every singer's measurements." She paused dramatically, drawing out "measurements"—this was important.

A hobo bumped her with his stick as he passed, and Sweetie hollered, "Hey!" Then she returned to her story. "So the singers are mostly all divas, but we've got this one diva's diva—she won't go onstage without a guy spraying a flit gun of Chanel Number Five on the curtains first."

Jane tripped on a crack. Heels were trouble.

"So anyway, she looks to be on a serious path of weight gain. And this is a problem, right? Her costume's ready, made just so, with all the right beading and trim, in exactly the size she was when we officially measured her. But now the designer suspects—heck, we all do—the diva's gained weight. So? In this circumstance, I'm the girth detective. You know, sneaking around, measuring the back sides of chairs she sits on?"

She heard movie patter in Sweetie's speech and was tempted to listen just to her sound without considering her content.

Against a red light and in front of a honking jitney, Sweetie ran across the street, Jane trying to keep up without turning a heel.

"So last night? I follow the diva and the rest of them to the Streets of Paris nightclub. On Mason?"

She'd seen signs for it on a wall a block back—LOUSIEST SHOW IN TOWN! COCKTAILS FIVE CENTS!

Jane nodded, distracted by columns and stone and flags ahead.

"When the diva sits on this stool, her belly pushing up against the bar, I drop my sweater on the ground so I can bend over to mark the floor with chalk at the edge of the stool's back leg, so I can calculate the distance between the stool back and the bar edge?"

She hurried, fearful of losing Sweetie in the throngs hustling toward a squealing bus.

"This drunk kicks me when I'm down there, and I tip over on this sticky floor. Ripping a seam at my waist? But I went back to work late last night? And got all the numbers entered into the bible! So, this morning, my sleuthing complete, all the numbers calculated—she's two sizes bigger!—we're letting out the seams so she can hit the big notes. Woo-hoo! But shush it. Nobody, most especially the diva, can know we know she's made it to a new category of fat."

Sweetie looked at her like she expected a response.

"Phyl Coe on the radio."

Sweetie laughed at the girl detective reference. "Sneak the measurements, record the numbers, do the math. That's the kind of artist I am right now, but not forever."

She saw Sweetie was good at her job.

By the time they entered the War Memorial building, she really wanted to work with Sweetie, who was so magnetic, so encouraging, the way she bubbled with support and possibility, such a cheerleader. It didn't matter if the work wasn't near as interesting as Sweetie made it sound. And there wouldn't be telephone or greeting work.

They entered the stone building, making their way to an

interior stairwell. Up and back and behind they went, Sweetie leading her through a mass of bodies.

"How long you been working here?"

"Started right after I met Rivka. After she fixed me up."

Let Sweetie be my Rivka. Let her fix me up, Jane thought.

Sweetie opened a door into chaos and began pointing, naming drapers, sewers, cutters, painters, dyers, accessorizers, milliners, tailors, stitchers, and shoppers. Rows of ladies hunched over sewing machines while men in shirtsleeves hollered at them. Other ladies cut fabric on room-long tables. Up and down the walls and on every flat surface were fur, lace, feathers, brocade, beads, and velvet. On dress forms to the left were a maid, a gladiator, a queen, and a dirty monk. And the white wigs and ship hats and fire swords from the pictures on the wall of their flat! Jane wondered if Sweetie had designed those, or if she had just drawn them after they were made.

In the middle of the room was a huge yelling woman with marble-colored skin, tall as Jane but wider, with a white shiny suit and matching fabric wrapped around her head.

"Diva?"

"Designer, my boss."

The big lady screamed in another language, cigarette in one hand, coffee cup and saucer in the other, a statue come to life, people shifting around her so that she looked like the center of everything, instructions flowing from her fingertips, conducting every movement in the room. Something about that, her control of these people, disarmed Jane, who believed in the possibility of a woman's success, but mostly her own. She tasted resentment.

Why did she feel a rising instinct to diminish this woman? Was it so she herself would feel bigger? Was it the momma in her? The daddy?

Whatever it was, instinctively, she found the quickest, most insignificant path to minimizing the woman's obvious importance. She turned her back to the designer and said to Sweetie, "Don't stand behind *her* in the potluck line," throwing her arms to the sides to signify the size of the woman's hips.

This wasn't the sort of thing Jane did. She *wanted* this job.

But when she did it, Sweetie's eyes bulged so you could see the whites all the way around. Jane's right hand hit something soft, and then it was hot and wet.

"Aaaaarrrr!"

The designer was right up behind her. Jane had smacked her coffee cup, spilling hot liquid down the front of the shiny, white clothes.

"*Tu es virée!*" the designer yelled, the veins at her temples pulsing, blue.

"She says you're fired."

"I haven't had an interview."

The designer seemed to understand English.

"*Eh bien, tu es embauchée. Maintenant, tu es virée!*" Spit bubbles popped at the corners of her red, red lips.

"You've just been hired, and fired," Sweetie said, her face frozen in an expression more of fear than sympathy.

Jane looked around the room and saw that Sweetie was now at its center, all eyes on her, not the designer, not Jane. Sweetie was the one who'd be punished. She'd brought the idiot into the workroom.

STRIPPED of her interview costume, back in the hand-me-down bathrobe, Jane sat on the flat's parlor rug, up against the sofa, cracking her toes.

"Disgusting!" Sweetie said, in her after-the-opera-interview mood.

"I maybe stood a chance at the costume shop, but the receptionist one had dozens of girls in line, and that was just for one morning's interviews. Those were the only two."

Jane rested her cheek against a bony knee. She hated to fail and hated more that she was to blame.

"I recommended you to Madame DuBois, put my name behind you!" Sweetie said, standing above her in the bay window. "When Rivka recommended me, I took it seriously, I did Rivka honor. What you've done to me there . . . I'll never . . ." She swallowed something and turned to Rivka. "And that all bounces back on you. I'm so sorry about that, dear."

Sweetie's lashes clumped, wet, into star sprays. She frowned at Rivka, who sat riffling through newspapers around her on the sofa and didn't look up.

"I'm so sorry I put you in this position, saying we should help Jane. You were right."

Sweetie'd turned on her.

Before Jane could interrupt, even before she could think what to offer in self-defense, Rivka said, "Jane is right. It is ugly, unfair world for unskilled women." She lit a cigarette in a series of tiny gestures. "There is more for unskilled men, of course."

"Why can't a girl do those jobs?" Jane asked, thinking of her picking work. She'd never been the only girl in the field. When Okies were hungry, everybody worked, even little kids, dragging burlap bags behind them in the dirt like tails.

You can do men's work, said the radio voice in her head.

"Those jobs require strength? Man stuff?" Sweetie sank onto the sofa and rolled her eyes. She'd shifted so easily from supportive to contemptuous, acting like she'd been truly injured in the opera mess, then jerking back, pretending she was most offended by the harm Jane had done Rivka—a harm Jane couldn't see—as if Rivka were Sweetie's main concern.

"Not all male jobs require male strength," Rivka said.

"What are you talking about?"

Sweetie looked like she had no memory of women doing backbreaking field work. Had Uno shielded her so well?

"There is one at *Prospect.*" Rivka circled something in pencil.

"The *Prospect?*" Sweetie sat upright.

"But testicles," Rivka said.

"Testicles?" Jane asked.

"Man job." Rivka read aloud: "Copy boys wanted for expanding staff of ambitious regional newspaper. Need smart, hardworking hustlers. Contact Jorge Cruz at MIssion 7- 2073."

"See? Copy *boys,*" Sweetie said. "She's ruined her chance. The chance I gave her!"

You can be a boy, said the voice in her head.

"Maybe she can persuade them," Rivka said.

"Why would they give it to a girl?"

"Boys," Jane said. "Copy *boys.*"

"So?"

"It says boys, not men."

"So?"

"I could be a boy." Her head buzzed with unfamiliar joy as she said it.

The girls were silent.

It was obviously true. It was easier to move and be in the world in overalls than the hose and heels a city girl required. In pants there was no limit to your gait.

"What are you talking about?"

"I'm six foot. My voice is husky. I've got no bosoms."

"She is right there," Rivka agreed.

"Listen to Laurel and Hardy," Sweetie said.

"No," Rivka said. "She is right. She is not idiot, we think. She is willing to work hard, we think. She is tall and deep-voiced enough to pass as eighteen-year-old boy, immature one . . ."

"She doesn't look like a boy!"

Jane thought of everybody at home who said she looked like Daddy. "Cut off my hair."

"I'm not!"

"She could get this," Rivka insisted.

Jane's skin warmed.

"You want me to cut that gorgeous hair?" Sweetie asked.

Gorgeous? That's a hoot.

"I know *Prospect* people." Rivka's voice underlined *know*. "I will cut her hair. I will make her boy," Rivka said. "I can teach her. I taught you."

"Taught me how to be a girl?" Sweetie shrieked.

"How to be city girl."

Sweetie got up and walked back to the window, facing away from the other two.

"We will see if she can be boy. We will have party. See if she can get job."

"You're inviting Mac?" Sweetie asked, her tone a dare, a tone Jane'd not seen her take with Rivka. There was something behind that.

"I can do this," Rivka answered. "I can make her copy boy. You think I cannot do this?"

Jane heard her say the word *I* three times and wondered if this was a moment of purchase.

"If I shave my head, you can get me a job?"

Rivka looked almost surprised to be reminded of Jane's presence. Then her eyes went up to the ceiling, looking for the answer.

"It is more than shaving head. It is becoming something you are not. Something higher. Something better. Can you learn to do this?"

"You think being a boy is better than being a girl?"

"I did not say that. You did not listen. You apparently cannot listen."

Grab hold. You're in a hole. Stop digging.

"I can do it. I can. I can be a boy. I can be better," she said.

Being a girl had always been a hard thing, so many layers

of subtlety on top of the obvious difficulty of just getting a job done.

"You think manhood's just some thing you put on?" Sweetie asked. Her cheeks were inflamed, making the whites of her eyes look too bright, almost fake, angry, maybe because she was no longer the one doing the helping, nor being helped.

"Precisely," Rivka said. "Manhood is some thing you put on."

CHAPTER THREE

DRIVE

That's more like it.

She patted her hair, an inch long and gummed up with pomade, admiring her reflection, a great pleasure welling up from deep within. She'd never been so interested in her whole nude self, never lived in a place with a mirror bigger enough than her head to make a real study of her appearance in the world. Now, running her hands over her shoulders, arms, hips, legs, she understood why Rivka had mocked her when she'd stepped from the bath that first night, a girl weirdly tall, with bone-shaped limbs, a concave chest. But now she liked what she saw in this new light.

This was how he would have looked, his newborn self stretched, divided, multiplied into a flesh-covered skeleton, like her. If he were here, breathing, talking, laughing at her side, they'd be a matched pair. Cutting her hair felt like letting that happen.

But still, he wasn't standing here with her.

She'd pushed out live and he had died.

Same with Daddy.

Both had gone into the ditch. Only she had come out.

She thought, Not my fault.

She straightened up taller, less dangly.

She pulled on a pair of boys' underwear, snug, stretchy, the same brand she saw in library magazine advertisements, with pictures of baseball players swinging a bat in their skivvies. These were nothing like her droopy, homemade panties. Nothing like the hose and garters attached to a girdle from her interview, making her feel sucked in, breathless, jury-rigged, as if the snaps might break, giving her scarcely any inclination to think what she thought, so aware was she of the rayon pattern scratching into the skin of her legs.

From this first new layer, she was comfortable.

She pulled on wool pants, her bare skin slipping into baggy, slippery-lined legs. They were too big, but she thought she'd grow into them and would step freely down the street, going where she cared to go, as fast as she wanted. She put on the crisp, ironed shirt, thick socks, wingtips, adding layers of protection, and finally left the bathroom for the parlor, where Rivka nodded, shook her head, nodded again.

"Let me teach you how to tie tie."

Sweetie cut through the room. "You look like your daddy."

Jane shuddered.

Rivka stuffed her pockets: a beat-up wallet with a dollar in change, a key to the flat, a handkerchief, a pack of Lucky Strikes, a pencil, and a pocket notebook—a moleskin.

"Ballast," Rivka said. "Man needs weight."

Daddy used to load his pockets with nuts, bolts, his pocketknife, when he didn't have money to carry.

Jane put on a gray wool cap, which warmed the top of her head, though she thought it made her look like the hopeful sucker in a comic book.

In spite of that, and in spite of Sweetie mentioning Daddy in this moment on the brink of the party, she felt good. Hands in her pockets, knees wide, she felt the freedom of spreading out. She'd worked hard for so long to hunch over, to hide the bigness that made her the butt of jokes, so that her very self was what stopped her from getting the things she wanted.

And now for that fact, her height, to make her more believable in this new role, with all its possibilities, was an amazement.

"About your voice," Rivka said. "Drop it to lower register, just little lower."

That wouldn't be hard with her damaged throat.

She had been thirteen when she'd breathed in valley fever's dust-borne spore and it had swum to the bottom of her lungs, circling up, filling itself with a hundred babies before rupturing, releasing them to repeat the pattern, traveling through her blood, spreading the fungus, turning her voice to a growl.

One morning that year she had woken in the car's back seat, where she'd slept so as not to keep her parents awake with her coughing. She'd trapped a fiddleback spider in a jelly jar and set it on the dashboard, where the sun shone into and out of its quilted glass surface, shooting little fragmented rainbows through the dusty sky. She could see the air where she lived had a graininess, and could understand why it was so hard for her to breathe there.

Seeing it so clearly had set her off coughing.

Momma had opened the car door in her nightgown—"Quiet! You'll ruin your throat. Sound enough like a boy already!"

Now that fever-ruined voice was a lucky thing, everything gone opposite.

"Stand up straight!" Rivka lectured. "Throw your shoulders back! Stick your chest out."

Jane did, taking up more space.

Rivka continued, "No one will believe in copy boy who does not smoke."

She taught Jane how to light a cigarette like a boy, how to let it dangle out the side of her lips, how to grip it with her thumb and two fingers, flicking ashes, rude, as if no one needed to sweep up after her, or as if she didn't care they did.

"All is fine now with body, voice. But I am as worried about *ain't* as the rest of it."

"And *fixin'* and *figurin'*," Sweetie said, her eyebrows raised, so superior to Jane, having banished the chopped-off *g* from her own speech.

"That is color. *Ain't* is error. There is difference."

"I ain't gonna say *ain't* no more."

Rivka looked at her sharply.

"Sounds like there is someone in there."

Jane smiled.

"Muzzle her."

JANE lit another Lucky Strike, sitting on the top step. Her cough had mostly calmed since she'd left the dust for fog, but she expected the cigarette to take her right back to hacking. She loosened the tie that had been choking her all afternoon, making her feel like a cow on a ramp, and took a long drag, feeling her throat itch. But the cough didn't come, so she settled, studying her neighborhood from the flat's front steps.

That stretch of Clay was swank. Nice old houses, fresh paint in pastel colors, respectable homeowners, flowers blooming in matching pots on stone stoops. No smell of piss, no tents, no trash can fires. Even the air was cleaner and brighter here than Van Ness, near the radio station and opera. Hard times hadn't made it to this Gold Coast block, which raised the question again of how the girls afforded it. Jane didn't understand money or class, only that she was at the bottom of both systems and planned to climb up. But she did know that the one with the dough had the power, and in this flat that was Rivka. She needed a job so Rivka would accept her and she could stay in this place. Selling herself as a city boy at the party would be a start.

Down the block two men approached, and, judging from how the downstairs neighbor peeked out her lacy curtains, they were hardly welcome. The shorter of the two, walking with his right foot on the sidewalk and his left in the street, said, "Oppie, I can't walk much more. Can't we just find a diner?" He stopped as he said this, lifting his fedora and smoothing dark hair that stood up in tufts. His cheeks were splotchy red and his glasses tilted.

The other guy, Oppie, was tall and thin, in a blue work shirt with a pack of Chesterfields sticking out of his top pocket and faded blue jeans with a big silver buckle. He walked with his feet turned out, like he was getting ready to dance. His bright blue eyes and wild brown hair made him look deranged.

"Please." Oppie stopped and pointed bony yellow fingers and a cigarette into Splotchy's face. "Quadruple digits, divisible by seven. 1428, 2128, 2821 . . . Ignore the landscape, focus on the math." A soft humming sound filled the space between his words.

"How many divisible-by-seven numbers before we reach the ocean?"

So 3528 is divisible by seven, Jane thought, as if she might need to know later, as if this information could be key to not failing.

Her fingers trembled. But when she saw their ridiculous wobbling, she figured these might be the best two to practice on. Besides, she was the jump-in sort, not a wader, so long as she suspected the water was lower than the top of her head, which she determined was the case just now.

"Howdy, mathematicians."

"Physicists." Oppie drew it out. "Theoretical physicists."

"Looking for Rivka and Sweetie?"

"Huzzah!" he cried, punching his pal in the arm, causing Splotchy to drop his hat. "We must not live in the emotions, brother, but in analysis."

He turned to Jane. "Do you see what I did there?"

"Physics," she answered, remembering eleventh grade, a test she'd studied for by Studebaker headlights.

"Brilliant!"

"Go on up. They're cooking."

Oppie flicked invisible dust off her shoulders and head, placed Splotchy's fedora on top of her cap and passed, saying, "*Ich danke Ihnen*, door boy."

"Thank God they don't live in the Sunset," Splotchy said. "My feet couldn't take it."

Lord almighty, she thought as they passed inside, her heart pounding from this first brief trial.

She worried the next guests would be a tougher sale, but then by the looks of it, nearly everybody was arriving drunk, so maybe she'd been given an easy first night. In twos and threes they dribbled in, Jane taking notes as they did, filling in their names throughout the party as she eavesdropped, thinking she might need flash cards.

Haakon, the leftist French professor, his wife, Barbara, an interior designer with an idea cabin at Willow Camp in Marin, and Harry, the charismatic Australian longshoreman leader, were dropped off by a driver with a broken nose and a black eye. A wild Armenian writer from Fresno named Bill and symphony conductor Pierre arrived by cab. Clarinetist and bandleader Artie came in a jitney with political lawyer and lumber heir Leland Sutter and Yolanda, a hatcheck girl who'd graduated from Pomona and was researching the red-throated loon on a small, private grant. The *Examiner* gossip columnist Victor Beauchamp arrived dripping copy boys, eager-faced kids about the same age as Jane. There were others, lots of others. With most of their arrivals she practiced a nonchalant nod or a tip of the hat, just to see if they registered shock or disgust at the sight of her, some kind of pretend-boy circus freak invited as a joke. But she hadn't yet gotten the raised brow or dropped jaw she feared.

The guests offered her a world of new physical details to study, the ways they walked, their dismissal of Jane when they approached, their city accents. She longed for a big, beet-stained notebook. Her moleskin was tiny, forcing her to compress even more than before. She nearly filled it that night with cramped information about San Franciscans, her impressions, what she should do to fit better with this jumbled crowd—"Jut pelvis out to look like cocky guy. Frown when I smile, to look more experienced/judgmental. Smirk, don't laugh, to seem bored of simple jokes." It went on for pages. She liked to break an impossible thing down to its doable parts, list making as an optimistic art.

She grew more confident as she stood in the foyer, near the open door—an escape route. From that spot she witnessed their many small embarrassments, a joke no one laughed at, a story the intended audience walked away from in the middle of its telling. Everybody failed a little. She studied how they recovered.

"Get in here," Sweetie hissed. "The point is to be inside."

Looked like she was unable to resist the drama of the situation.

Jane pulled the cap off, slipped outside to toss it into a bush, and settled Splotchy's fedora on top of her head. As she adjusted her posture, stretching to her full height, a silver V6 Cadillac convertible screeched up, parallel parking in rumbling jerks in front of the flat.

"He's here! The editor, H. R. MacDonald," Sweetie said, close to Jane's ear. "Call him Mac. Only been here a couple months, but he's discovered Rivka. Won't remember me." Her mood ticked upward even so.

"How could he not remember you? It's your party."

"It's Rivka's. His type likes the Rivkas. Secret restaurants, dive bars. They get sax'ed rubbing elbows with real creatives. Ups their credibility."

"You're creative," Jane said, in a kind of apology.

Sweetie smiled, grudgingly, tucking her arm into Jane's,

pulling her close. "They should make a guidebook to explain it to us immigrants," she said. Jane couldn't see a thing about Sweetie that would mark her as an outsider.

The buzz-cut editor jogged across the street and up the steps, his skin steaming like he'd run in from downtown, some fresh animal.

"Hello, Sweetie!" Mac hugged her hard, lifting her off the ground, and she squealed, her cheeks turning bright. He remembered her.

"Come in," she said.

Sweetie's hair shone, coppery.

They stepped inside, and the editor scanned the crowd.

Sweetie tugged on his sleeve. "Meet our new lodger."

"Benny Hopper," Jane said, nodding like a puppet.

His eyes swept up and down her, a grin on his face. "How old are you, fella? Looks like your mother was a rail tie, your father a redwood."

This was starting already.

"Ha! Yeah!"

Mac stepped away, into the crowd.

She'd made a regrettable first impression—"Ha! Yeah!"— but she didn't despair. Looking straight at her, Mac hadn't said, "It's a girl" or, "Why'd you invite an Okie?" No. He'd met her close up and come away with the brilliant conclusion that Benny Hopper was tall. The ordinariness of that observation made her giddy. He wasn't too high to climb.

Five foot ten with a sprinter's build, he was like a mountain lion prowling the party. White cotton shirt, cuffs rolled up on thick forearms, brown tie loose and swinging as he roamed, group to group. A half-dozen ladies quick-cut their eyes at him while they carried on conversations with other, less eligible guys, causing Jane to think, If I wanted to get his attention I'd stand there, just off-center, in the parlor . . . But then she pulled herself back—How should Benny get his attention?

At every conversation he interrupted, he said to call him Mac. "Goddamn reporters, calling me *Boy Wonder*! No dignity!" He roared and slapped backs.

With his arrival, the party's tone shifted, became more boisterous, his presence seeming to give them permission to push edges. Three guys moved couches into the entry, rugs against the walls, piano into the middle of the parlor. The doors to the other parlor were tied shut with a ribbon. Sweetie asked them not to scratch the floorboards, batting her eyelashes, but Rivka just kept cooking, sipping a clear drink with a baby onion at the bottom, stirring boiling pots as her guests took over. She didn't seem to care if things got scratched, which Jane thought strange—that someone would pay for things they wouldn't then protect.

Artie pulled out his clarinet, and Rivka's radio friends produced their instruments too. Rivka waved them off with a wooden spoon when they demanded she sit at the piano, and so instead they played along with a girl named Jim at the keyboard. The rest of the party danced to "Stompin' at the Savoy," "Darktown Strutters' Ball" and "Tiger Rag." Sweetie scooted into the mob, wiggling her round rear end and swinging a damp dish towel over her head near the corner where Mac stood talking to two other guys, the three of them admiring Sweetie's dance.

Rivka kept her back to the party, stirring the sauce.

Jane opened the living room windows to the cool because the air was getting thick and she was feeling dizzy. She'd started drinking beer a half hour before to calm her nerves, and somehow beer tasted more potent here.

Then a short guy who looked like he'd just climbed out of a boxcar—hair like a thistle—sat next to Jim on the piano bench and played his guitar, singing "Motherless Children" all by himself.

Everybody got quiet while he sang that song in a voice so ugly Jane's eyes began to leak. Daddy had sung that song, but this guy sang it better, more talky. That music in this place, right under the green tractor painting. Jane's chest tightened. The way he sat among them, wearing the Okie clothes, singing the Okie song, but acting like something else, like he had some kind of right. Like Sweetie, acting like a starlet. Jane looked around the room. Did Daddy have this effect? Was he a lesser version of this guy?

When he finished singing, they all clapped. Jim yelled, "Amen!" and others repeated it, others who'd likely never said "amen" before, even Mac. That hobo seemed above them. How'd that work? Was it something in him? Something about his audience here that made them more receptive to his roughness?

The group went back to dance music.

Mac took the singer aside, lit him a cigarette and poured him a whiskey from a bottle he got from the top shelf of a cabinet near the door. Mac knew where to find the good stuff.

Jane sat a few yards away with Oppie on the back of a couch in the crowded entry, nursing a beer and smoking one of Oppie's Chesterfields. He was very drunk and acted like he knew Jane—Benny, that is—which made her feel somewhat confident at his side.

"Why does Rivka look so dyspeptic in your direction?" he asked. "What's your crime?"

She stiffened at "crime " but then calmed herself, inspecting Rivka through the open kitchen door, chopping parsley on a butcher block, barelegged, in a black skirt and a threadbare white cotton blouse. She still wore the ankle bracelet and she'd put on red lipstick, but she didn't appear to dress a thing up unnecessarily.

It was true. Rivka did look at Jane with a cold eye, the eye of science: How's my experiment going? Is my subject failing? She couldn't explain that to Oppie, so she said, in her deepest voice: "She thinks I'm some kind of horse thief. In a bad way."

"She should talk." He blew smoke rings.

"She's made it. I'm on my way up."

The boy's clothes made her more openly opinionated, more sure of herself, less polite. "What do you mean, she should talk?"

"Doesn't it seem odd she would have this place, these parties, on a musician's wages?"

"What are her wages?" she asked. "And why do you care?"

"I don't. Just interested. Probably some old country connection."

"Old country?"

"Anyway, it seems disingenuous for her to judge. That's all I'm saying." He puffed. "But then, people do forget where they were and what they did after they've passed through it."

I will. I'll pass through it and forget everything, Jane thought.

"I always say, when you see something you want to do, do it. Figure out what to do about it afterward." He looked up at the ceiling. "Dust will settle."

"Focus on the future," she added, glad at their philosophical connection.

They each took a drag on their Chesterfields.

"Huzzah," he answered, blowing smoke. "But perhaps I ought to refine that, given you plan to be a journalist."

She'd told him she was a writer—all those notebooks qualified—and that she was aiming to do it at the *Prospect*, the idea gelling as she said it with her sense that things happen for a reason—that she'd lost her shot at the *Swale* because she was meant to write at the *Prospect*.

"As someone who has in the past been treated unfairly by the press, as someone who knows something about it, I think I am permitted to ask if you are comfortable writing about other people's private lives as part of your work. Does it bother you what might happen to these people after you tell their stories? I mean, does it make you uncomfortable to use their lives for your own advancement?"

She thought, He doesn't even see I'm a girl. Because he's drunk? Or am I that good?

And because that thought boosted her confidence, she challenged him.

"That's dumb. If you say, 'Go ahead and do it' about your job, you have to say, 'Go ahead and do it' about my job too."

"I guess it's a question of one's sense of the consequences."

Hogwash, said the voice in her head.

She'd swallowed two and a half cans of Acme Beer by now, as well as smoking four cigarettes without coughing, and the professor was blurring, even boring her a little. She'd tried Daddy's beer and hooch and cigarettes before, from age twelve on, same as the other picker kids, but that was nearly always around a campfire, near her pallet, where she could pass out without any trouble, not standing in costume at a party where she needed to keep her wits. She was proud of how she was doing at this new test, being a boy, not an Okie, not falling-down drunk on beer.

"New mascot?" asked a deep voice behind her.

"House pet. Belongs to the girls," Oppie answered.

She turned and saw Mac, his golden eyes trained on her throat.

"Have we met?" he asked, leaning against the wall, crossing one ankle over the other.

"On the porch." She wiped her hand on her thigh before extending it. "Benny Hopper."

She'd practiced for this, several times over, squeezing Rivka's hand hard as a boy would, numbing her own palm.

Mac gripped and squeezed with his right hand while slapping her shoulder with his left, pinching the slim muscle hard. He looked at her mouth. Throat, grip, muscles, lips. He suspected. She couldn't run away.

"I'm the new lodger."

"Breaking rules already."

She cooled, scalp to sternum.

"Blocking the liquor cabinet."

Maybe because her blood had drained so quickly from her brain to her gut, she felt she'd just gained a strategic advantage. While she stood between Mac and what he wanted—the store-bought liquor Rivka kept, maybe on his behalf—she had his attention. She wouldn't waste it.

"I'll be a reporter for you soon." She said it with the blunt confidence of somebody right at the sweet spot in the timeline of beer consumption.

"I can tell a story." She said that with the confidence of a guy blocking the liquor cabinet.

"Ahhh . . ." Mac smirked and rocked up onto his toes, then down, looking over her shoulder at the bottles behind glass.

"I'd be glad to start in your advertised position, as copy boy, sir." She straightened—a boy was better off tall. "If that ain't too rude to say." She heard *ain't* right after she said it and felt hot all over at the mistake, her emotions so volatile, turning always on the success of the thing she'd said or done last.

"Mac. I said to call me Mac." He'd missed the *ain't*.

He drained the last drops of his icy drink and looked at her.

"City's a ship, boy." He tilted his glass in her direction, his voice loud. "Water's choppy, yes. Things are not so good, the poor and all. But those of us in charge, we need to flush out the old, the tired old guys. Focus on the positive, the new. Speak up, man, speak up and make plans! See the possibilities!"

Daughter of Abraham, she had experience judging degrees of drunkenness and saw right now she was standing at an unlatched shed.

"I can take this city, Mac. I can write!"

Her face felt hot, but she knew he didn't see her clearly enough to judge. This was the time to say things, a narrow opening through which she could make an impression uncorralled by logic, his or hers.

He rubbed his hand down his forehead and pinched the bridge of his nose. "I'm sick of pussyfooting. I don't know what's wrong with everybody, so afraid something bad'll happen." He wobbled. "Take risks. Take the right risks. You sound good to me, man. You should move ahead, full steam, Bob!"

"Ben," she said, "Benny."

"Benny, yeah. The lodger? Yes? Well, blaze trails, you know. I've always done that. I understand a boy like you. I started with nothing, too, nothing." He spilled ice on the linoleum, as his red, muscled-up arms slashed through all the somethings he'd had nothing of. "I was the bastard child of an aging beauty and a titled Englishman. He died before he knew me. She deserted me. I raised myself." He took a big breath in preparation. "I was a farmer, a coal miner, a logger, a prospector, a sports shop owner, a golf pro, and a banker—I learned it out of a book!" He said this all in a singsong, like a monologue memorized for class—the Gettysburg Address or something—delivered out of context. Though, she thought, its being rote didn't mean it wasn't true.

"Then I came here, as a financial writer. President Hoover wanted me, but our publisher, Mr. Mercer, saw something in me and outbid him, and here I am, youngest managing editor in the country!" He tilted the glass up to his mouth but got nothing but ice cubes slipping off his chin. He licked his lips. "About the only thing I never was? A sailor! Damn! I hate to swim!" He roared at that.

He was so vain. Completely vain. She knew it was easy to manipulate the vain.

"Me too!" she hollered. "Only swimming I ever done was in an irrigation ditch. My knees touched bottom!"

Her throat constricted at having said that word, *ditch*. She was making mistakes left and right, but Mac laughed again, threw his head back, exposing his throat. The ditch didn't mean anything to him. He didn't care what she did in that ditch. She was handling him.

"How old are you, sir?"

"Mac," he corrected her again. "Twenty-six."

Could she be like him, successful, in just nine more years? If she were still a him?

He pointed his elbow at Oppie, who'd wandered off. "Careful whose advice you follow. Professor poisoned his tutor. Over in England? Talked his way out of it."

"Shit," Jane said, intoxicated by *tutor* and *England* and *poison* and happy with a boy's freedom to say anything, at least when everybody around him was drunk.

He put his arm around her neck and breathed chemical mist into her eyeballs. He was shorter than she was, though it seemed like they were nose to nose.

"Hard to know who to trust in this town."

But he trusted her. She was winning this night. The arches of her feet tingled. She wanted what he had—fame, popularity, money. Judging by the quiver she felt where his arm circled her shoulders, maybe she wanted him too. She straightened herself up. She wanted the job. That's what she needed.

"Thank you, sir—I mean Mac."

"Terrific!" He pounded her in the middle of her chest, creating a moment of panic. "You'll be terrific!" He gave her a big smile, his teeth white and square, his eyes red.

Her lower belly lurched. Why did his look go straight to her gut? Then he turned and walked away through the crowd, wobbling.

She yelled, "Wait!"

A trio nearby turned to look, but Mac didn't notice, just kept moving between clusters, slapping backs, laughing toward the door.

She whipped her head around to the kitchen, to Sweetie, who was watching, and spread her arms in the air—What should I do?

Sweetie turned to Rivka, pouring spaghetti into a bowl,

steam clouding her head, and Sweetie spoke in Rivka's ear.

Jane turned away from the girls before she could read any mouthed advice. She wanted to stop Mac herself, stop him and get a job.

She pushed through toward the door. She couldn't see his head above the crowd, which surprised her as he seemed so big, but she caught a flash of that white shirt, those muscular arms, between clumps of other people.

She saw the front door open, yellow hair flaming on the threshold. She was stuck. She couldn't squeeze between the radio people laughing and another trio circling the Australian, talking loud.

She panicked and gave a big shove, and the Australian—who was reaching out with one arm, indicating something a distance away—fell over in one of the few open spaces in the party, just fell over, onto the ground. Two men squatted to help him up, another started to laugh, and the last one turned to her, balling up his fist.

"Sorry! So sorry, sir!" she yelled, jumping through the opening where the Australian used to be to push through to the door.

"Hey, string bean!" somebody yelled.

She kept pushing and the crowd parted, and she got to the door and saw Mac climbing into the convertible.

She ran down the steps and across the street, where Mac was trying to steady his hand enough to get his key into the ignition.

"Mac, sir, why don't you stay, have coffee?"

"Meeting somebody for drinks." He jabbed the key all around his target.

She thought about teaching herself how to drive on the Golden State Highway, Daddy in back, her hands on the wheel, crowbar on the seat, headed for the ditch. And then she thought about escaping from that night, driving herself here, to this moment.

"I'd be proud to drive you, Mac."

"Don't need a driver." He dropped his keys and then fumbled to regain them on the floorboard.

"It'd be an adventure I haven't had, driving you around."

Mac looked up. She widened her eyes, raised her brows, sincere.

"See things, people, I couldn't otherwise, sir."

"Mac, I said."

"Yes, sir."

He grinned. "You're funny."

She was flooded with warmth. She could get this.

"Sweetie's lodger?"

"And Rivka's."

He handed her the keys. She couldn't breathe right. He pushed up out of the driver's seat and swatted her on the rear end, sending sensation down and up. Then he weaved to the passenger side, leaning against the Cadillac. She rushed around and opened the door for him, and though she acted calm, her heart was beating as hard as it did when she broke tape at a finish line.

He tumbled into the passenger seat, yelling, "My kingdom awaits!"

In that moment, seventeen-year-old Jane, tomato-picking, cross-dressing, beer-drunk Okie, felt a shiver of embarrassment for the managing editor of the *San Francisco Prospect*, seeing how even a high-up person might reveal too much out of uncontained vanity.

She decided to ignore that so as not to tamp down her success, and the doubt passed.

She looked up and saw the girls on the porch.

Behind her, Mac yelled, "Got the kid! Heading to Breen's!"

She turned back, saw him wink with the whole left side of his face, a stage wink.

Then she saw Rivka shaking her head no, staring at Jane,

her hand on the doorknob, the look of a naysayer—Don't drive after drinking. Don't head to a bar after midnight. Don't leave with a man you don't know. Don't throw out your well-laid plans.

Sweetie hollered something inaudible, rushing down the steps toward them.

The machine in Jane's head began to blend memories of risk and reward—a ribbon she won, a pie she stole—with the nagging of her prefrontal cortex—These are unfamiliar things. You don't know who to trust—mixing it all up fast, calculating "leap" or "stand" an instant before the chasm, helping her choose the thing she'd do, which had almost never been just to stand. Some of it was built in—a cellular confidence that she had it in her, that the seeds would sprout and the dog wouldn't bite, a natural optimism that shrank thresholds. The gorge never looked as wide to her as it did to others. But it seemed like more than that now, like an accelerant had been added to the spark of her natural confidence.

She climbed into the Cadillac, tasting an acidic tang of anxiety. Then, as so many seventeen-year-old boys before her have done, she put the key in the ignition and released the brake.

SHE woke on the hardwood floor of an unfamiliar apartment in the sky.

Her right cheek was crushing a brown leather shoe. In the background she could hear the repeating crack of a bat connecting with a ball, a guy yelling in Chinese, a whining bus, horns, all kinds of horns, and the pounding of construction. She pushed up, raising her head a foot off the ground, and then she lay back down on the shoe, moaning, and pressed her thumb into that almond-shaped lump, to stop the throb. Whatever healing her head had done since the ditch seemed ruined now. She'd been dragged through a knothole backwards. She rubbed the hair on the back of her head and remembered she was Benny. "Unhhh."

"Shut up, hayseed!"

She looked toward the sound, which came from a long brown couch pushed against a white wall covered with taped-up pages from the *News*, the *Prospect*, the *Examiner*, and the *Call-Bulletin*, a wall itself like a busy front page. She squinted through an alcohol scrim at "Quentin break plotted," "Dempsey pushes stroller up thirteen flights," "China Reds Menace SF Missionary," "Hungry Hobos."

On the couch below the wall lay a growling man in wrinkled gray slacks and one shoe, his suit jacket over his head and shoulders.

She stood and looked out a picture window over water.

"Telegraph Hill. Hundred-thousand-dollar view there, son."

She turned to see Mac standing near the newspaper wall, his buzz-cut shiny in the morning light. He'd showered and smelled, even from a distance, like brushed teeth—the minty smell of apartment dwellers, not the baking soda smell of a person who rubs his teeth with a rag over a tin cup. His flannel suit and dark tie were pressed, like his white shirt. Movie star handsome. Even his bumps and scars looked designed, not suffered. She'd grown up to respect a certain amount of scarring, proof of what a person had accomplished, though that obviously wasn't true for a woman.

Her mouth was parched, her lips gummy. She turned back to the window, rubbing her hand through spongy hair, embarrassed to look bad in front of him.

"The Russian stuff's great," he said. "No smell. That's what they're drinking in New York. Harder to get here, but everybody loves it. Next time, don't mix." He pulled at his sleeve cuff. "I'll get coffee. Then breakfast. You two can hitch along if you're hungry." Then he passed through a door in the newspaper wall, where his kitchen must be.

She'd never known anyone who spent money easily, who would pay for breakfast out, other than a weekly donut at Elthea's, which she'd never seen Daddy actually pay for. She would ask for crackers and a coffee. She had a dollar in her wallet.

Folding over to get a knot out of her back, she saw her own still-red toenails, painted for the radio interview. She hadn't removed the polish before Rivka's party—her transformation was incomplete.

"Loudmouth jackass," muttered the guy on the couch, his jacket falling to the floor. He had a square head, oily black hair, eyebrows like caterpillars above black-framed glasses. A mud brick of a body, an old brick, maybe forty. He opened his eyes wide, squeezed them shut and opened them wide again, looking like he might lose last night's supper.

He was completely drunk. She might not wreck things with her toenails since she was only a quarter-drunk, at most half-drunk, compared to his more complete condition.

"Morning, sir. Benny Hopper." She curled her toes under.

"I know, turnip." When he rose from the couch to a surprising height—no more than five foot three—Jane went the other way, dropping to the floor and sitting Indian style, her feet tucked under her thighs. She tossed him his shoe. He burped as he reached to catch it. "You don't remember. I'm Lambert. Derek Lambert. Say it right. Lamb-bear."

"Lamb-bear," she repeated, groping under the sofa for her shoes, trying to remember having met him last night.

"Riveting, your ambitions." He lit a cigar and sat back on the couch to tie his lace. "So unique. Taking the city by storm. Good-thing you've got no competition. The rest of us'll just step aside, avoid the force of your brilliance. Too bad we've been wasting all our time here, waiting for the potato truck to make its delivery."

She thought, Okay, he doesn't like me. Yet.

Her fingers found a wingtip.

Mac came out of the kitchen with three mugs, leaning down to hand the first to Jane, before Lambert, violating the obvious order of things. Mac didn't like him, was trying to unsettle him. Okay then.

"Longshoreman pal gets me pounds of it, green. Bags fall off the boat."

"Hunh," Lambert said. "Fall off the boat?"

Mac kept looking at Jane. "Best in the world. I roast it on the stovetop." The nutty smell overcame the general stink of alcohol. "Anyway, it's free."

"Right. Free," said Lambert.

The feeling was mutual—he was openly contemptuous of Mac—though Mac acted like he didn't see it. He must have a use for him.

She got the one shoe on her foot, untied, no sock, and groped for the second.

"Rooms are cigar boxes. No closet. Elevator shakes like the big one. But I can't get over the view." Mac jerked his head toward the window. "Soon I'll get the same view, with better quarters." He said it like he was bragging—to her. Why would he bother?

She turned back to the window. To the left was the prison, Alcatraz—the girls had told her about it—on a rock in the bay between the two new bridges, surrounded by sailboats, ferries, and freighters under an alarmingly blue dome. All that beauty, so close to criminals.

Lambert said, "Every stupid citizen's gonna be smug all day, like they personally filled the bay, dyed the sky."

She knew this kind of guy, who talks down everybody and everything. Nobody was going to sneak up on him with a nasty surprise. *He* was the nasty surprise.

She saw her shoe sitting under the window in the corner.

Lambert dropped ashes into a crystal boat on the coffee

table. "You want a view, you gotta go to New York. Lemme explain about views and vodka."

Mac rolled his eyes. "Yeah, New York, so you say."

Get the shoe on.

"Any city where the creatives commute to sand dune suburbs for chicken fried steak and pre-mixed Manhattans . . ."

"I don't live in the Sunset. I don't drink canned Manhattans, at any rate."

Jane looked at the newspapered wall and interrupted. "Studying the competition?"

Mac turned from the window to the wall. "Revolving exhibit. Figuring it out."

She hopped up, grabbed the shoe and sat with her back to the other two, slipping it on. Discovery avoided.

Lambert said, "If we're gonna eat, let's do it, children," stubbing his cigar in the candy bowl.

Jane was queasy, needed the crackers, so she stood and slipped on her jacket, feeling at once it was too light—fully loaded, a suit was heavy, she'd learned yesterday. She patted her hips and found no wallet, cigarettes, keys, or notebook. Checked her breast pockets. Nothing. No ballast.

"Don't tell me," Lambert said. "You're the kid who loses things, right? Oh my God. Didn't Mommy sew your money to the inside of your jacket?" He was hoarse with joy. "I know your type. Seen it a million times! I could write an encyclopedia on your type!"

But that wasn't her type.

The keys—the apartment and Uno's car—and the wallet, her only cash. But worst was the moleskin. She'd written in it all yesterday, about cutting and pomading her hair, learning to smoke, aiming for the *Prospect*, assessing people at the party, planning how to act like a boy. Someone had stolen it, maybe read it.

"You must have dropped it at Breen's," Mac said. "We'll find it at breakfast."

Explosions went off behind her eyes.

"Don't worry about last night. Forget it."

The headline taped to the edge of the wall nearest her face read, "Ragged, hungry, broke harvest workers live in squalor amidst death," over a picture of a pathetic-looking Okie family, like any one of them she knew.

Lambert leered. "Missing something special, kid?"

She had to make Mac like her before somebody read that moleskin, found her out, reported it, made her Jane again.

"Mac, sir, want me to drive?"

"We'll walk."

She picked up their mugs to carry them to the kitchen.

"Leave 'em," he said. "Girl's on her way."

She rubbed her smooth cheeks.

"What's a matter, Boy? Need a shave?" Lambert's face cracked open, grinning. Between his top and bottom teeth, it looked black, like he had no tongue.

She saw then, in her mind, vivid as life, Lambert laughing, his thick arms wrapped around his belly, rocking back and forth: "Oh my God! He's a girl! He's a girl!"

A twenty-four-inch jar of pickled pigs' feet sat at eye level on a dark wood bar as long as a football field. The jar was working its magic on her head and gut, neither of which needed it, especially since Malachi, Breen's barman, had found neither her wallet nor her notebook.

"What're you trying to preserve? The founding family weren't exactly paragons, were they?" Mac used his eggy fork to punctuate, looking straight ahead at Lambert's reflection in the mirror over the bar where they'd bellied up for breakfast. "Killing each other, incest, all that. It's the Barbary Coast. If we want readers, we gotta turn up the lights!"

Lambert smiled, ugly, everything—his teeth, mouth, head

—block-shaped. "I know. I've been here. I've been studying this market since you were in shorts."

"We're booooorrrrrring! We gotta expose their secrets. Tell 'em and sell 'em." Mac chewed three bites of Hangtown fry before looking up in the mirror again at Lambert, who had half an oyster dangling on his lip. Mac winced. "I've done the math. We're last of six. Newsroom's full of stiffs, except you." His voice got quieter, almost intimate. "We gotta tell the secrets, the right secrets. This paper's gonna die off some day, but I don't want it jumping off the bridge on my watch."

Lambert's nostrils flared. "Sure, we can gossip our way to first. Show every shitty thing everybody does. Readers'll eat it up. They'll love you. I know you want that. Who cares if some big fella's caught ass-up on the front page? But I'm saying we don't have to do it that way. There are better ways, ways that'll position us. For the future."

Mac set down his fork and rubbed a napkin across his lips and chin, back and forth, getting all the imperceptible grease, laid it over his plate, and turned his stool to Lambert. "I understand. We have to be strategic. Tell certain secrets, which are smart to tell, not the others, which are not so smart to tell. Those we keep. Use 'em later. But don't mistake me. Don't think I don't know the future. I know the future. That's why they hired me."

"Aw, you got this gig too young." Lambert shook his head. "That's the tragedy. You don't know what you need to know to be good. You're gonna fuck it up!"

Mac waited, looking in the mirror. "I give you rope."

He let it hang.

"All right." Lambert rubbed his stubbled cheeks with both hands.

She had no idea what they were talking about but understood they were doing it in front of her because she didn't matter. This was the way people on top did, in front of people on the bottom, confessing bad behavior in front of some guy sweeping the sidewalk, wiping the counter. But it didn't matter because she was going to be ruined as soon as somebody found her notebook anyway. None of this pig slop mattered if she was found out.

"Malachi!" Mac waved at the potato-nosed bartender. "Telephone."

Malachi wiped his hands on a towel, carefully refolding it and hanging it on a rail before delivering the phone from the end of the bar, stretching the coiled cord at least fifty feet. He wiped the mouthpiece in five precise motions with a cloth before pushing the heavy black machine in front of Mac.

"MIssion 7-2073," Mac said. "Mary, send Jorge," and then he banged it down.

Jane moved to the back of the bar, opening the door to the toilet.

"Hey!" the bar boy yelled. "Gents is open. Leave the ladies' alone. Do I really gotta wash up after you again?"

The toilet. She remembered a shrieking woman and Lambert laughing—"He's a girl!" A roomful of strangers laughing. That's what happened last night. She'd used the ladies'.

It was time to get good at holding her water.

She entered the men's room, taking a stall, and sat behind the latched door with her head between her hands. Lordie, the notebook. Small hexagonal tiles spun at her feet.

When she returned, Mac was talking to a guy, his belly against the bar, craning right and left.

"I led Benny astray last night, Jorge, kept him out late, left the bar tab open. Kid's suffering consequences." Mac looked like he might rub her head—Who's a good boy? "I'm gonna make it up to him. Get him on the bench."

Jorge raised a sausage finger to Malachi as he returned from the kitchen with a tub of clean glasses. Then he looked Jane up and down, his brow furrowed. "How awful for the boy. He's really earned the job." Sarcasm pooled on the bar.

Malachi poured Stolichnaya into a short glass over ice and handed it sloshing to Jorge. Its antiseptic smell made Jane's belly twist up more than the oysters or pigs' feet.

"I can pick a horse," Mac said. "Train him." Mac turned to her. "Benny, this is your boss, Jorge, best in the business. He *is* the *Prospect*. Knows everything. Mind your Ps and Qs around this guy."

Lambert slid off his stool and slammed the door on his way out, no goodbye.

Mac set a short pile of bills on the bar. "This should cover breakfast and whatever. Talk to Jorge." He hit Jane's back and followed Lambert.

She looked down at the cash. Too much. Why'd he do that? She should slip it in her pocket, get out, buy gas and drive Uno's car south, maybe to Los Angeles, where she knew no one, no one knew her. Try again, far from her stolen moleskin.

"Malachi!" Jorge held up two more fingers and headed to the far-corner booth. Then he yelled, "Boy!"

Malachi put their plates into a tub while Jane counted out breakfast money.

"About the contents of your pocket," Malachi said. "Lambert took 'em."

"What?"

"Saw him do it. You was passed out in the corner. He picked your pocket. He saw I saw. Told me, 'Stay quiet.' Said it was a joke." She looked hard at Malachi, trying to tell whether this was him playing a joke on her.

"Why'd he do that?"

"Dunno, son." He kept wiping. Then he refilled her cup of coffee. "Somebody over there ought to see straight. How do they put out a paper, everybody drunk?"

Jane left the tab plus a nickel on the counter and gripped the rest in her pocket with a clammy palm.

She joined Jorge in a back-corner booth, sliding onto the leather bench where the old editor hunched, his white shirt-sleeves soaking up table spills, bow tie askew, dotted suspenders holding the getup together. His liver-spotted hand clutched the glass. A pair of spectacles magnified the spider veins under his eyes. Big as a mountain, face like a mudslide.

Malachi delivered two more glasses of vodka as Jorge started up on the ice.

"Boy," he said, phlegmy.

"Yessir."

"You are lucky to have a patron in our editor." He slurped and rattled the ice in his glass. "Must see something in you." Another sip. "Probably ambition. That would be enough for him. Maybe you got the loyalty gene."

"Sorry for the trouble, sir . . ."

"Don't interrupt, Boy." He took out a handkerchief, blew his nose with a blast, folded it up and put it back in his pocket. "If I were in charge, you would not jump ahead of more obviously qualified boys."

Jane knew every job had a Jorge—the wall between you and what you wanted, protecting the old way from the new.

"But apparently, for this hire, this time, it is not up to me."

He held his glass in the air, empty but for ice. Jane slid her drink in front of him.

"Not drinking today, Boy?"

"Don't like the clear stuff."

Jorge took a sip out of her glass and wiped his wet chin.

"As I previously noted, you are a lucky fellow to have such a friend. A friend in high places. Nonetheless, let me tell you about the very low place where you will begin."

CHAPTER FOUR

PROSPECT

J ane practiced herself into an excellent liar.

The seed of that skill had been planted long before, but it sprouted and grew and blossomed with constant tending at the *Prospect*. Only three months after her arrival, people looked at her and saw a copy boy, at the bottom of the ladder but capable of climbing.

She'd been hazed, yes, like any new boy, sent to the basement, told to fetch "the long weight," made to stand there with the press running for an hour before she got the joke.

It was nothing compared to the things she saw happening to girls in the building, pushed into closets, groped, laughed at by clusters of men. She never heard the details—she was just a copy boy, not privy to the inside talk of the girls or the men —but she did see one or two of them run out of the building crying, with a new girl to take her place two days later.

Her boy hazing wasn't so bad. It sharpened her ability to smell a rat, made her try even harder to apply herself to what she needed to learn.

Before work every morning she went to the South O' Slot Diner on Fifth, where she ordered black coffee and crackers and read the *Prospect*, the *Examiner*, the *Call-Bulletin*, and the *News*—a tomato picker surrounded by longshoremen, policemen, artists, an Okie among Orientals, Italians, Irish, and Coloreds. She became interested, less intimidated, by the people around her, wanting to master their differences, their similarities.

She read the politics, police blotters, sports, even the society pages, and listened to everybody talk, heard their opinions and their accents and their gossip. She wrote it all down to study because she planned to use it soon, when she had her own column. She'd believed in such a goal even before the ditch, but now she saw a clear path leading her to it and she loved a clear path.

Rivka bought into the goal too. Jane's getting this job and caring about it made Rivka like her better. She hadn't said anything about kicking her out ever since. Every week she'd restock a pile of books next to Jane's bed—Charles Dickens, George Orwell, Ernest Hemingway, newspapermen all—and Jane loved them, but none as much as the syndicated articles of Martha Gellhorn, which Rivka would put on top of the pile.

Martha was a beautiful lady, and young, who wrote from war zones all over the world. She said plain, honest things, saw who people were, what was in them, even in children. Jane copied into her new notebook one of Gellhorn's lines about a little boy in war-torn Spain—"Between his eyes, there were four lines, the marks of such misery as children should never feel. He spoke with that wonderful whisky voice that so many Spanish children have, and he was a tough and entire little boy." When Jane read those words she saw the faces of kids she knew, saw her own tent living self, "tough and entire," her own "whiskey voice." She underlined sentences like these throughout Martha's columns and read them out loud, trying them out with different accents in the mirror.

That's who Jane would be, the second Martha Gellhorn. Plain, honest, smart. Though she was obviously willing to forsake the honesty. Momma always said she would *do* something, after all, not that she would *be* something—like honest—which liberated her from some of the rules, so long as she was working toward the main prize.

She'd won a spot on the long copy boy bench, her new starting line, where six guys sat waiting to be sprung by a reporter's shouted "Boy!" When that call went out, the boy at the end of the bench hopped up and ran, eager for his twenty-minute adventure up or downstairs to hustle copy or out on the street to fetch coffee or whiskey. They weren't supposed to have names on the bench. They were all "Boy." It was efficient. The ones who'd studied at Stanford or Berkeley or Columbia felt worse about that than she did. "Humiliating" or "unconscionable," they said, angry not to be known. All that schooling hadn't taught them how to make the best of the worst.

Unburdened by education, Jane just introduced herself to everybody anyway—"Hello, I'm Benny Hopper"—willing to break rules to be remembered. As for being a boy, she'd fix that when the time was right, after she proved herself. Identity was a decision subject to timing, not a solid fact, after all, she thought.

Lambert was the only stink in the tent. The whole first week she worked at the *Prospect* she worried about her missing moleskin, expecting him to spring it on her. On the very first Friday, she waited until he left for lunch and then sneaked over to hunt through his desk, finding the moleskin and her wallet there, shoved to the back of a filthy top drawer. Not her keys though. Uno's car was lost to her now. She'd have to ask the girls for another key to the flat. She went through every page of the moleskin, looking for clues, but couldn't tell whether he'd read it or not. She stewed through that lunch hour until he returned, marched to his desk and confronted him—"You stole my stuff at Breens!"—hissing like a beetle, which for some reason she was unafraid of doing in front of him.

He laughed in her face.

"Yeah, I took your shit! You're lower than a rookie! You're a rookie on the bench! What'd you expect? If you're stupid enough to pass out in a bar, then you've fucked your own self, dummy."

She didn't know how to react, other than to hate and distrust him and worry every night that he'd read the notebook, that he knew her story. But if he knew, he hadn't done anything with it. Was he saving it, to use at the best, most humiliating time? Was he all hat, no cattle, or a real threat? She kept her eyes on Lambert.

She hardly ever saw Mac anymore. She'd obviously been nowhere near his apartment or even his stool at Breen's since the second day she'd met him, and now at work he was always in his office in meetings, door closed, on the telephone with the publisher, Mr. Mercer, or out of the building, attending functions, confirming for her the desirability of social busyness. His absence was a disappointment. He was the sun, her cheeks toasting when he passed through the room, even if he didn't glance her way, so she worried that, because she didn't see him, she'd lost his interest, that he'd found another more deserving underling on whom to gift opportunity. That thought weighed heavier than almost anything else in this otherwise happy season.

But finally Mac rewarded her patience.

Catching her on the stairs after she'd finished a run, he grabbed her elbow and leaned in.

"I need you to do me a favor."

A bubble of hope bounced in the spot where her throat met her clavicle.

"I need you to pick up my Cadillac—it broke down in Berkeley, I had it repaired there. I need you to bring it back for me."

He put an envelope in her pocket and patted it, and she felt a shiver on the back of her neck.

"This should cover it."

It was simple, nothing personal, but still it separated her from the others, put her out front. And he'd said, "I need you," three times.

SHE picked the car up and paid for it with the wad he gave her. This was the second time he'd trusted her with money, so she counted it twice, thinking it might be a test, before pulling away from the repair shop, over to the pier, where she waited with the other parked cars in line to cross the bay on the auto ferry.

Jumpy with coffee and sprinkle donuts, she got out and walked to the rail's edge. Seagulls flapped all around and over her head, squealing like they do. She watched a dozen dirty birds malingering on wood gone white with ammonia droppings. They all faced one direction and stood on one leg. She'd heard they kept themselves warm that way. She tried it herself, standing on her own right leg, pulling her left one up as high as she could get it, extending her arms like wings. This was another good thing about being a boy, the freedom to look stupid in front of strangers when you wanted to. She thought the bird warming method was working but then had to grab the pier rail to save herself from tipping over.

That's when she saw a girl walking her way, slim and pale, a large coat cinched around her waist, ending just above her bare ankles and thick-heeled black leather shoes. Though she wore no makeup on her eyes, her lips were painted black-red. Platinum hair blew all around her head. She had a thin neck, and her bare, ridged collarbones were exposed where the coat stood open.

The girl walked straight toward her in a rush, stopping a couple yards away. Then she closed the remaining space, moving slower, rolling her eyes. "Sorry. That was cuckoo. I thought you were someone else." She tilted her head to the side, squinting.

Jane couldn't think of anything to say.

"Can I bum one?" the girl asked, pulling her hair back to stop it from flying in her face. Her voice was scratchy, with a trace of West Texas. She jerked her head toward an unhappy group standing three cars behind them. "They're crazy-making."

A short-haired woman in a khaki skirt and black beret was at the center of three sobbing boys of grade-school age. The oldest of the three cried least dramatically, but his face looked most miserable. With one hand he held his gray wool cap on his head against the wind. The smallest of the three slapped the back of the middle boy, who ignored him, crying to the lady instead. She leaned down to their heads, talking, her face serious, the way a person looks when talking to an adult. The older boy looked pinched, like he was trying to be who she wanted. The other two didn't. They just looked a basic sort of unhappy.

Jane fumbled in three jacket pockets before finding the Luckies pack in the last spot, empty. She said, "Sorry" in her deepest voice, hoping to be believed.

"Share?" the girl asked, tilting her head toward Jane's mouth, and then she looked back over her shoulder at the quartet.

Her right hand was still holding her hair, her left grasping her coat collar, covering her throat, so Jane put the burning cigarette in the girl's mouth, touching her bottom lip.

The skin on her face looked thin, but it was thicker, chapped, bumpy on her mouth. Odd. Was it scarred?

Jane shuddered at the strangeness.

The girl pointed and asked if she minded stepping behind a big red booze truck with her, to get out of the wind. Jane followed.

"That your family?"

"My boss and her sons." The girl hugged herself.

"Y'all headed over to see the sights?"

The girl didn't answer for a second. "Y'all?"

It was hard to be perfect all the time, to always remember, in every spontaneous moment, never to say "y'all" or "ain't" or "might could," when those were the words that popped out of your mouth when you were nervous or when you were relaxed.

The girl shrugged. "I do that too. Where you from?"

Jane didn't want to get into that. "East. Heading to see the sights?"

The girl nodded like she got it—Don't mention Texas.

"She's putting me and her boys on the boat with their foster father."

"Foster?" Jane leaned in, getting her ear closer to the girl's mouth. The seagulls and the kids were so loud.

"She boards her kids during the week, when she and her husband are working."

Jane glanced back at beret lady to see if she looked relieved or guilty but couldn't tell at this distance.

"Sometimes they come home on weekends. This week's a change." She looked back over the truck hood. "I'll ride with them, settle them down." She nodded her head and marched in place, closing her eyes, inhaling again. Her face was a little lopsided, pretty, but the left cheekbone was higher than the right.

"I'm a reporter," Jane said, feeling the need to assert who was who and what was what, though a reporter wasn't what or who Jane was, and she was surprised at herself for saying it.

The girl dropped her ashes with three sharp shakes. "Really?" She handed back the cigarette.

"Rookie, but, yeah," Jane said, sounding casual, thinking, Soon. She exhaled smoke to the side, but the wind blew it back in her face and she coughed.

"I've got a story for you, rookie."

"Pardon?"

"Vee!" beret lady yelled, and the girl looked around the

truck at her boss and the kids just as the ferry blasted loud, approaching the pier.

"I gotta get back." She held the cigarette out and Jane accidentally took it like a girl, between her pointing and middle fingers. Then she rearranged it awkwardly.

The girl looked hard at her.

Jane thought, You don't look at people you don't know that way. This girl was breaking some kind of code.

"Do you want to meet for drinks tonight? Hear my story?" the girl asked.

Something was off about her—seeing Jane was a liar, offering her a story anyway. And her thinness. There was something off about this girl.

Jane didn't know how to get out of this, so she said, "Of course," polite. "How about Breen's? Eight? Benny Hopper."

The girl pulled a card out of her pocket. Jane loaned her a pencil and watched her write "Breen's, 8," pressing hard, so that the pencil end snapped. Then she wrote "BH," lightly with the broken tip under "8," and returned the pencil.

"Vee! Come on!" beret lady hollered, not seeing the two of them as she hustled her boys onto the ferry toward a black sedan.

"Thanks for the smoke," Vee said. "See you tonight. Breen's at eight." She shook Jane's hand before she walked to the car, her fists clenched.

Jane watched her rejoin them, urging the three boys into a back seat. A big man with gray hair sat behind the wheel, facing the boys. Beret lady walked away from the car to the parking lot, her arms folded across her middle, her head down, dragging her right leg to the side.

Jane climbed back into Mac's Cadillac and wrote "8, Vee, Breen's" into her own notebook.

There was something interesting, sharp-edged, about the way Vee didn't bother with fussy girl things. Jane imagined looking like that when she got to be a girl again. Smart, more corners than curves—like herself. But not *off*, definitely not *off*. She was done being on the outside.

She pulled forward into an open spot on the ferry, handing Mac's dollar out the window to the attendant—collecting the change, putting it back into her pocket—and watched the other commuters pull in all around her, blocking her view of Vee's ride.

The white boat's motor groaned and its horn blew as they began to move.

Jane got out of the car and walked to the rail to admire the skyscrapers.

As the ferry cut through the waves, she looked up at the new Bay Bridge. A few helmeted figures walked up high on cables, nothing tying them to the span, inventing that bridge with every unharnessed step. Just last month one had fallen to his death, the twenty-second man killed in the project. She'd read that they planned to lose one man for every million dollars they spent. That made sense—only a couple dozen men dead to make this miracle bridge.

What fine work brave, smart men did in this place. Jane lifted her chin and filled her lungs, feeling brave and smart too.

I can take this city.

Then a gust of wind blew her stolen hat off her head and into the churning water below.

"BENNY!" Linda called from the switchboard where she sat with eight other girls, each in front of boards controlling cords that connected calls. "Look here!"

Linda was maybe twenty-five, a normal, healthy size, about five foot three and comfortable in her body. She wore a stylish wrap dress with ruffle cap sleeves and a tie around her waist, fashionable but cheap to buy and easy to sew, practical for a working girl who'd arranged no social plans after hours but who liked to look good in case something came up. Her dark hair was neatly pin-curled the way girls' hair was styled in the magazines. She had a dimpled chin and blackened lashes. She regularly pinched her cheeks throughout the day to avoid the cost of rouge. Jane wondered how it felt to be normal like Linda.

"Boss said to give you this." She handed Jane an empty envelope with "Mac" scrawled on the front. Jane knew it was for the leftover car repair money. She pulled the cash out of her wallet, slid it into the envelope, sealed it, and signed her name over the seal. Linda put it in her top drawer. "You can trust me." She dimpled and said, "I'll give it to him," causing the other switchboard girls to giggle.

Jane did trust her with the money. She wasn't interesting enough to distrust. As she walked away from the switchboard, she noticed how true that was of most of the girls who worked there, the typists, telephone girls, receptionists, and executive secretaries. Everywhere she looked she saw girls who looked healthy, like they had no history of hunger or illness, or even doubt. Sure, they were living in a depression and everybody felt it, drawing lines down the back of their legs instead of springing for hose, repairing lost buttons, trimming worn fringes rather than replacing them with something new. They grew carrots and peas on their back porches, drank home-made wine, put extra pallets in every rentable room. But still, they maintained an acceptable, middle-of-the-road normalcy because they had their jobs and their paychecks. And because of who they came from. They wore normalcy like skin, un-aware of it. That was the way most of the *Prospect* girls looked, frayed but fine. Not like the people standing in the soup line or sleeping on the sidewalk. Not like the Mexicans—except for Jorge. Why was that?—or the Chinese or Coloreds working in the basement on the presses or on the trucks delivering papers. Not like Jane used to look. Not like Vee.

Vee had a too-bare neck, like she had no clothes under her coat, like that was her only outer layer. Either way, whether because she didn't have anything to put below the coat or because she just didn't choose to, that wasn't normal. Her hair was so white, too white, like she'd bleached it in the sink. And her mouth so bumpy. Scarred. How would a girl get scars like that? Then she thought of the way Vee looked at her, like she knew her, and that seemed weirdest and most worrying of all.

She thought about Rivka and Sweetie. Rivka was completely authentic. Though she had weird in her, she wasn't showy or fake. Her thick accent put Jane in mind of onions, cooking onions, not spicy and raw but warm and savory, Jane's idea of what it must be to come from the Old World. Sure, that marked her as different, but in a familiar, earthy way. And she never seemed insecure about that difference. She'd been accepted at high levels, made normal by merit. *Was* it her merit that did that?

Sweetie wasn't normal, but she was an A-plus fake. She costumed herself so well that she was like the collector doll version of a real normal girl: hair, clothes, makeup, all recreated from the movies and magazines. Nobody ever eyed Sweetie and thought, What's she doing here? At least not until Jane herself had drawn their eyes at the opera workshop, when her mistake may have made them reconsider whether Sweetie fit after all.

The weirdest, least normal girl was Jane herself, pretending to be something she absolutely was not. Faking everything about herself. Hiding when she dressed, when she washed, when she peed. Hiding her body, her voice, her past, her family. She, who wanted to be seen as normal almost as much as she wanted to win. She wanted to be completely inside the *Prospect*'s machinery, its cogs and chutes, to pass through it easily and come out a well-known writer, one of them. And because she'd been succeeding so well at faking so hard, she had a good distance to fall. Anything could topple her.

Don't mess this up.

Jane didn't keep her eight o'clock date at Breen's with Vee.

She couldn't risk losing what she'd worked so hard to gain. Joining up in public with a girl like that, no matter how interesting she might be, would put eyes on the two of them, maybe make people see there was something off about Jane too. She didn't want to hurt Vee's feelings, but she had to protect her own position. She had almost no choice.

She went to Breen's with the bench guys at five thirty and stayed until seven, when she left to walk home with a safe amount of time to spare before Vee would cross that threshold.

LAMBERT performed his front-page story about a girl who'd been choked, beaten, and lay in a coma, reading aloud in his version of an Okie accent—"'The dust gets in yuh. Yuh cain't wash it off. That guhl was always cawfin' it up. Now she's choked on it.'" He clutched his throat, rolling his eyes back in his head. Then he slapped the half slip the quote was written on into Jane's chest, yelling "Giddyup, Boy!"

Ass, Jane thought, hustling with the paragraph through two dozen desks and the rolling chairs of coughing, barking men blowing clouds of smoke—cigarette, pipe, and cigar— yelling into telephone handsets and banging out paragraphs.

She ran with the half slip to the spine, the spiral staircase at the core of the building, skipping steps without touching the wrought iron rail, up into the barn-large third-floor composing room, where twelve operators rode the keyboard seats of gawky mechanical beasts, linotype machines, seven feet tall and two tons heavy, somewhere between a typewriter and a backhoe.

Three men in, she found Fred, a reedy, hunchbacked compositor whose gray skin said he normally ate his Spam sandwich right where he sat.

She passed Fred the half sheet. "Hope your fingers are loose, 'cuz Lambert's loquacious." She liked to use her new words here.

"Goody," Fred growled. "I love the sound of Lambert's voice." He stubbed out his cigar in a half-full coffee cup at his feet. "A little less than he does."

Fred put the paper on the dish over a three-color keyboard, capital letters in white keys on the right, lower case in black keys on the left, spaces and punctuation in blue keys in the middle.

Transcribing Lambert's copy, each of Fred's keystrokes called a letter down the beast's slide. They lined up into a die, which a black metal arm injected with 550-degree molten lead, refilled every so often from a boiling bucket at Jane's feet. The week before, a copy boy had kicked the bucket, really kicked it, burning his legs and creating an infection that killed him two days later. Jane kept her body parts a smart distance from that danger.

The metal letters became a slug, a single line of type another guy would pull out and place in a galley frame, together with all the other slugs, to make a column and then a page—*click-click-clink, shshshshshsh, clunk*—and then the tinkling of brass on brass as the matrices dropped back to start over.

Fred checked the first line's die, released it to the process and returned to the next line, all in a nice, natural rhythm. Fred was the meat in his machine, part of the bigger machine, and so on.

Fred said, "Shit," feeling a typo, and ran a finger on his right hand down two rows of keys, calling down the metal capital letters "ETAOIN SHRDLU" in the middle of the die, which would be cast into a bad slug, a sign to the proofreader to toss the line. It was faster to do a run-down like that than to fix his mistake when he made it. Jane aimed to rise in this place before somebody figured she was a bad slug and did what they had to do.

"Back to the mouth," Fred said, and she hustled toward the spine. She'd have to repeat this run between the second and third floors several times—the story was MTK, more to come. But she was glad for the gap between the last paragraph and the next, glad to move on to another idea. She didn't want Lambert looking in her face and thinking she was like the choked girl, with the dust in her.

The girl's friend was wrong, anyway. You could wash it off. And what did get in you, you could push right out, send it down the pipes. Some poor hicks didn't know how to do it, but Jane did. She'd cleaned herself thoroughly. She was smooth running now, in spite of the grit she'd had between her teeth and in her nostrils and under her nails when she got there, before she made herself new. She wasn't like the coma girl.

Lambert's next half sheet was sitting beside his typewriter by the time Jane got back. She read what she could as she ran it up to Fred. The girl had been found Saturday morning in the alley outside Breen's—Breen's! Where Jane had been that night. Where she went almost every night, with everybody else. Her body had lain just outside the door Jane passed through twice a day.

Seven times she ran up and down the spine with the little half slips of that story, reading the bits she could while she ran, short phrases, not sentences or paragraphs. In half an hour, she'd delivered the last half sheet from Lambert to Fred, growing more anxious as she went.

Fred pointed at the mess on the floor, and she gathered the discarded papers and reassembled them in what seemed like the right order so she could piece the whole thing together— Okie . . . eighteen . . . photo . . . unidentified man . . . crowbar.

Crowbar was a word she didn't like. Similar to *ditch*.

She tried but failed to stifle a coughing fit, valley fever reasserting itself.

"Get that checked, kid, jeez. Nobody wants to catch that."

"It's the smoke," she said, stuffing Lambert's half sheets into her back pocket.

Her fingers remembered the crowbar's feel.

Tucking her chin and blowing in and out her nose to stop the cough, she went back downstairs, sidestepping copy boys descending on the wadded half sheets, sandwich crusts, and cigarette ashes that covered the *Prospect's* floor at the end of the day.

She stepped behind a tall stack of boxes to reread the story without anybody watching. The girl's skull had been fractured, a crowbar left on the ground next to her body. The article said the girl—Vesta Russell—had been photographed before by a lady photographer working for the Farm Security Administration.

Jane had seen FSA people poking around campsites and fields, with union guys, stirring up trouble, nudging people to strike. The story said the photographer had hired the girl after taking the picture. It said the girl had gone to Breen's to meet someone at eight o'clock. Someone named BH.

Jane's throat and mouth burned yellow.

She had to see the picture.

She ran back to Lambert's desk, where she found him on the telephone, his back to her, pulling the cord as far as it could go for privacy.

She feathered piles of paper across his desk until she found the picture that went with the story. Holding it in her hands, the noisy room went silent, nothing but her fingers gripping the corners of a photograph of a man with two women and a baby.

She knew before she looked that she'd find a picture of Vee, and she did, but her eyes pulled her to the man.

She couldn't breathe.

The girl she ditched was in a coma.

Hit by a crowbar.

Pictured with Daddy.

Fuck!

She'd thought she could live in this new city, with a new name, new job, new body. New everything, but he'd returned to remind her who she was, who she'd always be.

She tried to calm her breathing, in and out her nose.

The dust gets in you, and you can't wash it out.

LET'S say you're some farmer, peas or spinach, and you've got yourself a tractor to work good soil near the coast. You inherited that land, that tractor, in a state where the banks aren't running people off dried-up dirt. You're a lucky man, you think. So you keep that tractor running every day, keep it well tended, because you're responsible, you take what you've inherited seriously. But the salty sea air all around your land gets inside your tractor's works, where you don't even see it, not your fault, salt rubbing every internal surface. And that salt air, laid on the cogs of a good, well-tended machine, doesn't dry up or blow off. No. It rusts out the interior of that tractor where you can't see it, so that one day it locks up, broke, and finally, all at once, you see how bad things have always been, even while you were riding that tractor in your rows in your fields in your state, all in spite of how carefully you thought you'd tended it and how well that tractor seemed to be running.

That's how it works, Jane saw.

DADDY stood in the middle of the picture. He wore a soiled white shirt, rolled at his elbows, and overalls, one strap hanging. His arm was wrapped behind the girl, his big brown hand cupping her shoulder, his fingers indenting her skin, his other hand gripping a banjo by the neck. His hair was pushed back, under a cap—she'd never seen that cap—his eyebrows raised in a question or a dare, the wrinkles between them like mountains on a map. He looked thinner. Also his mustache was gone. Maybe that's what made him look younger, like her, like Benny. When had she seen him last without his mustache? But there was that shovel-curved scar.

Somebody came right up behind her, and she went cold and turned to find Walt, the copy boy from San Mateo, looking over her shoulder, breathing heavier than usual from running up and down the stairs. He put his finger on Daddy in the picture. "I didn't know you played banjo."

"Go on!" She elbowed him in the ribs, and he ran off.

That *was* the face she saw in the mirror every morning. It looked like Jane-as-Benny standing there next to Vee. A taller Jane-as-Benny, minus the scar. She'd thought a lot about whether she looked like her brother, like Benjamin would have looked if she hadn't killed him, skipping over the more obvious thing—that with her hair cropped close like it was, dressed as a man, she looked like young Daddy. Anybody who saw the picture would know it.

On his left side was a weathered, hard-eyed woman holding a naked baby. On the right, the pale girl, Vee, glowed bright.

In the picture, Vee's hair was brownish-blond, pointy chin, bare neck, her dress fabric a familiar, washed-out floral, one lots of Hooverville women chose for sewing, the prettiest of all the cotton- or feed-sack patterns. Scraggly-haired, thin— too thin—one bare arm dangling, her hand empty, the other hand at her throat, her fingers wrapped around it. There were those scars on her full, chapped lips. Her eyes were light, blue or gray, and she looked straight at the photographer, blank.

Beautiful and blank. Not blank like she was empty, just like she wasn't giving anything away.

Lambert yelled, "Goddammit!" into the telephone, and Jane dropped the picture, shoving her hands in her pockets, turning her shoulder.

He poured a shot of whiskey, standing at his desk, drank it fast and slammed the glass down in a bang. Then he stepped away to the coat rack to put on his tie and jacket.

Wake up! Grab it! Go!

She slipped the picture in her pocket and ran for the spine.

———————•———————

CHAPTER FIVE

COMMUNICATION

Rivka stood at the top of their Clay Street steps with her hands behind her back.

"You are very late. We were supposed to meet Sweetie thirty minutes ago."

Jane had forgotten her own birthday dinner. She didn't want to go, couldn't act normal now. But she had to perform. Sweetie'd arranged this dinner, and Jane still needed to tend their relations after the opera interview. Getting along, having the acceptance of both her roommates was part of her plan.

"Let's go," she said, her gut burning.

Rivka bent and set a man's cap on the planter.

"What's that?"

"Somebody dropped it here on step. Leave it, in case he comes back."

It looked like the cap Daddy was wearing in the photo in Jane's pocket. She wanted to grab it, take out the picture, compare them right then, but she didn't. She couldn't let Rivka know about this, so she left the cap on the planter and the picture in her pocket and walked with Rivka, silent, to North Beach, feeling she might combust at every street corner.

He'd come to the door where she lived, looking for her.

She saw him in her head as she swung the crowbar the last time. She'd hit him, knocked him into the ditch. He'd never hit her. Could he have attacked Vee? Would he? She felt a sharp pain over her eye, that almond lump.

What are you afraid of?

She thought she was afraid that picture was recent, that Daddy was alive, that he was looking for her, that he'd beaten up Vee one block from the *Prospect* as a message to Jane. That somebody who looked at this picture would say, "Hey, that guy looks just like Benny Hopper." Afraid that Sweetie would see Daddy in the paper, think he was a killer, think Jane was a liar —"Your papa killed Daddy over Momma," Jane had told her. That Vee had chosen to talk to her on that pier because she recognized Daddy in her and that Jane had gotten her attacked, maybe killed by now. Everything Jane wanted, everything she'd earned, would be garnished.

But nobody else was going to see that picture because she'd taken it.

Still, she had to find out when it had been taken and where, who Daddy was to this girl, where he was now. If it had been taken recently, then she hadn't killed him in the ditch. He was alive, a suspect in this killing. If it had been taken, say, a year ago, it didn't change anything—no one would see it, and he was dead. No, wait. The cap on the porch. Either way, he was alive and looking for her. But either way, she wasn't a killer. Then she remembered her brother. Either way, she *was* a killer.

Still, she had to find him before he found her. She settled that in her head. She couldn't risk the *Prospect* and the girls and the flat.

This was what she considered on the walk to Isadore Gomez's Café on Pacific, so that by the time they arrived, she'd confirmed her plan—first find Daddy and fix it with him. She'd figure out what fixing it meant later.

AS they approached the café, she wondered why they'd worked so hard to go so far. It didn't look like a place you'd bring anybody for a special dinner. Up a narrow flight of stairs, they entered a smoke-filled room, broken plaster on the ceiling, wobbling chairs, and cracked oilcloth on the tables, no better than a truck stop. Then she got the fatty smell of steak and fries, and her mouth began to water.

The Portuguese owner, Izzy, sat down with them, belly hanging over his belt, the burnt citrus smell of sweat overtaking the table. Rivka asked him if he had the Russian stuff, and he said, "For you and your friend, sim!" He rolled his three hundred–odd pounds back behind the bar and returned with a bottle of vodka and poured it for them at the table with ice and lemon. Jane sipped, frowning at its bite, wondering why everybody loved the stuff.

Izzy said, "You'll have the fried chicken, son. She'll have the steak."

"I was thinking . . ."

"Don't think," he said. "Take it easy. Save thinking for old people."

Rivka told him, "Sweetie will be here soon."

"We'll set her up fast if she comes." Izzy pushed off the chair for the kitchen.

Rivka frowned. "She is coming."

Jane said, "I wanted the steak."

"Take the chicken. He never charges us, except two bits for grappa. Do not jinx it. Your accent is risky enough to damage his business."

"You have an accent."

"Mine is Prague. Better than Texas. Completely better."

Izzy came back around to refill their glasses, and they sat in an awkward silence for a few minutes until the vodka broke something loose and a wave of appreciation overtook Jane.

"I want to say I'm sorry. I know my being here stops you from doing things the way you . . . do them."

Rivka's face reddened. "What do you think you are interrupting?"

"I know y'all are close."

Jane said it plain. She'd heard about girls like them before. There were two Sacramento schoolteachers who lived together—Momma called them friendly sisters. She didn't care. Rivka and Sweetie had been pretty good to her.

"Do not say *y'all*." Rivka's mouth puckered up. "I practice at home in mornings."

"I've heard you."

"You have not heard what I mean." Now her cheeks puffed out like her mouth was full and she was choosing whether to spit or swallow. "Your being here has changed it. It has."

Jane had to work hard to keep things on an even keel with Rivka. Sweetie'd moved from easy, warm, friendly, accepting to pissy, in a general snit. Now Rivka's criticism hurt. Rivka could be hard work, and right now Jane was tired of it.

A plump girl delivered steak and green beans for Rivka, chicken and mashed potatoes for Jane, the smell of which took her back to Granny's table, with an oilcloth like the one here. She wanted to eat with her hands.

Rivka said, "I like, I need, to start in quiet, with what is simple, with just my thumb under my hand, and then my hand over thumb, a few movements each way, to get ready for scales and *arpeggios*, for thirty minutes."

She stopped to sip her drink, and Jane sipped hers too. The clean, harsh taste shaved fuzz from Jane's tongue, and she wondered if it did the same for Rivka, cleaned what she was saying. Jane picked up her fork. She couldn't wait.

"That is how I like to start."

"Simple. Every day." Jane nodded, chewing salty fried flour and flesh.

Rivka's skin darkened.

"It is important. I need my hand to respond to music but also to tone I want. Do I see red? It has to make that." Rivka closed her eyes and held out her hand, showing Jane. She hadn't touched her plate. "Do I see blue? Then it is this." She opened her eyes. Jane looked at her hand. "If I am after melody, I want weight of my arm on key, everything relaxed, this caressing pressure of fingers. Outstretched, flat, caressing fingers. I want to get this right. See, melody is story. If you want to tell story, your fingers go flat. But you make arched hand to tell something under story, something subtle, something maybe composer did not intend. But you do."

Jane couldn't see why something so abstract would upset her. Rivka made everything so precious. Jane knew about practice! Everybody did! And her stupid, fancy accent.

Rivka moved her head toward Jane, interrupting the fork in its path to her mouth.

"That is what practice is for. For applying your experience to reach your intention. That is what you are interrupting. You are ruining my expressive intent, and you are starving your own." Her normally dark eyes fired, glints of gold in the brown.

Jane set down her fork, her throat tight. "I'm a hard worker."

"I did not say you are not hard worker. I am saying you do not practice meaningfully."

"I practice. I've been writing my journal for years. Years."

"Journal, ha. I hum while I wash dishes, but is not practice. Is not purposeful. You are not purposeful."

"You never wash dishes, never! We always wash them." Jane flushed. "And I am purposeful. I always have a plan, always."

Rivka sneered. "You waste my time and resources."

"Waste? How am I a waste? What am I not doing?"

"You have plan for things you want, yes, anyone can sense that. But you do not attend to small things to get there. You are not disciplined. You are not careful or intentional. I hate to see how you fail to work intentionally. You have everything you need . . ."

"Everything I need? Really? You don't know what I have. You don't know what I need."

She felt something dangerous, tears welling.

"Is true. I do not know your history. But I know you have almost everything you need to be great writer, except character. Something essential is missing in you. You will never be great unless you grow this."

Jane shoved her plate away, banging it into Rivka's. "I thought you were trying to help me, but this is for you, not me. You're a bully. You think you can make me who you think I should be, like you're the one who knows. You think because you made Sweetie a junior assistant you can make me a writer? Well, how's that working for Sweetie?"

Izzy appeared at their table. "Speaking of . . . Sweetie called. She's booked tonight. She'll see you tomorrow."

"She planned this dinner." Rivka sounded suddenly weak.

He shrugged.

"Did she ask for me?"

"It was so loud in here." He looked away.

Rivka's lips quivered, changing the shape of her face.

Izzy slinked off, surprisingly nimble.

Jane didn't care how Rivka felt. Daddy's cap was the emergency.

"Has anybody been by the flat, asking for me?"

"Who would look for you?"

"No one, then?"

"No." Rivka rose from the table.

As Jane stood, Izzy handed her a short, corked bottle. "Happy birthday, Boy. Eighteen—you're a man now. Here's some Vitamin V, for the road," he said, and he slapped her back. She slipped it into her pants pocket with the picture and the half sheets.

Was she a man now? Manhood seemed so hard to earn, so easy to lose.

Izzy's fat hand squeezed the back of her neck. "When you come to a pool of water on a long road, don't make it muddy. If you pass that way again, you may be thirsty." He laughed, much bigger than the joke deserved, and returned to the bar.

"He says that to everybody. That is his thing to say."

Then Jane followed Rivka on the long walk home, fuming at her critic.

The downtown fog filled the air with actual drops, suspended, so that the smells from everybody and everything collected in each drop and what Jane didn't inhale wet the skin of her face like sweat. They walked down that crowded-at-night sidewalk all the way to their front steps on Clay Street, where Rivka turned to Jane and said, "He came back for his cap."

SHE slumped against the cabinet, her eyes closed, waiting for milk to warm in its pot.

He'd left his cap on her porch and returned to take it back.

He was talking to her.

She had to find him, not be found, had to go on offense.

But that would be tomorrow. Now she needed sleep. She'd drink her milk, drop into bed. In the morning she'd figure things out, adjust her plan. She poured her drink and headed to the sunporch.

It wasn't a proper room by other people's standards, she knew, no closet to speak of, but she only had one suit and one white shirt and one tie, and those she hung on nails she'd hammered into the wall. She kept her wingtips on the floor under the suit.

With the help of a kid she paid a nickel, she'd lugged her hope chest up from Uno's car to her room the first week she was there, and that's where she kept her Jergens, which she only used right before bedtime, so she wouldn't smell like a girl at work. That's also where she stored her clean skivvies and the cloth bandaging she wrapped round her breasts, which had begun to grow—all those years of wishing, and now they decided to sprout. She also kept the box of Venus Junior sanitary pads and the sanitary belt Sweetie bought her at the Owl Pharmacy in the hope chest for her time of the month. And her notebooks.

The presence of these things made the room personal, which she liked. But the door gave her privacy, which she'd never had before, and she relied on it, having a safe place to think. Her ideas about herself had gotten bigger in this place.

She walked through the door to her room to find Rivka hunched over the desk where she'd set Daddy's picture and the half slips.

"What are you doing?"

Rivka looked up, her cheeks flushed, standing in front of a big black typewriter, Jane's other stuff moved to the side.

"What's that?"

"So you can practice."

"When would I practice?" Her voice sounded like there was a row of tomatoes still to pick after her wrists above the gloves were already swollen with itch.

"Now," Rivka answered. "Nights. I told you. Practice. Intention."

"I don't know how to type." Jane spit it out.

"You will figure it out. So you will be ready." Rivka laid both hands on top of the machine, her long fingers pale against the black metal. "I see something in you, *tupý*. You need to be ready when moment arrives."

Jane looked at the typewriter, with its wide stance and forty-six-tooth underbite, the lever like a pencil behind its ear.

"You will succeed," Rivka said. "That is given. How good

will you be, is question. What are you aiming for? Where are you going with all this? Go further. Start now, practice."

Jane wasn't sure about the difference between being good and succeeding but felt swayed. It was powerful to be seen as special. Where *was* she going with all this? Despite what she wanted right now—to sleep—she wanted other things more. She sat and laid her fingers on the keyboard.

"Quick brown fox jumps over lazy dog," Rivka said. "One hundred times."

In spite of her tiredness, Jane began typing that stupid line, struggling and slow, with many errors, but intrigued. When Rivka left her room, she laid Martha Gellhorn's columns on top of a book under the hanging bulb and typed every word of every sentence, over and over, and after a while she heard piano music and knew Rivka was practicing, too, and they both kept it up until Martha's sentences came out of Jane's fingers, almost as if she'd chosen them herself—which she had—and then she began to write things not on the clippings, things about Daddy and Momma and her, and with Rivka practicing in the living room, her own words started to sound like a kind of music.

It went on that way until the window light changed to pinkish gray and the piano stopped.

She went down the hall and saw Rivka standing in the bedroom, her face in her hands, her shoulders shaking. Sweetie'd hurt her by not coming to dinner, then not coming home. Jane searched her memory of the things she'd seen in this flat, slights, messages forgotten, questions unanswered. She hadn't paid attention before as it wasn't about her.

She had little history of giving comfort or receiving it, having no real friends at home. It just wasn't possible as a white trash girl who wanted so crassly to move up above the others like her, a girl who hadn't had the things or the time she'd need to do it. Momma never showed her what comforting looked like.

There was only her Granny for that, when she was little.

≡ ≡

JANE would lie on her belly under Granny's kitchen table, sunshine lighting up the floor from the window over the sink. She'd color over Granny's old newspapers, arcing three-color rainbows of brown, orange, and blue, the only colors she had, neat and waxy. When she came across a word she liked, she wouldn't color over it, but would leave a white box open so that when she finished the picture she'd be left with a kind of mystery code she would then aim to crack.

Granny would crawl under the table with a glass of thick milk, look at the picture, pull Jane on her lap, and kiss her ear. "You'll get up over the buzzards."

SOME of Granny must have gotten in Jane because she felt sympathy for Rivka, who looked shrunken into a third of herself. Jane wrapped her arms around Rivka's shoulders and Rivka let her, turning her face and sobbing harder, loud and hoarse, her tears wetting Jane's shoulder for what seemed like quite a time, making Jane feel awkward. What was she supposed to do about this? Just stand there, waiting?

She thought of the few times she herself had really cried this way. Mostly she'd done it alone. But when she was young, she'd cried in front of Granny, who had rubbed her back until she stopped, then sat her down, said something simple, inviting her to spill the beans if she wanted. So she did what Granny had taught her, rubbing Rivka's back, whispering, "Must be awful bad." She felt Rivka nod her head, yes, and then shake it, no, as if she didn't know if it were bad at all. She wanted to pull away but also to do this comforting well, to be good at this moment. So she didn't rush, just kept patting Rivka's back and nodding agreement that what Rivka was upset about was either really bad or not.

Finally, after a good amount of tears, Rivka pushed away from Jane, who pulled a handkerchief out of her pocket, giving it to Rivka to wipe her eyes and blow her nose. Rivka stuck out her bottom lip and took a deep breath.

"I think you are in trouble."

"I am."

Rivka lifted her head, her eyes wet.

"A man is looking for me. I need you to tell me if he comes. He looks like me."

Rivka blinked twice, looking over Jane's shoulder. Jane turned and saw Sweetie standing at the door to their room, showered, in yesterday's clothes.

She couldn't read Sweetie's face—it was closed down, immobile.

Sweetie broke the silence. "You two are up at a strange hour."

"Ironic," Rivka said, wiping tears with the back of her hand.

Good, Jane thought. She's still got her edge.

Sweetie headed to the kitchen, and they followed her. She dropped the *Prospect* on the counter and started coffee.

Jane read the headline, "Beautiful Blonde Bashed at Breens."

———◦———

CHAPTER SIX

NEGATIVE

P ictures sell! You shoulda lost the story instead!"

She sat one spot off the hot seat, down the hall from Mac's office, where he was yelling.

"I'll fix it!"

"She gives it only to us—exclusively to us—and you lose it!"

The door flew open and Lambert plowed to his desk, Mac on his heels, his face red and unshaven, his eyes bloodshot.

Lambert looked about to eat the telephone receiver. "Gimme Grete Wright, the photographer, W-R-I-G-H-T! Grete Wright!"

He paced around his desk, knocking a coffee cup off the top as the cord whipped around.

"Hello, Mrs. Wright? Yes. No, we didn't. That was a mistake."

Mac squeezed the skin of his forehead—grip, release, grip, release.

"Could we trouble you for another print off the negative? Or the negative itself?"

Mac kicked a trash can.

"No, ma'am. Not a third time. Thank you, ma'am." He hung up and began making notes on a half sheet. "Boy!"

Hank Ikeda hopped up, scarecrow lanky. "Sir?"

"Get over to Berkeley, the lady photographer's house. Pick up the picture. Again!"

Hank beamed with the chance to cross the bay on an errand—any boy would—standing at attention at Lambert's desk, his fingers spread wide, ready to grab.

"You'll take the ferry and then the jitney when you cross— two bucks'll cover the round trip. Get it from Jorge."

"Yes, Mr. Lambert. No problem."

"Stop hovering!"

Hank sat again beside Jane.

They'd replace the picture. She'd only stolen a copy of it. Daddy would be in the paper. Someone would put Jane and him together, ruin everything.

She leaned in close to Hank. "Let me do it."

He swatted her away. "What's wrong with you?"

"Lemme take that job."

"Are you crazy?"

"I want that job."

"Forget it. I was up, he called me."

"What do I have to give you to let me take that job?"

"Stop it." He shoved her.

"I'll pay you." She was desperate. She'd borrow from Rivka to pay Hank.

"You'll get called up any minute."

Wally, on her other side, said, "Yeah, what're ya moanin' for?"

"Shut up, you!" She shoved him like Hank had shoved her.

She couldn't let the picture get back in Lambert's hand and on the front page. She had to get the original, the negative, so there could be no more copies.

Hank leaned into her, whispering, "I'm gonna sneak over to the diner, see my mom before coming back." His longish, shiny hair formed black points on his forehead, raking his eyelashes. His mother worked at a diner by day and cleaned offices at night at Castle Steele. He didn't get to see her much, and that seemed to bother him. He mentioned it sometimes. Jane did feel for him. But that wasn't her problem.

"I can help you get to your mom. You can count on me," she said, though he couldn't.

"Benny!" It was Mac, still at Lambert's desk.

Everybody on the bench looked alarmed at Mac calling Jane by name, not "Boy."

She was at his side immediately. "Sir."

"Mac. You're doing the errand."

She felt heat on her back from the bench. He was jumping her over Hank.

Lambert spit in the waste can. "We have a process."

Mac grabbed the half sheet on Lambert's desk, slapped it into her bound chest, and headed to his office. She followed, afraid, hopeful.

"You heard him, about the picture?"

Jane nodded.

"Get to Berkeley, pick up a new one from Wright, government photographer, the girl's boss. She's a ball buster, but it's no great thing."

Jane tried not to look surprised. Here was her chance.

He walked behind her and slammed his door.

"Then something extra." He scratched his nose. "After Berkeley, go by Sweetie's, pack a bag for her, put in her dresses, all her stuff in the bathroom, like that. Got it?" He blinked several times, fast.

"I, I don't . . ."

He blew out a big breath. "Don't be a drip, kid. All she's done for you? Just pack her bag. It's on a shelf over her closet. Take a cab—here's the cash, all the cash you'll need, and extra—leave the bags with the doorman at my place. Got it?"

So that was it.

Sweetie was his girl now. This was where she'd been when she hadn't come home, why she was preoccupied, absent. Sweetie liked powerful people. She'd liked Rivka, but now she'd replaced Rivka with Mac. Jane calmed herself. None of this mattered if it made it possible for her to get what she wanted. First the job, now the picture. So maybe Mac wouldn't be some boyfriend for her when she became a girl again. There were other men, lots of them.

"Make tracks!" Mac yelled.

"Yes, sir," she said, on purpose.

He squeezed her shoulder in a familiar way, and then she stepped out of his office, guilty, grateful, resentful, all of it.

She walked over to Altha, queen of typists. "I need a press pass."

Altha popped her gum. "That needs to come from someone higher on the food chain."

"Mac said."

Altha cocked a heavy-penciled brow and curled a card into her typewriter.

Jane grabbed Hank's hat off the hook where he'd left it.

THE jitney dropped Jane at a two-story house at the dead end of Virginia Street in the wooded hills over the university. The house was under construction, its doors and windows gaping holes. Two-by-fours, pipe, and corrugated tin were piled in the middle of the yard with drag marks from the pile to the street —hobos making use of scrap. She knew it didn't take much to make a one-season home.

The address out front didn't match what Lambert had given her, but she saw the right one dangling on a board on a waist-high metal gate to the right side of the wrong house.

She opened the gate, stepping onto a path of damp mulch, fruity and rot-smelling. Trees arched low. She put her hand on her head so she wouldn't lose Hank's hat to a branch.

A wailing sound blew through the path and through her, too, spiking doubt.

Still, she walked the length of the construction site's front and back yards to a second gate, passing through, pretending she had a right, thinking, This is what a reporter does.

She entered a sunlit lawn sloping to a house of redwood and stone with peaks, towers, flowerpots, brick trim, and leaded windows open to the breeze, a fairy-tale house.

An awful harmony of cries flowed out its windows.

She considered turning around, heading back down the hill to University Pier to catch a return ferry to the paper—she could make an excuse, explain it.

Baby, baby, suck your thumb, said the voice in her head.

"I ain't some baby," she whispered.

Shoulders back, chin up, she climbed the porch steps.

The door opened before she could ring the bell.

"Saw you coming," said the girl at the door.

She had wavy, bark-colored hair in a messy bun. Her eyebrows were thickly disheveled over irises nearly as dark as her pupils. It was hard to tell her age, twenty, maybe. She wore a black cotton dress, an apron, and low shoes, scuffed. The maid, Jane thought.

"I'm Benny Hopper." She could barely hear herself over the caterwauling.

The maid looked her up and down.

"Give it back!" pierced the air inside, but the maid didn't wince.

Jane continued. "I'm a reporter."

The maid let two of Jane's heartbeats pass before saying, "What? At the *Berkeley High Jacket?*"

Why'd she think she could do that? A maid to a reporter?

Jane pretended not to hear the insult. "The *Prospect*." She tipped her stolen hat with its fake press pass tucked into the brim.

The maid smirked, backing up, sweeping her arm behind her.

"I'm sorry about Miss Russell's trouble," Jane said, aiming to get back on track.

"I just got here," the maid said over her shoulder. "We never met."

She was not like maids in the movies.

Jane followed her into a woody entry, then down into a sunken living room.

They passed a wall-wide stone fireplace, over bare floors, waxed to a high shine, like some kind of chapel. The heel clops of Jane's discard-bin wingtips echoed.

The maid paused to pick a pencil up off the floor below a white canvas chair—canvas, like her family's tent—next to a small table with two big books, under a painting thick with dark colors and a framed photograph of shadows on a building. Jane picked up a piece of driftwood that sat on top of the books.

"Don't touch that," the maid said. "Mrs. Wright won't want you touching her things."

A piece of wood?

She hadn't studied for this, didn't know the rules that would govern the choices Mrs. Wright had made, furniture so plain in a place like a church. It drew her. She thought, Maybe this is how it'll be when I'm famous. I'll have a home that's beautiful and strange, like this.

The girl led her to double pocket doors, where the noise came from, and turned to look at Jane again, at her mouth and throat, the places people always looked. Jane never knew she had a pretty mouth, a smooth neck, until she became a boy and wasn't supposed to have them. When she was a girl, people'd always looked at her feet and hands.

"Once more unto the breach." The maid opened doors into a room writhing with life.

In the middle were a large table and a dozen wood chairs —it was a very big kitchen—two of the chairs knocked over onto an Indian rug. On the table's top, two boys wrestled, the bigger one on his back, holding a wooden sword up away from his body, the littler one on top, grabbing at the sword and slugging the kid who had it. Both of them were crying. No one got between them to stop it. They were the boys from the auto ferry.

Jane felt the walls move in around her, giving her less room to breathe or move. So many unconnected things gathering in this way. She'd known these people were related—she'd seen them at the dock—but now she felt that connection, close as a pillowcase over her head.

A compact man with short, fair hair and rimless eyeglasses stood in the room's right corner, bouncing the third boy, the littlest, too hard. The boy was howling, his face wet with snot. The man's khaki pants were pressed, his cream shirt spot-free, for the moment.

In another corner, near the stove, was a doll-sized, pixie-haired woman in a long, white belted dress with colorful, flowery stitches along the top, like Mexican women in schoolbooks, silver beads at her neck and a wide silver band around her wrist, her face bare but for red lipstick, the tiny lady from the pier, the mother. Was she the one who earned the money for all this? Was it her pictures that bought it all? Or did the money come from the beige man?

Grete tilted her head up, emphatically directing a second man, tall, with a gray beard and a high, round forehead, who gestured with a smoking pipe in his hand. He hunched down, getting his ear closer to her mouth.

A big-tongued retriever ran around the table, happy, as retrievers are, no matter the circumstances.

The maid yelled to the tiny woman, "Mrs. Wright! Reporter –name of Hopper!"

The dog ran over and jumped on Jane, its two great paws hitting her belly and knocking her hard to the floor, so that she was a little bit hurt and a good deal embarrassed.

"Down!" the little woman, Grete, yelled at the retriever,

and she moved around the table, sliding her right foot beside her. "Passion controlled is power, stupid dog! A poodle might understand that!"

The dog ran off and Grete grabbed Jane by the forearm and pulled, all six feet of her, until she was vertical again. Jane blushed to be helped by this little woman.

Everybody—the three boys and the two men—looked Jane's way. The attacker boy hopped off the table and stood, sniveling, just before her. The victim boy sat up, removing owlish glasses to wipe his eyes, and then replaced them to stare. The littlest boy clamored until the tidy man set him down, and the dog rushed up to lick the snot off the kid's face. The pipe-smoking man crossed his arms and puffed.

"I'm from the *Prospect.* Sorry about your assistant, Vesta Russell."

"Obviously I know the name of my assistant, Mr. Hopper."

She's mean, Jane thought. But that don't make her special—*doesn't.*

"I'm here for the picture," she said, not letting her voice rise or drop on "picture," trying not to let on how much she wanted it. She couldn't track everything that might happen because of that picture.

There was a second of quiet before Grete yelled, "Quincy! Paul!" She waved her arms. "Get the boys to the car."

"Darling," said the tidy man in glasses. "Why don't you let me . . ."

"I'll take care of it, Paul."

"I hate for him to waste your . . ."

"I am honest when I say, I can handle this. Then I'll get back to work."

Paul glared at Jane. "Please don't waste any more of my wife's time than you absolutely must. You don't understand what you're interfering with."

She did a lot of interfering, it seemed.

Paul's eyes darted between Grete and Jane.

"Quincy." Grete turned now to the bearded man. "We're agreed?"

Quincy looked like a big kid costumed for a play—pipe, beard, wool cap, patches on the elbows of a tweed jacket. He arched one eyebrow high into that shiny forehead, and Jane's sense of his faking it made her even more aware of her doing the same. Of everybody faking really, everybody but the kids. They seemed real.

"Of course," Quincy said, showing gray, crooked teeth through his smile. "The boys need distance from the crisis." He folded his hands over his belt buckle, in an almost prayer. "We'll spend some time near the shore, air out their troubles."

His smile raised Jane's hackles.

He stepped closer, took Jane's hand and shook it, covering it on the knuckle side with his other big, soft hand. He looked her in the eye, the appearance of respect. "So nice to meet you, Mr. Hopper," he said, though they hadn't really met.

He made a little bow toward Grete and turned to the beige man with a salute—"Professor." Then he put his arm over the older boys' shoulders. The shorter of the two shimmied free.

Quincy rolled his eyes. "Come on, stinkers."

The kid turned toward Jane, his cheeks furious red.

Quincy said, "They're sensitive."

"Bear up!" Grete said. "We'll see you next month."

Paul and Quincy together ushered the boys out of the kitchen and the house.

"Thank God," said the maid. "A person can finally think."

Grete said, "Go!"

"Cropped out entirely. Such is my lot." And she left.

"What was your name again?" Grete asked.

"Benny Hopper."

"Hopper." Grete tilted her head. "From the *Miner*."

"The *Prospect*."

"Right. Sorry."

Sorry she misspoke? Sorry Jane was from the *Prospect*?

"You lost the picture?" Grete asked.

"I didn't lose it."

"What did you do with it?"

"I mean, I have nothing to do with it. It is lost. By some-one else." Grete was blaming her, like she knew it was Jane's fault.

"Little inconvenient for me, having to make a new one."

"Mr. Lambert said you could give me the negative," Jane said, making quick work of it.

Grete squinted. "Is that what he said?" She turned and walked toward the back wall, sliding that foot, talking as she went. "The negative is mine. I'll give you a picture—again— not the negative, obviously. I'll want brownie points in return."

The picture wasn't enough. She had to get the negative to stop this.

Grete reached into a leather bag on a hook near the back door.

"Sloppy operation you've got over there." She shook a big ring of keys—making a jingly sound like the look of her jewelry and belt—and opened an interior door into darkness, pulling a string overhead, lighting a stairwell.

Jane followed her down, ducking her head, gripping the rail. At the bottom, they made a U-turn and faced a small, square basement with a set of piers in the middle. It was dark and cool. On the two sidewalls were casement windows close to the ceiling, so Grete didn't need to pull the second light string. The space was full of stacked boxes, creating little walls, little rooms. There was one door in the middle of the back wall, with a padlock, deadbolt, and handle lock.

Grete led Jane there.

Each box-walled room they passed had a label scrawled in chalk on the concrete floor before it—"sidewalks," "fields," "machines," "architecture," "portraits." The last entry, just before the darkroom, read "bodies," provoking a whole-body shiver in Jane.

Grete used three separate keys to unlock the door, which opened to a long, shallow, pitch-black room. She pulled another ceiling chain that turned on an overhead light, over a counter with a sink. On the left on the counter was a pile of blue leather notebooks. Next to those were three rubber bins marked "D," "S," and "F" and dark brown jugs whose labels Jane couldn't read. There was also a tall machine that looked like a monster camera. Over the counter, where the fourth casement window should have been, the wall was hung with dark fabric. Pinned to the fabric was a piece of paper with blue handwriting: "The contemplation of things as they are, without substitution or imposture, without error or confusion, is in itself a nobler thing than a whole harvest of invention."

Grete said, "Francis Bacon."

"Ma'am?"

"The philosopher."

"You contemplate things as they are down here?"

"It's what I'm aiming for. Mostly. I mean a photograph isn't life. It isn't fact. If it's good, it's closer to truth."

"How can it be true if it isn't fact?"

Grete nodded, smiled, as if surprised to find Jane had a thought in her head.

"A photographer is like a historian, really. We choose how to frame what we look at. Fact is what we aim at. But by choosing to include some facts, and not others, we alter our viewers' understanding of the facts. We show them what we find to be true."

"So your pictures tell half-truths."

Grete shook her head, disappointed. "I find it nobler to distill something important than to clutter a picture with irrelevant facts."

That's convenient, Jane thought. But she understood the concept, of course. It was familiar.

Grete turned, blocking Jane's view as she opened a file drawer, thumbed through it, and pulled a negative framed by stiff white paper out of a waxy envelope. Then she flipped a light switch and pulled the chain, turning off the regular overhead lights. The room glowed golden. She slid the negative into a slot in the machine, put paper below, pushed a button, and shone the negative's picture onto the paper. An image immediately appeared on the paper at Grete's fingertips and then disappeared. Grete carried the again-blank paper to the tub labeled "D," dropped it in, swished it with tongs, and the picture reemerged. She picked it up by its edges and dropped it into the "S" tub, swirling it around. Then to the third tub —"F"—rinsing it. She took it out and shook a four-by-five-inch print of Daddy, Vee, the baby, and the other lady.

"*Family*," Grete said. "That's what they called it."

"Who?"

"The *Examiner*. When they published it."

Grete clipped the photo onto a wire hanging over the counter.

"Things as they are," she said. "Or were."

She returned the negative to a drawer. Jane couldn't see which one.

"Without substitution or imposture?" Jane asked, carefully pronouncing the last word so as not to give it too many syllables.

"Always."

"Things ain't always black and white," Jane said. *Ain't* again. She hated the way it popped out, disruptive. "Are they really a family?"

"Good question. Very good." Grete smiled. "You'll find all kinds of gray in my photographs. Which is a way of suggesting the truth—people are so unknowable."

Jane looked at the picture, thinking of the last time she'd

seen Daddy—of his being so willing to turn on her. Was it the drinking? Her swinging the crowbar?

"Would Mr. Bacon consider you more a facts fellow or an inventor, Mr. Hopper?"

"I'm a copy boy," Jane said, piercing her own balloon, sensing that was the move.

"Copy boy . . ." Grete nodded, looking up above Jane's head, squinting. "As Mr. Browning says, 'A man's reach should exceed his grasp, or what's a heaven for?'"

Jane gave nothing away, though she agreed with Mr. Browning.

"Or did you lie about your job before because you're concerned about being judged? Don't worry! I know something about that! I hate being judged, but I rely on it too. I love to find out I've won!" She laughed again, a high laugh.

Bitch, said the voice in Jane's head, and she winced, but the word prodded her.

"Is one of the men upstairs your kids' daddy?"

"Ah, my marital history. That would take too long to explain." Grete unclipped the photo, shaking it and then tucking it in her pocket.

"You farm your kids out?"

"Why would you ask that?"

She couldn't admit seeing them at the pier.

"You said, 'See you in a month.' You said, 'Bear up.' Is that because you give them to the bearded guy?"

Grete narrowed her eyes. "I have them cared for so I can work."

Jane's jaw ached. Though she'd seen and experienced much worse than that, Grete's sending her kids off when she didn't have to got a steep rise out of her, maybe because she'd like to live Grete's life, have her home and her choices. Or maybe she related more to the kids than to the mother.

Ain't right.

"Most women wouldn't make that choice."

Grete's eyes narrowed on Jane. "You would be surprised what they would do if they had the choice. But then you're a man, so you know nothing about it."

She reached out and rubbed Jane's cheek with her thumb. Jane jerked her face away.

Grete puckered her lips, nodding decisively. "Do you have a cigarette?"

Her hand shaking, Jane reached for her Luckies.

"Not in here, never in a darkroom."

Grete left the negative in its drawer and locked up.

Jane followed her through the basement, up the stairs, into the kitchen.

Grete returned the keys to the bag on the hook and led Jane out onto the lawn.

Grete inhaled as Jane lit her cigarette. "Marriage, families are complex. My own father left when I was twelve. It was my polio." She lifted one dark-booted foot out from under her gauzy skirt, twirling it once, slow. A silver bar climbed up its leather sides, glinting in the sun. "My mother was too self-interested to do much for me."

Jane thought of Momma, who'd always expected something of her but hadn't explained what or how.

"So. Because I wanted to get out of that household, I walked all over New York, by myself, all day, every day, with my bad foot. I skipped school to do that. School was never as useful to me as my walks."

Jane put Grete's beaky face on the body of a soft, limping girl. Something shifted slightly when she did that.

"That created me. Entirely. My polio, my walks and my disinterested parents created me." She shook ashes into the breeze. "Walking in the terrible parts of my city, I learned how to see what things are." She looked done, as if she'd explained everything.

"You mean your idea about what things are."

"I have a strong sense of what things really are."

She looked down at Jane's feet, then up at her hands, making Jane want to put them behind her, protect them from evaluation.

"A very strong sense. As much as any other photographer, really. I know that must sound wrong, a woman saying such a thing."

It is *wrong.*

"But if you lay my pictures down, side by side, with any of the others—Walker Evans, Arthur Rothstein, Russell Lee, the rest of them—without putting our names on the pictures, I think you might find that mine, comparatively, show very well what things are. I think you might even judge me the best at what the group of us do."

Jane's heart pounded. So ambitious. She said these things aloud, like she believed it acceptable to say them.

Jane's own desires shimmered, possible. Still, Grete was awful.

She's working you.

"Where was *Family* taken? And when?"

"I sold it to the *Examiner* a year and a half ago. It brought in a lot of government money, I might add."

A year and a half. Jane still might have killed Daddy. No— the cap.

"Who are the people in it?"

"You mean Vee? That's who the story's about, isn't it?"

"You told Lambert about her already, that you hired her after you took the picture. What about the other ones?"

"Makeshift family."

"What do you mean, makeshift?"

"Spontaneous, transitory grouping, I think."

"Grouping?"

"Why do you want to know?"

"For the story."

"Right," Grete said. Then she pulled the picture out of her pocket, looking at it. "He looks a lot like you."

There was almost total silence, just traffic in the distance, birds in the big tree.

"I don't see it."

"You don't see it."

Take control.

"How'd you find them?"

Grete dropped the picture back in her pocket and clasped her hands.

"I work slowly, come on a picture one step at a time, looking for the person with a secret. The noisy ones, so eager to tell me everything, they're fine. I enjoy taking their pictures and talking with them." Grete waited then. "But the one who looks at me out of the corner of her eye, standing outside the circle, that's the one I want. I just stick around. Sit on the ground with people, let the children touch my prop camera, get it filthy with their dusty hands, smudging the lens." She began to grimace but stopped herself.

Was Daddy the grimy one? The interesting one, looking out the corner of his eye?

"Then I ask for a favor, a bit of cloth to clean my camera, a drink of water. And while they watch me use these things, I tell them about myself. I show them I can be trusted, long before I ask anything of them. Before I take even one picture. Because I know if I behave in a generous manner, the pictures I get are worth it. Usually the outsider centers the picture."

Jane put both hands in her pockets, clenching her fists, like she had coins to protect. "This is how you trick poor people into giving up what they got?"

"That's funny," Grete answered. "You should know better. The fact they're poor doesn't mean they're stupid. Vee made a deal that I would take her on as my assistant. The man was

more efficient. Wanted money right then and there to b̲e̲ ̲.̲.̲.̲
the picture." Again she squinted at Jane.

Would he ask for money? Yes, he would.

"Of course I don't do that. This is documentary work. I am
a conduit. I deliver a real moment in time to art, through which
people can see what's real. Payment would ruin it, put everything, its use, at risk. When I move people with my pictures,
like this one"—she patted her pocket—"I help hungry people."

"I've eaten guv'ment guilt." Jane let her accent all the way
out, wanting to puncture Grete's preciousness, all that hot air,
like hungry people didn't need money. Just needed their picture taken and the gift of a meal.

"Yes." Grete smiled and nodded. "So you have. You understand then, it would be wrong for me to stay home, stop sharing what I see with the world." She said it as if she cared what
Jane thought. "And you can see how my children can, themselves, become who they want to be, who they should be,
without relying every day on me to spread things out before
them. You see that, don't you, Benny?"

"I know people who get what they want without their parents doing anything to help."

"Not in spite of their parents' distance. Because of it."

"That's handy."

"And true. You are entirely what you make yourself. That's
it. If you point yourself at a truly fine ideal, then your hard
work and focus will lead to excellent things."

Jane thought of Grete's boys, carted away by Quincy. She
saw it was strange, the time Grete was taking with her.

"Where'd you take that picture?"

"Along the Sacramento River."

"Did you see the other woman or the man again?"

"Never. They're probably traveling the highway, probably
all the way south, to San Diego, by now. No way to tell."

Jane got out her notebook, started scribbling.

"Someone like you must find it hard, Benny, bumping up against the ceiling over at that inferior paper."

Ceiling? She was one step up from the basement.

"You could do good work with someone like me, in a line like this. I'm looking for an assistant."

Vee's spot. She could benefit from Vee's attack.

"I have a job."

Grete laughed and dropped her cigarette on the grass, crushing it. "You are a strange, unlikely boy. But that does make you interesting."

I'm interesting, she thought.

Don't be a sucker.

She'd moved the conversation too far from the picture again. Jane pulled herself back to something they hadn't spoken of but which now seemed important.

"Where's the baby?" she asked.

Her own sister or brother must have arrived months ago. Her twin dead eighteen years.

"How would I know?"

"Don't you . . ."

"Good luck at the *Examiner*, Benny." Grete plucked the picture out of her pocket and let it flutter to the ground. "Go in over your head, if you want to be good."

"It's the *Prospect*."

Grete walked away, her voice floating back to Jane—"You'll have to keep showing me your hat so I'll remember who you are. Benny Hopper. Benny Hopper. Benny Hopper." Then, when she was stepping back onto the porch, Jane heard her say, "BH."

HER breath quickened.

She saw a frog on a rock at the edge of the lawn, heard a bee in a tree overhead.

Things got unnaturally clear.

It was the way she'd said, "Good luck at the *Examiner*, Benny," that did it, the way she'd called Jane's paper by its wrong name—the *Examiner*, not the *Prospect*—right before mouthing the fake name Jane gave her.

Like the preacher going on about the sin of pride while she sat in the first pew next to Granny, polishing a painted-gold track medal in her pocket with her thumb.

Grete knew she was a fake.

She'd been caught lying before, naturally, lots of little things. But this was different. This was a challenge to her job, her reputation, her family.

Fine, she thought. She knows you're a fake. This is good, better to see that. She may pretend to like you, may see something in you. She may even be like you. But she's your enemy. Now you know it for sure.

These hormones flowing through her body, this almost rage of righteous self-defense, clarified things.

I won't run, she thought. I'll fight.

She picked her second copy of the picture up off the grass. As long as the negative existed outside her possession, somebody could call it back, summon the spirit, and everybody could see at any time she was connected to Daddy, who was connected to Vee.

She looked up at the house and saw through a stairwell window that Grete was on her way upstairs, moving fast with that lame foot

Jane pocketed the photo and walked to the kitchen door, turned the doorknob, and entered the house, no squeaking, no echo, through the entry, the living room, to the kitchen.

She opened the leather bag hanging on the hook, took the key ring from a pocket inside and headed through the basement door, down the stairs, without turning on the light, feeling the wall as she went, so cool and earthy she tasted dirt. At the bottom, casement windows lit her way to the darkroom.

She was scared but excited, too, not at the danger but at what she was doing to Grete, beating her. If she'd looked at it directly that way, she might have turned back, seeing how much of this was unrelated to what she really aimed to accomplish. But things underneath were more powerful than what lay on top.

She tried three keys on the padlock before one worked. Next she hunted for the key to the deadbolt, which she found after four tries. Then she had the door lock open after two keys, and she finally was alone in the darkroom, feeling almost better it hadn't opened easily. She'd earned her entrance.

She waved her hand in the air in front of her, and when the hanging string brushed her fingers, she pulled it, turning on the overhead amber bulb, and closed the door.

There on the counter were the notebooks. She picked one up and flipped through it. In one section, each graph-paper entry started with a code—SRH0336, OH0135, SH0836. Below the codes were a few sentences, recorded in a tidy, up-and-down script, in pencil.

"Who we gonna fight?"

"Every damn bird's got a nest."

Just some sticks, twine, leaves, could do it. She knew that nest longing. The words sounded like her people, before—Not anymore, she thought, exaggerating the diction scrub she'd achieved. The cadence of their words, the wrong verbs with the right nouns, made her melancholy, and she wanted to take the notebook but denied herself, putting it back where it belonged without looking further. It wasn't what she'd come for.

She turned to the drawers below the counter on either side of the sink, pulling open the one on top left. Inside, date-labeled folders were full of envelopes. She picked one up and saw it held negatives, transparent, brown, framed by white cardboard. Two of the folders in that drawer were labeled "09/12/35" and "09/29/35." She closed it and moved to a drawer one below it. "1936." She opened the drawer and pulled out the first file, thick with envelopes, pouring them on the counter. She tried to see through blurry covers little bits of time, vague behind wax and amber, smelling of dissolution.

Thump—the back door to the kitchen opened overhead, a male voice asked a question, a high female voice answered, both laughed. Jane leaned in to the counter, searching.

She heard the front door open and steps echoing from there to the kitchen.

She moved to the corner of the counter and thought she'd found the right one, but when she opened the envelope, no, another dusty family. She put those back in the envelope.

Thunk. Thunk. Feet overhead, in the kitchen. More voices. One louder than the rest.

Be more mechanical, more logical, she told herself. This is something anyone can do.

She touched an envelope, glanced at it, moved it to the right when it was wrong, again and again, moving envelopes to the right, before she finally saw it. There he was.

The voices upstairs grew louder, arguing.

She put the right envelope in her jacket pocket, the others back into the file folder, the folder back in its space in the drawer.

She heard Grete's high voice overhead, agitated, "Keys."

She pulled the string and darkened the room.

She locked the padlock, the deadbolt, the door lock, and left the keychain hanging in the door. She rushed over the chalk word, "bodies," into the closest box-walled room. She climbed up three boxes to reach the latch of a casement window. She'd come to steal the negative of Daddy, but now she wanted more of what was Grete's, wanted Grete not to have it. She slipped her hand into the open top box, grabbed a handful of envelopes, and put them in her breast pocket.

What Grete had was what Jane had come for.

She hoisted herself up and out, into the side yard, pushing

the window closed after her, and ran through the yard and the shady path, past the first house and into the street, all the way down the hill, loot in her pockets.

Waiting at the Berkeley pier, she pulled out a negative, holding it up to the light. A little girl, maybe five years old, riding a horse. Her hair was wild, long, curly, flying behind her. No saddle, her legs and feet bare. In the background were dirt and tumbleweeds and mountains.

She looked at the next one.

A foot, held aloft in the sky, as if its attached body were lying on the grass. The foot had soft, tended-looking skin. It was curled up into itself, fetal. It reminded her of a girl in a story she'd read, a girl whose feet were bound to make them look smaller, prettier in shoes, to keep her from walking far. That foot hadn't stopped Grete.

She pulled out another.

A skeletal man on an overturned bucket, propped up against a tree, his face turned to the side so you could see every bone in his cheek, his jaw, around his ear, even the shape of the teeth under his lips, gray, like he was part of the bark. But his eyes faced the camera, directly level with his face. Grete must have knelt on dirt to get him, eye-to-eye, that way. Jane turned the negative over and saw the word "Hunger" in pencil on the frame.

SHE'D had to take the risk. The greater risk lay in not getting the negative. Of course that didn't mean she also had to take the extras, but she wasn't going to consider that now, bogging down like some people did, worrying over what was done.

She wanted to really go through the pictures but not on the ferry or the jitney to Sweetie's for the suitcase, per Mac's instructions. While she was there, she'd spread the pictures out, see what they were, figure it out, make a plan.

She paid the driver from Mac's wad of cash and stepped out, entering without a sound, like a burglar.

Inside the door, at the bottom of the stairwell, she heard the girls in the kitchen.

"You promised!"

"No! You promised!"

Why weren't they at work?

Should she sneak up to their room, take the suitcase, with them next door in the kitchen? Could she do that? What would he say if she came back without doing it?

"I do care!"

Jane took two silent steps up the stairs.

"Used me!" Rivka cried.

Jane took another step, ashamed of them for having this fight, ashamed at herself for listening. Maybe she should get out, explain her failure to Mac, honor the streak running through her that hated useless displays of emotion. She stepped backward once on the stairs.

"Please!"

Another step.

Sweetie said, "You have Jane."

Jane stepped back wrong, into space, nothing beneath her foot, and felt herself fall. She grabbed at the rail before she went all the way down, clattering.

She looked up at both girls at the top of the stairs, Rivka's face ashen, Sweetie's glossy pink.

She did the math, got quickly to the bottom line.

"Sweetie, let's go."

SWEETIE sniveled into her kerchief in the cab's back seat.

"Mac needs me to settle him, make sure the world doesn't take too much. People take from him all the time. He needs me to be the one who doesn't."

"What in Sam Hill does that mean?"

"You're young. You don't know . . ."

"I know cow pie when I step in it. You're quitting Rivka after she did everything for you, got you a job, paid for your home, your food, clothes! Stupid!"

"Then why are you taking me to Mac's place now?"

"Because you're what Mac wants, and it's best for me to do what he wants." She hadn't said anything more honest for months. "It's best for me. That doesn't mean I think you should do it. What about your job? What about designing costumes? You ain't quitting work, are you?"

"Aren't! Will you never learn? And this is not a choice!" She turned and said this to the window. "It's . . . it's like I'm submitting to gravity, only a thousand times stronger. To try to pull myself up would be impossible."

"Oh, gawd. Does Mac feel the gravity too? Does he?"

Sweetie sighed and dropped her hands.

She disgusted Jane now. All that helper talk was claptrap. Sweetie was moving up by abandoning Rivka for Mac.

She didn't compare that to what she herself was doing.

Mac had never been Jane's, not even close, but she'd liked being near him, the senses that rose up in his company, wishing he would choose her, someday. She'd known it was all but impossible, given the Benny charade, but she'd seen him, underneath, as a potential someone for her. A trophy. Instead he'd used her to get Sweetie. She'd used him, too, to get this job. It got confusing when she spread it out. That's why she rarely did it. Why she tried to keep things in their own piles.

Never would have worked.

Then Rivka. Sweetie said Rivka had her? Rivka didn't have her! Nobody had Jane unless she decided they did. She felt some guilt about the typewriter, about Rivka's guiding her, but still she knew it did no good to linger on things.

When the car stopped at Mac's, Sweetie turned back to

her. "What you've done can't last forever. A person can't go on being what she isn't."

"You make costumes, Sweetie!" Jane yelled. "Costumes!"

"Make fun of me all you want. I don't care! I don't even care about your lie—you know what I mean! I gave you a chance, knowing the people you come from, but the apple doesn't fall far from the tree. I never believed you! You're not believable! This is going to come out!" Then she slammed the car door and ran into the foyer of Mac's apartment.

She don't matter.

Jane gave the driver the *Prospect's* address.

She had more important things to think of.

As the cab rumbled over potholes, she pressed negatives against the backseat window but kept returning to *Hunger*, the man so eerie, exposed. She saw the picture was beautiful, but even its beauty seemed dirty. Grete had done what she said— captured a real moment in time and delivered it to the viewer. A picture like this would affect people, probably already had. It made her think of Granny, in the hospital at the end. It was tiring, keeping so much stacked away. She'd figure it out later.

SHE ran up the spine, past the second-floor copy bench and reporters' desks, to the third floor, hustling past the compositors—"Got something?" "Nah!"—straight to the corner, where a photo guy, Fleming, sat at a desk in front of the darkroom, hunched over a comic book.

Jane straightened her hat, fake pass still in its brim, identity in place.

Fleming threw a newspaper over his comics when he heard her approach, but then smiled when he saw who it was. "Hey! Promotion!"

"Can't keep a good man down," she said.

"That's the spirit! A little surprising . . ."

"Fleming, I need some darkroom instruction. I'm writing something where the picture itself is the story. The art and science of it. Can you show me how you do it?"

"Art and science? Heck yeah! 'Bout time somebody paid attention!"

He opened the door to the darkroom, and she followed him in.

"You gotta use your whole brain for this."

"Show me." She held out the negative.

He held it up to the light. "How'd you get your hands on this?"

"Turn it into a picture."

Fleming's enthusiasm filled the darkroom with bubbles of delight—*glisten, pop.*

"Wright—oh man! She's good. I mean, not at developing. She's no artist there. But taking the pictures? Yeah. Used the Graflex for this one. Single-lens reflex camera. See, she looks down through this black leather hood." He hunched his shoulders and dropped his head to act it out in the posture of a buzzard. "She looks through the lens that'll expose the film. A mirror projects the image up, and then it flips out of the way when she presses the shutter. It's got film packs that can be exposed real fast, by pulling paper tabs. Makes these nice big negatives, four by five, two times bigger than her Rolleiflex, which . . ."

She found it hard not to stare at his bobbing Adam's apple and pimply cheeks, growing redder the more excited he became about the Graflex. He had a face for the darkroom.

"Actually, I don't need all the details. Just the simple steps."

"I thought you wanted . . ."

"Later."

He continued, a few degrees less bubbly than before.

"So, mostly we get the unexposed film and have to develop

the negative, but not in this one. This negative's already exposed. So if you wanted to change it, you'd do it when you make the print. You'd dodge or burn it."

"Burn it?"

"Not burn, burn, though, yeah, these are nitrate, so they'll burn." He took a slurpy breath. "Wanna see?"

"Nope."

Now his complexion just looked pasty with isolated red spots—this wouldn't be the diversion he'd hoped for.

"Turn on the amber light. Go ahead," he said.

She did, and then started a list in her notebook.

He flipped off the regular lights, turning the room gold.

"Put it in the enlarger." He pointed to the machine.

She wrote this down too. She heard her own breath as she slipped the *Hunger* negative into the square slot in the camera enlarger, pushing until it clicked.

"Now put the photo paper below, there."

She wrote it and placed a piece into the squared-off tool on the counter below the enlarger.

"Just flip the switch, shine the picture onto the paper. Twenty seconds."

Right away, the image shone onto paper at her fingertips.

"I remember when this one came out," he said. "Surprising she loaned you the negative. It's kind of famous."

She rolled her lips over her teeth and pressed. Did she hear a challenge in that?

He continued.

"Turn off the light and move over there, bring it up on the paper." He indicated the counter behind her, and she carried the blank-again photo paper to the liquid in a tub labeled "developer."

"Drop it in, swish it," he said, unemphatic. The picture reemerged.

"Okay, now the stop bath," he said, his voice flat.

She picked it up by its edges and dropped it into the second tub, swirling it around before making her note.

"Move it to the fixer tub, make it last. Then you'll rinse it off and let it dry."

When she'd done it, she had a four-by-five-inch print of *Hunger*.

"She wants the negative back, right?"

He was nosy.

"Can I turn on the overhead now?"

He turned it on and looked down at the picture. "Work of art, man, work of art."

Her resentment tasted briny.

"This is a starving man. You think he wants her camera in his face? Think he cares about art? He wants food! He needs money!"

Fleming lowered his eyebrows.

She calmed her voice. "So how's the dodging and burning work again?"

He quarter-turned his body away, his shoulder toward her as he answered. "You dodge by reducing the light that hits the paper. You can use a paddle, piece of cardboard, even your hand"—he looked at hers—"anything to come between the light and the paper. It keeps that part of the photo lighter. When you burn, you protect the other parts from the light and burn the spot you're aiming to change. Like a sunburn."

"Got it."

It was so simple to change the way things were or looked.

Family had been published at the *Examiner* over a year ago.

"How long do newspapers hang onto pictures?"

"Not long. They're flammable. Especially as they age. Like I said, the nitrates . . ."

"I appreciate your help here. I'll name you on the article."

He crossed his arms over his chest, frowning, looking down his long nose at her.

Darkroom judgment. She did hate to be judged, unless it ended in a prize, like Grete said.

She unlocked the door and started to step out of the dark-room, but then she stepped back.

"I'm gonna try again, on my own."

"Don't mess anything up," he said as he exited in a slump.

She relocked the door and spread the negatives from her pocket all over the light box, a gritty mosaic, which she studied through Fleming's eyepiece.

Then she put all the negatives into a film box, behind two others, under the counter, keeping out the two developed pictures—*Hunger* and *Family*.

She looked at *Family* on the desk, unable to tell if Daddy was older or younger than when she'd seen him last. The photograph, its light, caught the essence of him, not just him then or him now. Eternal him. Grete was good.

She guessed she did love him. He was her father. She'd never hated him at all, really, before that night of the ditch when the new voice spoke in her head.

She'd think about that later.

She put both pictures in her pocket and headed out of the darkroom, past Fleming's desk, where he stood with a couple other guys, talking, shaking his head, looking disgusted.

It didn't matter what he thought about her. He didn't matter. He was some nobody who worked in a dark corner of a vast place. He was never going anywhere. What mattered was finding Daddy, making sure no one had the idea Grete had—that Jane was BH. What mattered was getting where she was going.

SHE hunched over her notebook, the telephone cradled between her chin and shoulder, at the desk of a reporter, Pete, who'd been out on a one-week bender.

"Security Administration? Farm Security?"

She rechecked her notes. The agency had visited camp-sites she'd lived in, fields where she'd picked, making her parents suspicious—"What do they want? They trying to get us fired?"—acting sincere, though everybody knew they were the government.

"Who can I speak to about the pictures that come through your program?"

"I can help you," said a lady in a thick, unfamiliar accent.

Jane was silent.

"Though I am a woman, I am an actual professional, I assure you."

Jane lowered her voice. "What's your policy on fixing photographs, if something's wrong?"

"We don't do it."

"Even . . ."

"We don't do it. Mr. Stryker has rigid rules about that. We don't want to risk the legitimacy of our documentary work in any way."

"Could you explain . . ."

"The point is not to take beautiful pictures, though that's desirable—it increases the reach of our photos—but the point is to accurately document conditions so decision makers can respond appropriately." She popped her gum, then continued. "Mr. Stryker kills any photos he finds at all problematic in terms of objectivity, factuality, punches holes right through the negatives. Thousands of photos. He won't risk unprofessional work."

Manipulation was unprofessional.

Nitpickers.

"What happens if a photographer breaks the rule, poses the picture or changes the picture when he develops his own?"

Silence, not even the popping of gum. She'd gone too far.

"We get the negatives."

"What if he burns something out of a negative?"

"He would be fired."

Jane said nothing.

"Is there something you'd like to tell me, sir? It is sir, isn't it?"

Before she'd hung up on the question, Lambert said, "Gimme the picture," like a ghost over her shoulder.

"I don't have it."

His face flamed. "I don't have time for your hick do-si-do. Gimme the picture."

"Wright wouldn't give it to me."

"Idiot! We sent you on a simple errand, entirely arranged in advance! Are you trying to ruin me? Or are you just so incompetent . . ." He shoved her shoulder.

Jorge stepped between them. "What's this?"

"He came back without the picture!"

"She wouldn't give me the negative. Said it was hers."

"Who asked for the negative? We just need the picture."

"I thought you said the negative. She wouldn't give it to me."

Jorge yelled, "Boy!" A pig-eyed kid in a frayed tie jogged over from the hot seat and took a quarter from Jorge, who said "Three Danish," and the kid hustled downstairs. The other copy boys scooted down the bench, closing the gap.

"Those are real copy boys," Jorge said, his eyes bugging. "They know what a ladder is and they climb it right, don't knock other guys down, one rung at a time. That's how civilizations are built. That's how it works. That's how to be useful, how to get ahead. That's how you do it!"

She saw massive bricks, one set atop another, for decades, centuries, to build a thing, guys like Jorge doing it.

Make-work.

"We're not just making rules to annoy you. We have knowledge about how things work. You think because you're young, think you're smart, you can just turn over all the tables . . ."

"No, Jorge . . ."

"The reporters," Jorge continued, pointing at a group of them joking, playing cards, one asleep on his desk. "Split their infinitives, mess up *their* and *there*, pronoun reference switching . . ."

Lambert rolled his eyes. "Gawd! Now?"

"Most of them?" Jorge continued. "Worthless. Complacent. Got in the door by natural talent or connections, not work. But they aren't going anywhere else without the work. You," he pointed his fat finger at Jane, "are obviously aiming to graduate up off of the bench into that tribe of assholes. You know how I can tell?"

She didn't answer.

"Because you fail to do what you have been asked—no, told—to do."

"It's just . . ."

"You were told, Boy, to bring back a picture. And you failed at doing what you were told to do, the way you were told to do it."

Lambert yelled "Goddammit!" and ran to his telephone. "Give me Wright's house! *Again!* Grete Wright!"

"What are you . . ." Jane started.

"I'm gonna get the fucking picture!"

"Wait, you can't bother her again today. She'll say no!"

"Don't you tell me, Boy!"

"I'll go back in the morning. I'll get it for you. I'll tell her I messed up, not you. I'll do it."

Jorge yelled, "For Chrissake! Hang up, Lambert! We'll send somebody back to do it right in the morning. Too late to use the picture tonight anyway."

Mac broke into their circle. "What's this?"

Lambert slammed the telephone into its cradle. "You'd think this kid could do one thing right!"

Jorge said, "Boy got confused on the difference between a negative and a picture."

"I'll go back to Wright's in the morning. I'll get it!" She went all the way. "But I have something better."

"Oh Gawwwwddd!" Lambert wailed.

"I think there's something wrong with her pictures. I think she's been scamming the Feds, the FSA, staging things, faking them."

Lambert moaned, "And you know this how?"

"Reporting! That's what I've been doing. That's why it was harder to get the picture."

"The picture is what we *told* you to get!" said Jorge.

Lambert said, "We're on a murder story, dummy!"

"Is she . . . dead?"

"On her way!"

"But I think this is part of it. If the victim's—Vee's—boss is involved in a federal scam, and it's connected to her attack . . ."

Mac interrupted. "What?"

"Wright cheats the government, fakes her pictures . . ."

"The ones we run?"

"Everybody runs them. I think Vee knew. And I think that's why she's dead—not dead, coma!" The idea was forming as she said it.

"Kid's a bad slug!" said Lambert.

"Pipe down!" Mac pounded one fist into the other palm. "All right! You've got one day. But we're not going to use your story if we don't get the picture too! You hear me? The story and the picture."

"Yes, sir!"

"What'd I tell you?"

"Mac, sir. Mac, not sir."

"Tick tock, Boy. Tick tock."

SHE took over Pete's desk again, which was jammed up against Lambert's. He'd stomped off, so she used the chance to look in his desk for the keys to the red Chevrolet he kept parked on the street in front with about a thousand tickets on the windshield. Tit for tat, she thought, pocketing the keys. She'd make trouble for him in return for all his trouble, not to mention the moleskin theft. That wasn't a grudge she'd forgotten, and it felt good to take his key after he'd unloaded on her just now.

"I already talked to you people," said Detective Mel Toledo.

"Different section," she said, checking over her shoulder to make sure Lambert hadn't returned to hear her messing with his story.

"First we thought it was all about the crowbar. On the ground, next to her body. Turns out that's not it."

"Another weapon . . ."

"Sort of. Cerebral hypoxia. She had petechiae—little red dots in her eyes. Contusions and abrasions on the right side of her throat. Fingernail marks show he choked her first, hit her second."

"He choked her? *Then* hit her?"

"When she was already out, face up. Hit her on the right side of her head with that bar. He was a leftie. Made a circular fracture to her skull."

She hadn't thought about Vee's body, what it meant she'd been attacked. Hearing it now made her see yellow, so she sat. She tried to picture Daddy choking Vee, swinging a crowbar down on her head, thinking of Jane while he did it, but she couldn't, didn't want to.

There were other possibilities—he did it for Grete, or someone else did it, to make it look like it was Daddy.

He wasn't a leftie, but he was a two-hander, like Jane.

"You there?" Toledo asked.

"Why would he hit her after he thought he'd killed her?"

"Sometimes, something like that, maybe it had special meaning to him."

"Anything else?"

She heard rustling over the telephone line.

"Crowbar, wallet with her license, two bucks." Toledo laughed at somebody in the background before continuing. "Wright's business card with 'Breen's, 8, BH'—in pencil. That's it." Jane wrote it all down. Then he asked, "What's your name again?"

"Ja . . . Benny. Wheeler."

She heard a scratching pencil in the background.

She hung up, flushed. It was hard to keep lies straight.

Raggedy ass. Don't ruin this, said the voice.

"Shut up," she answered.

She pulled the crumpled half sheets of Lambert's story toward her on the desk and reread them. On the last one was the line that would have gone below the photo she stole —"Vesta Russell, taken by FSA photographer Mrs. Grete Wright, near Sacramento's federal labor camp."

Tumbleweed. This picture happened when Jane lived a couple miles away.

Though Daddy might be dead, he might not. He might still be living back there in Sacramento, near that dark-haired woman and the baby.

There was too much in her head. She couldn't contain it.

She got a notepad, turned it horizontal, and made a chart, columns left to right, with everything she knew, questions she had. Then it got to overflowing and she redid it, neater, so it was clearer what she had to do next. Everything in its numbered box.

All the day shift were gone now, so she went back to the darkroom, locked the door, climbed under the desk behind the film boxes and slept for a few hours, newsprint crumpled under her head, before the morning guys began to arrive. She took a hobo bath in the men's room and went out to the diner for coffee and to reread her chart before taking care of business.

CHAPTER SEVEN

THANKS

J ane walked through the open door to a house packed with people, the living room decorated for a day-early Thanksgiving party—eggs, potatoes, sausage, champagne, juice, other drinks on a table in the middle. Leaves, feathers, sticks, and ribbons hung in garlands on the walls.

The Wright boys were acting crazy, hanging on the arms of a guy in a cowboy getup who swung them around, threatening to shoot 'em up. One of them squealed, "I'll scalp you!" They looked ecstatic in the presence of the man who must be their first father. He was wearing a white linen suit with a bolo tie, silver belt buckle, and sharp-toed boots. None of the farmers or ranchers she'd known wore clothes like that. His fingers were stained, blue, orange, red.

Then there were the guys who looked to be from Professor Wright's university department, gray-suited men using big words—three- and four-syllables—milling with Grete's arty friends in corduroy jackets and messy hair. Everybody looked their own kind of arrogant, preening, everybody fake, she thought.

She could hear Grete and Paul in the back of the room, their voices rising and falling dramatically—"tragic," "heartbreaking," "institutional poverty."

Apart, in the corner, were a woman and three children,

their clothes ragged but clean. The woman had fine, wavy strawberry hair pulled back into a bun. She wore a faded floral dress. No makeup or hose. She had to be Vee's mother. Jane turned away.

She moved to the kitchen, gateway to the basement.

There, a red-haired girl sat at the table, her cheek resting on one arm, her wiry hair in disarray. She'd need a rope, not a rubber band to tie that hair back. Her skin was pale, the kind that gets dark in the summer when all her freckles run together. She wore a faded plaid shirt and overalls. She neither smiled nor frowned, just watched Jane, as if she'd been waiting.

It was mostly her hair, brick-colored, rough, untamed, prairie not garden, that reminded Jane of the difference between the place she'd been living and the place she was from. It was a difference in texture. The tips of her fingers tingled, remembering the roughness, the realness of home.

Not that the city was smooth and slick. She knew its pebbly concrete, its thick sludge of fog, the almost physical smell of fish on the bus, the clang of metal in the basement where the printing press worked. That was texture, too, obviously. But it was different.

At home things were granular, made of particles she could feel, so that if she were to take a strand of that girl's wiry hair between her fingers, she'd touch the many little moving bits gathered to build it, and under a microscope those bits would look like grains of dirt. The same was true of the loose-weave dresses made of cotton sacks, and the canvas wrapped over tent poles, and the wood grain of a homemade banjo. Even the cornbread, especially the cornbread, which was why she loved it, that graininess, soaking in buttermilk.

Looking at that wiry red hair brought it back. She was homesick.

"Mind if I join you?"

The girl sat up, bringing her fists to her chin.

"You her boyfriend?"

"No. But I thought she was pretty."

"Pretty ain't nothin'."

Jane shuddered, having said something so stupid.

"She sung me awake every day."

"What'd she sing?"

The girl started up, no self-consciousness—"Wake up, Jacob, day's a breakin'. Peas in the pot and hoe cakes baking."

Jane joined her—"Bacon's in the pan and coffee's in the pot. Come on round and get it while it's hot."

She nodded, wiped her eyes with her sleeve. "She did some things not a one other person mighta done."

"What sort of things?"

The girl looked out the window at the lawn. "Why you asking?"

"I'm trying to find out what happened to her."

The girl chewed on her lip. "Wouldn't it have been better to do something before?"

The sorest spot.

The kitchen door opened and the maid came in, carrying a tray of dirty coffee cups and champagne glasses. Her mouth opened as she looked from Jane to the girl.

"Get out, Hopper. She's coming."

Jane rose and looked at the red-haired girl, who said, "She ain't dead yet."

SHE hadn't been to a hospital since Granny and didn't know what to do.

She followed the signs that read "Emergency/Maternity." Two cop cars were parked in front of that entrance, and she hurried past them. One of them, leaning out his window, yelled, "I guess they'll let anybody be a daddy these days!" and the other one laughed.

She rushed the wrong direction through the maternity ward and the children's ward and the cancer ward until finally she came back around to emergency, passing through all the miserable people waiting for attention, and asked a round-cheeked nurse, "Where will I find Vee Russell?"

"Vee?"

"Vesta, I mean."

Her starched hat concealed her eyes. "She's been moved." The nurse wrote directions on a scrap of paper without asking questions, too many people wailing all around to care about Jane.

Up the elevator, she found the pea soup–colored waiting room she'd been directed to, where a couple of worried people in work uniforms stood with a pale-skinned doctor and a ruddy, athletic-looking nurse in starchy white. Jane sat in a chair against the wall and hid her face in a *Saturday Evening Post*, listening, trying to plan. She wasn't catching much—"patient," "trauma," "coma." But also, she heard them say "he" instead of "she."

The smell of the room—antiseptic floor cleaner—brought her back to the room where Granny had passed, and that was enough to start a prickling in her eyes, which she rubbed with the back of her hand.

Over the top of her magazine, she looked at the dark-haired woman holding a handkerchief to the lower part of her face with both hands. Her eyes were puffy, no eyelashes or brows. A tall man with spiky hair, in denims and a heavy work jacket, held his arm tight around her as they faced the doctor.

He answered their questions in a voice too quiet for Jane to hear. But after he walked away, the nurse took his place in the center of their group, leaning in to put a hand on each of their shoulders. "Really, in spite of the shock of his being unconscious, a coma is the best thing for him. It reduces the trauma while the swelling goes down. The doctor thinks that's good."

The couple hugged each other, and then the woman hugged the nurse.

For some reason, Jane thought of Hank Ikeda, the copy boy who missed his mom. Maybe his mom was like this woman.

Her cheeks warmed. She'd made a coma happen to Vee, ruined everything for her and her family. How would she fix the rubble collapsing all around her? She'd be held to account.

She was in one corner of the waiting room. In another, the nurse continued comforting the couple. In a third, an impatient doctor tried to talk with two men who didn't speak English. And near the fourth corner were a pair of swinging doors under a sign that read, "Hospital personnel only."

She'd crossed so many borders. She put down the magazine and walked past everyone else, entering those doors into a wide, quiet hallway, expecting someone to stop her, though no one did. No one ever stopped her.

A nurse's desk loomed ahead on her left. Beyond that was a chalkboard with names and room numbers on it. She couldn't read it from where she stood. Just to her right was a cart of dirty laundry. She dropped her suit jacket into the cart and brought out the only white jacket in the cart, stained with blood on its right arm. She slipped it on and walked toward the chalkboard, her head down, past the nurses, who were circled up, whispering to each other, gossiping, toward the chalkboard—Room 437, Vesta Russell. The line below her name was blank.

She made a right down a long hallway, the wrong direction, and then doubled back and found 437 at the other end of the hall. She waited outside the door, looking both ways, but heard nothing, saw nothing, so she entered.

There were two narrow beds, the one closest to the door empty, unmade.

Vee lay on the one near the window, in a blue hospital

gown, her head flat on the mattress, no pillows. Surrounded by that antiseptic smell, which was also, still, somehow earthy—sweat and urine—Vee seemed so delicate, more so here than on the pier. Her cheek and forehead and eye were blackened, swollen, bandaged. Ruined. Jane wanted to lay her hand against her cheek, wanted to be bloody herself instead of Vee. She made a loud coughing sound, shocking herself, and stopped it with her hand.

Vee was a real person, really harmed, by Jane.

Mind your row.

There was no clipboard or chart hanging off the end of the bed like in the movies. Nothing on the side tables. No papers anywhere. She looked on the chair backs. Nothing. In the drawers, nothing but jars, cotton balls, bandages. Finally she looked in the closet across from the bed, where a canvas bag hung on a hook. She opened it and looked inside to see Vee's clothes. She pulled them out, spreading them on the foot of the bed, on Vee's feet, her coat, chunky shoes, a summery dress, not right for this city.

No evidence. No explanation.

Was she just a desperate mother, like so many others, who'd take whatever work she could get at almost any cost?

Was she a normal girl who wanted to escape terrible circumstances, get to the city?

Was she someone like Jane, with visions of a great big future? A would-be photographer?

A do-gooder?

Jane felt angry at the absence of answers, almost angry even at Vee.

Why'd this happen? Who are you?

She said it out loud—"Who are you?"

"May I help you, Doctor?"

She turned and the athletic nurse gasped, staring at Jane's arm, the blood all over her sleeve.

"I'll, I'd better . . . take this off."

As Jane crossed the room to the door, the nurse asked, "Who are you?"

Jane pushed past her, out to the hall, past the ogling others.

"Who are you?" the nurse yelled.

Jane ran through the double doors and into the waiting room, directly into a circle of people who'd migrated into the hallway. Running, she knocked the grieving lady—Hank's maybe mother—to the floor.

The nurse yelled, "Fake!"

Someone else yelled, "Security!"

Jane ran toward an exit sign leading to a stairwell, down four flights, through one last hallway, passing women in labor and their pacing husbands in the waiting room, and out the door of the maternity ward. She ripped off the white jacket and threw it into a trash can at the exit in front of the cops, busy in conversation, laughter.

She ran around the corner and leaned, panting, against a building.

She found a pass on the ground near the garbage and used it to board a streetcar, pushing through the smokers in the open-air rear of the car into the center. It was full of people coming from the market, standing and hanging onto the overhead bar, their shopping bags dangling. Jane felt sick, surrounded by the smells of fish and spice. She wanted to spit out those smells. Every clanging bell alarmed her—Fake! Security!

She felt a bunching at her waist and saw her wrapping had come loose and was gathered just over her belt, allowing the small rise of her breasts to show beneath her sweaty man's shirt. She had no jacket, so she wrapped her arms around herself. She couldn't fix things here.

She jumped out at Market and Fifth and walked to Mission, where she found Lambert's red Chevrolet, parking tickets covering the windshield. She wiped them off into the gutter and used the key she'd stolen from his drawer to unlock the door, rolled down the window, started the ignition, and pulled away from the curb, spreading a glove compartment map on the steering wheel as she drove.

Entering traffic, she heard, "Hey, that's not Lambert!"

She pushed on the gas—right on Fifth, left on Market, heading east, the window partway open—and pointed Lambert's car out of the city.

SHE smelled home before she saw it. Silt and pesticide—arsenic, sulfur, kerosene.

She watched the gas gauge drop until she was just a few miles west of Sacramento. She pulled into a closed Texaco station, peeling sign out front: Beer, Beans, and Gas. Nobody was there at this hour to fill her tank. She drove around back, rolled up the windows and closed her eyes, waiting for morning.

"HEY! You can't sleep here!" A jumpsuited attendant rapped on her window.

She rolled it down, gave him two dollars, and pulled the car around to the pump.

He looked at her suspiciously as he filled her gas tank.

She saw it was already late, noon. She'd slept hard and long out back. How had she wasted so much time?

"Abyssinia," she said in a low voice, and pulled out of the station.

She crossed the I Street Bridge, exiting onto the frontage road where the American and Sacramento Rivers meet, a space filled with the familiar tents of canvas, tin, cardboard, plywood, just a little above her family's old campsite, a mile or two above Tumbleweed.

She parked along the levee, patting her pockets. Without a

jacket and hat she felt bare, her hands burning with cold, but glad she'd rearranged the layer of breast binding between her undershirt and skin, girl-hobo armor.

She walked down the slope toward the river, her wingtips sinking in mud. Only three months before, she'd slept in such a place. These people could know Daddy and Momma, might even see through this getup, recognize her. She was a confident fake, but in this place, without a hat and jacket, she doubted her disguise. She crossed her arms over her chest, protective.

In a flat spot next to the river, near a trash can fire, a guy played mouth harp, another banjo, singing along, and about a dozen men, women, and children danced around them—"If y'all's house catches fire, and they ain't no water 'round, throw the jelly out the window. Let the doggone shack burn down."

A song she knew, a song she'd sung.

Apart from them, six men stood in a circle around another fire, drinking out of bottles, a couple wearing coats, not just shirtsleeves, kids playing tag around them, running through tree branches and rocks and bushes, like Jane used to do, stirring up smells of wet, rotting leaves.

She thought about what Grete said she did when she approached a group, how she found the story through the outsider, how that had irritated Jane, but she decided to try it. She walked up to the one guy standing back from the fire, apart from the circle of drinkers.

"Happy Thanksgiving, sir," she said, dipping her head.

He nodded. His face was leathery, his body short and wiry, his hands safe in his pockets.

She took a deep breath. "I'm looking for information about a woman." She pulled out the *Family* picture and pointed at Vee's face. "I was told she came this way."

He looked at it, and then back at Jane.

"That you in the middle?"

"No, it ain't. He's a lot bigger! I'm looking into her," she said, and pointed again at Vee's face. "I was told she came this way."

"You were told?" he asked. "Or did you read it in the paper? You know we read out here, son. We know she's dead."

"She's not dead." It felt important to say that.

"Near dead."

"Did you know her?

"Who wants to know?"

The men around the fire rearranged themselves around the two of them, so that this man she was talking to was no longer the outsider but the center of a new formation.

"Benny Hopper. I work for the *Prospect*." Her ears burned with cold.

"You're from the paper but you don't remember her name?"

"Her name's Vee Russell."

"Y'all sold a lot of papers with her and Noreen's pretty faces before, but Noreen didn't get a dime from it. Even her name in the paper." Through his shirt his arm muscles looked hard, squared off.

"I'm sorry . . . The other woman, her name's Noreen?"

"Sold all them papers with this picture? Big, big deal, they said. And they didn't put her name in there?"

"Another paper ran the picture at first, not us," she said, trying to sell that as an excuse. She saw herself the way he'd see her—as a low-level agent of an untrustworthy institution. Such a person sometimes got hurt as a scapegoat for the bigger, badder guy.

The man's face glowed, like he was getting hot out there in the cold. "Noreen never wrote home and told her folks she lives in a ripped-up tent. She told 'em cotton grows high out here and she can pick them oranges right off the tree. She didn't want her people worrying about her. But they saw her picture in the paper. Just a poor lady. Just poor. Nothin' but that. Paper didn't pay her." He drew out *pay*.

"She wasn't in our paper. We didn't run it. Besides, I'm not here about her."

"What are you here about?" His voice sounded rougher now, and the group of bodies around the two of them seemed to thrum. He dropped his bottle, clenching his fists, stretching his fingers.

Hold your ground.

"I need your help," she said, standing in the cold wind off the river, tasting salty sweat.

"You need help? Why don't you sell that car, like Noreen sold hers? For scrap?"

"Not that kind of help. Not money."

"Oh," the man said, looking around at the group. "He don't need money!"

The pack laughed and she saw tongues, teeth, gums. Her own people, dangerous.

"Photographer said she was gonna help Noreen. How would she do that, if she never even took her name?"

"Look, someone's been attacked." Jane's voice cracked.

"You think Noreen has somethin' to do with that? You think any of us does?"

The circle pulsed, contracting and expanding like a living thing.

"Pretty boy's making claims," one of them said, and others laughed, hacking laughs.

Jane closed her arms tighter over her chest and looked at the faces, dirty, lined, some young men, some old, hard to tell because of the time they'd spent outside.

"I think the photographer is in on this." She hadn't planned to say that. It just came out.

"You think the lady photographer did it?"

"Maybe, yes." That wasn't true. Grete wasn't a brute. She was an artist, an intellectual.

"You think Noreen wants to get messed up with her again?"

Messed up with Grete? Vee?

"Noreen!" He turned his face up in a howl, his chin and throat where his face had been.

Jane looked toward the car but didn't run. She'd see it through. The dancers and musicians close to the river stopped.

One of them, a woman in a blue dress over a longer slip, walked over, her hair down around her shoulders. It was the other lady from *Family*, but different in life, smiling, the corners of her eyes turned up. She had a good, strong figure. As she walked toward them, she moved her body like a sensual person, like Elthea walked, unlike the way she looked in the picture, downtrodden.

"Yes, darlin'?" she said in a low voice, pushing off a trailing dance partner.

"Ma'am," Jane said, tilting her head. "Benny. From the newspaper."

"Hello, Benny." She brought her hair up off her neck with one hand and wiped her brow with the other.

"Yes, Mrs. . . . ?"

The woman looked at the man and then back at Jane. "Noreen."

"Noreen . . ."

Get 'er done.

"I'd like to ask you about Vee Russell, and . . ."

"Want a drink, Benny?"

She didn't, not at all, but she said, "Thank you," because she knew not to insult Noreen if she wanted to find out about Vee and Daddy.

Noreen led her to a boulder, where she picked up a jug, took a swig, and handed it to Jane. It went down bad, oily as gasoline, so that Jane coughed, making Noreen laugh. She patted a spot on the boulder next to her and Jane sat, near enough to smell Noreen's yeasty scent.

"Now you listen," Noreen said, then took another drink.

"And I will tell you all the lies in that article and the lies in that picture."

"Yes, ma'am."

"But you gotta pay me first."

She couldn't pay, shouldn't pay. She felt a roiling in her belly, as she had when she was a girl, thinking about what Momma'd do for money.

JANE had been walking home from school when the public address system crackled, "Would the Hopper family report to the camp office to make good on their late rent fee? The Abraham Lincoln Hopper family, please report to the Tumbleweed Federal Camp office at your earliest convenience? To set accounts right."

Uno's tinny accent bounced all around town, a loose ball bearing, so everybody outside, or even inside with a window cracked open, heard. In the bank, in the diner, through the truck windows of teachers and coaches. This was the third Thursday in a row.

This time, he'd done it when Jane was walking home from school, just behind the popular girls, who were themselves just behind the baseball players. She was following close on their heels so she could keep her eye on the muscled-up first baseman with a snub nose, a boy several lengths out of her reach, thick shoulders, sharp cheekbones, and a perfect knob of an Adam's apple.

Right in that space between algebra and tomatoes, Uno announced, his voice calm and businesslike, "Would the Abraham Lincoln Hopper family make good on their rent?"

She'd always thought his physical injury made him mean. He couldn't do the camp work his job description required, couldn't carry things that required both hands. He mostly sat in his little electrified office, wires snaking in and out of his cabin only, with the fan on his desk and the one radio in the camp playing Los Angeles Angels baseball, out of Mr. Wrigley's self-named South Central field, for nobody but him. He'd sit there, chewing on a pencil and looking out his window, one hand rubbing short hair on a narrow skull, frowning at folks walking by. Sweetie'd already run off by then. He was all alone, so he got others to do the work for him, move folks in or repair a fence or post signs about meetings or new rules, sweep up dirt in the common areas, so they wouldn't mess up the community hall. He was persuasive, as representative of the government, and most people were glad to pitch in, hopeful they'd be invited in to listen to baseball, or provided with beans or cornmeal. But he did his figuring and communication himself. He did not delegate that. That's where he excelled. He always knew who paid for what and how much.

When he called out Daddy's name that day, three girls ahead of Jane on the sidewalk locked eyes, confirming prior conversations, and giggled, poking each other—"Abraham Lincoln Hopper family, please get your no-count, white trash butts to the . . ."

"Shut your mouth, catfish!" Jane yelled, and ran. The last thing she heard as she passed was the first baseman's voice, a scrap in a sentence—"Okie picker."

She ran past camp to the big oak. She wouldn't pick that day. She lay under that tree in the weeds, looking at the sky, wheezing from the valley fever, which always acted up in the heat when she was mad. She wanted to talk to Daddy, but he was in Turlock, performing at the Play Pen. So she headed back to camp.

As she stepped up to their cabin door, Uno stepped out, smiling, in wrinkled shirtsleeves, and tipped his hat. "Well, good afternoon, Miss Hopper. How pretty you look today."

Through the open door, in the dark, she saw Momma, putting the kettle on, her face blank.

When he'd gone, Momma held out a fist of change. "Get us a bag of flour, eggs, coffee. Choose something you want too."

Jane did what she said, and the two of them ate on that for a week. And for four afternoons straight, on the walk home alone from school, two blocks ahead of the mean kids, she sucked on a different color piece of penny candy, pretending that made up for it.

Sometimes it had been hard to love Momma. But she did know the price of things. She had a sharpness, a practical nerve Jane respected, even when it cut her.

SHE saw that in Noreen, too, the edge of her need for money.

But still Jane said, "A reporter don't pay for information," feeling the grammatical error after it slipped out.

"Where you from?"

She didn't answer.

"No mind. Pay me." Noreen smirked, patient.

Jane sighed, checking her pockets for what she had left of Mac's money. "How much?"

"Everything you got." Her face was hard now, like in the picture, worrying Jane. She handed her all Mac's bills, six dollars.

"That's not enough," Noreen said.

Jane gave her the bottle of Izzy's vodka, and Noreen opened the lid and took a sip. "Okay then!" She tucked it into her bra.

"It was a good picture of you," Jane said, wanting to open up the right topic.

"I look like failure. That was the point."

"It was moving that way. Made people care."

Noreen squinted at Jane, her nose, her chin. "You related to the guy in the picture? That why you're lookin'?"

"No relation."

Noreen rolled her eyes. "Whole damn thing's a lie anyway."

"What's the lie?" Jane got out her notebook.

"Make you a deal."

"Are we gonna have to do this at every step?"

"I need your car."

"It's not mine."

"Whose is it?"

"A friend's," Jane said, thinking Lambert was the opposite of a friend.

"Alright then," she said. "Drive me."

"Ma'am . . ."

"Or I ain't gonna budge."

Jane pushed off the rock. Noreen picked up a dirty bag, and together they walked up the road to the Chevy.

"You okay?" somebody yelled.

"Doin' the pickup."

They got in the car and Noreen told Jane to drive up the road, about four miles.

Jane worried that would put them at Tumbleweed but didn't ask.

Noreen set her bag on her lap and pulled out a frayed newspaper. "This," she said, pointing to the back page, "fries me."

Jane saw her finger on a boxed story, set in italics, near the *Examiner's* article about Vee's attack and the photo of Daddy and Vee and Noreen. They'd rerun the picture they'd published a year before, after all that trouble Jane had gone to hide it. Wasted. The box headline read, "Photographer's Journal—taking a picture that saves."

Noreen changed her posture, the tilt of her head, making her body small, and read aloud as Jane drove.

*It had been a long seven days of driving and getting
out of the old Packard and waiting and getting back
into the Packard, and driving more. And now, in a
surprising June rainstorm on a valley afternoon, with
all that behind me, I still had hours of slick roads
ahead before I got home to my family.*

Noreen read well, her accent all but disappearing into her
version of Grete's voice.

*In spite of the ache in my bad foot, I felt good. In the
passenger seat was the box I would send to Roy
Stryker the next day. I was proud of what I had done.
As I drove, I looked down at that box and knew I had
been productive.*

*The rain pounding on the sedan's roof made me feel
clean. There were no other cars on the road, and I
considered turning off the wipers to watch the flow of
water down my window. Then I saw a sign: TOMATO
CAMP. Another invitation to shoot.*

Had Jane ever seen that sign, on that road?

*But I had a full box. No need to stop. I kept driving.
Ten miles on, I began to feel irritated. Why did I care
about that sign? I had done more than enough for this
trip.*

Jane believed Grete had these thoughts.

*I drove on, thinking I wanted to get back to my family.
The children were all home. They would be asleep by
the time I got there, but I could tiptoe into their rooms.*

Push David's damp hair off his forehead, hold my hand
there, feeling the pulse in his temple with my fingers.
Smell the cut grass scent of Jacob's skin. He can never
wash it all off. I wanted to be with them. And my
husband. And his children.

"What a wonderful mother." Noreen broke character. "Ain't
it nice how she'll tuck them in when she gets home?"

The kids probably weren't in those beds at all. Probably
farmed out.

Noreen continued.

Ten miles further and I knew I had trouble. I wanted to
turn around.

I told myself I did not need more pictures. I said if I
stop now I will be tired driving later. I will ruin my
equipment if I take it out in the rain. Don't be
ridiculous, Grete, I told myself. I was already proud of
the work I had done.

After ten more miles, I made a U-turn on the empty
highway. Those miles back took forever. And then I
saw the backside of the sign. It was painted with the
same message, by a different hand: TOMATO CAMP.
That was it. No directions. But I knew where to go. I
did not doubt myself. I just drove straight, did not
consider turning left or right down this or that gravel
road leading to another muddy field. I just drove
straight for three miles. And that is where I saw them.
The rain had stopped. I got out of the car and went
around to the passenger door. I opened it and got out
my Graflex. I walked straight to the starving
grandmother.

"Liar!" Noreen said.

She wasn't a grandmother.

It took me five minutes to reach her. My right foot slowed me when I was tired. I saw her look at it as I came through the rows on the inside edge of my sole.

Injury's her ticket.

I do not remember the exact words I said, but she understood I was there to help. She didn't tell me her name. She said they had been living on found vegetables. And birds they caught and killed. Her man didn't have work—none of them did—but he played banjo to get their minds off it. I said I would help. I shot them five times, each one from closer range, until at the end I was close. I took care to let them know we were equals.

Noreen dropped the paper onto the car seat. A vein pulsed blue at her temple. "Equals? She changed everything about us to look right for those pictures. None of it true."

"Changed what?"

"She wanted 'noble savages.'"

"Noble . . . ?"

"That's what the guy with the banjo said. Stop here!" Noreen pointed to a white farmhouse on the left. As they pulled over, she rolled down her window and leaned across Jane's lap to honk the horn, four long blasts, causing a load of children to pour out of the house.

"Ma!" they screamed, maybe a dozen of them, including a toddler in the arms of an older girl, running from the house, across the lawn, to the car.

"Did you say, 'Thank you?'" Noreen asked the big girl.

"Yes, Ma."

The back doors opened and the car filled with kids. Jane counted ten, sitting on each other's laps and the floorboard, smelling woolly as wet dogs.

"Benny's givin' us a ride back to camp."

They all cried out hellos, and the biggest girl, about thirteen, with frizzy black braids, handed a few dollars up to her mother.

"How was it?" Noreen asked.

"Just helpin' her get ready for her big dinner," the girl said. "She was okay."

"Thanks dumplin'." Noreen smiled at her daughter and turned back to Jane.

"Photographer didn't think it would look good to show my kids. People wouldn't care as much if they saw the variety."

In the rearview Jane saw towheads, brunettes, redheads.

"Anything to eat?" asked a crusty-nosed boy with a black buzz cut and dark skin.

"Tomorrow morning," Noreen answered. "There'll be something in the . . ."

"I can get you dinner."

The backseat crew cheered.

"But you've got to answer my questions. No more deals."

"Okay," Noreen said, having already gotten a deal she liked.

Jane pulled the Chevy onto the highway, heading to Tumbleweed Federal Labor Camp.

THOUGH they'd wrestled and fussed on the highway, the kids acted almost holy as they pulled up to the arched wood Tumbleweed sign, their hands folded on their laps, their voices whispers.

Jane parked on the side of the road, just past the sign. "Wait here," she said.

She got out and walked up the drive, under the sign, past the men's showers and women's showers and vegetable garden—winter spinach and collards and beets—dozens of canvas-sided cabins raised up on wood foundations, porches and water pumps out front, all of them dim and quiet. She walked past the community room, lit up like a bonfire, every open window glowing, the sound of fiddles inside. Loud voices, all turned inward toward each other, not out at her, celebrating the holiday.

She passed that, heading to the biggest cabin with a sign out front: MANAGER.

When she knocked on the door she got nothing, knocked again, still nothing. She turned the knob and pushed, but it was locked, so she pressed her face against the crack and said, "Momma." Nothing.

She walked around to the side and pushed her hand between the curtains—no glass, even for the manager. She went over to a pile of cardboard and pallets stacked next to the fence and got an orange crate and stood on it to climb through the opening into their bedroom, and jumped into a room with a nice-sized bed, Granny's quilt, flowers in a jar on the dresser.

She opened the dresser's top drawer: store-bought underwear, panties, bras, girdles, slips, hose, garters, a couple each of some things, all clean. She lifted them up, moved them around, disturbing the neatness. In the back of the drawer she found a folded stack of ones, dirty, bound with a rubber band.

She was the reason Momma had this cabin, these flowers on the dresser, this money in her underwear drawer. She'd gotten rid of Daddy so Momma could live here with Uno. She unbanded the bills, counting twenty-three dollars, put the money in her pocket and closed the drawer, balancing accounts.

She walked through the bedroom into the main room—kitchen, table, chairs. Against the far wall was a desk, a calendar on top, four lockable drawers, a telephone. Momma lived someplace with a telephone. This was far nicer than the Tumbleweed cabin Momma, Daddy, and she used to have, which Uno had evicted them from.

She unlocked the door, walked back to the Chevy, and told Noreen's family to follow her, silent, if they wanted to eat. They followed her orders exactly, silent past the community room party, where she could hear Momma's loud laugh. She felt sick with fear she'd be seen.

She got them to the Manager cabin, ushered them in.

"Pretty," said the black-haired girl, looking at a clean quilt in pink and blue—the Okie star pattern, Momma's favorite— folded on a kitchen chair.

Jane spread it out so they could sit on it.

In the icebox she found potatoes, onions, celery, carrots, and leftover chicken thighs. Only a little hesitant, she shredded the chicken and chopped vegetables and added them to salted water in a pot on the stove, still warm from the fire beneath. From jars on wood plank shelves over the stove, she crumbled in sage and red peppers. She mixed flour with water in a cup before adding the thickener to the soup. This was a dinner Granny would make.

She got down a jar of homemade biscuit mix and Noreen added water, stirring the dough.

"We need help," Noreen said. "But I don't want nobody looking down on us."

"I know," Jane said.

"That in the newspaper makes it seem like we're gypsies. We ain't gypsies except by circumstance. We want to own land again, settle our own land, stop wandering."

Jane took a bite of the dough, liking its salt.

"I bent for that woman."

She looked at Noreen, at the planes of her tanned face, and felt a pang. Momma was a proud woman who never bent for someone else. But Noreen had a bruised look her mother didn't have.

"I looked pitiful. More pitiful than I am. After she left, I unbent myself, had fun when the others come back to the campsite where she took our picture. Nobody wants to take my picture having fun. I like to have fun. I ain't no dog. I have some wolf left in me."

Jane took the bowl from Noreen to drop spoons of dough onto a pan and put it in the still-warm oven with a small lump of lard on each biscuit, feeling silence would work better than questions.

"Back in Sayre, the dust got everywhere. Inside the house, inside the stove. All over me. All in me. I breathed it in. It's a part of me."

The dust gets in you.

Noreen was Vee's unnamed friend in the newspaper.

"Now, in California, rain gets under the tent walls, makes all of us muddy. I eat that mud. Any baby I may yet have . . ."

Jane gasped and Noreen laughed.

"If I *ever* have another baby, she'll inherit that dust and that mud, even if she lives the rest of her life in the city."

Jane wanted to disagree.

"I'd like her to inherit other things too. Oranges. Grapes."

"You don't inherit that stuff," Jane said. "You pick it."

"Some people inherit it."

Jane thought, She doesn't see it there for the picking.

They got out cups and bowls and filled them with soup and biscuits. On the porch, Jane pumped water into an urn, and they poured it into jelly jars for everybody to share. The kids sat on that quilt on the floor taking bites and passing cups.

The music on the other side of camp was lively, fiddle driven.

"Anything else you want to tell me about the photographer?"

Noreen put her hand over her mouth, rubbing it, and then dropped it to her lap. "I'm used to folks lying. But I hate when they lie and pretend it's good for me." She fished around in her cup for a piece of potato.

Jane felt the tightness of the bandages hiding her breasts.

"Which lie?"

"She tried to clean the campsite of everything that looked like us? The bottles and the trash and the diapers? Made up who we are."

"Don't you think she was protecting you, your dignity?"

"When she told my big girl to get out of the picture, to keep the other kids out? When she posed me and that guy and Vee and her pretty blond baby? When she promised to help me but never gave me nothing? When she said authorities don't like to know about a drunk mother with ten kids from different daddies, different skin. A woman who puts her children out to work!"

"She said that and you still let her take your picture?"

"No, she took the picture a long time ago!"

"When did she say it?"

"Night after the first articles in the paper about Vee. When she come back."

"Came back? Why?"

"Vee had come to see us, worried. Then, after, when I read that about her being attacked, I called the photographer. I told her she owed us. For the picture."

"This happened when?"

"The day after Vee was attacked. I called the photographer in the morning. Then I stood all day in line at the cannery. When I come back to the tent, after stopping in old town, she was there, sitting with my kids, like to bite my head off."

"Why?"

"Didn't want me talking about the picture to anybody, telling about her pushing me around, paying the guy. She gave me twenty dollars, said she wouldn't give me no more. Said if I knew what was good for me, that'd finish it."

"She paid you?" Grete was such a liar. She wouldn't want those payments getting out. It wouldn't have looked good.

"Wasn't nothing, what she gave me. Compared to what she earned."

Jane thought a photographer probably didn't get paid much. But then Grete's house was so nice, and she seemed in charge of her husband, like she earned the dough.

"What do you know about what she earned?"

"Nothing. Just people talked about her, that she was different than the other photographers."

"How?"

"Said her pictures were more important. That's what she said."

Uppity.

"What about Abraham and Vee?" she asked. "How well did you know them?"

Noreen looked at the toddler, sleeping on the big girl's lap.

"That's her baby there, P. B., Potato Bug."

Jane looked at the girl's chubby cheeks, sticky with soup, the only one in the group with store-bought clothes.

"The baby in this picture?"

"Vee's baby."

"And Abraham's?"

"He was a prop."

Jane winced. A thing, not a man.

"Just for the picture. He does look like you. Do you see it?"

Jane breathed through her nose. "Did you know him?"

"He was just standing there, watching, up against the tree. Then he come up, trying to bargain, said he knew the photographer takes money."

"What do you know about that?"

"Nothing. I didn't get anything from her then. Didn't occur to me then."

"Why do you have P. B.?"

"After the picture, Vee asked the photographer for work. When she got it, we made a deal. She was gonna come back regular with money, for P. B. and us. Which she did. She kept her promise."

"Where's P. B.'s daddy?"

"Young fella. Don't matter."

Jane looked at her picture. "Abraham's not the daddy?"

"You're fixed on Abraham."

Jane frowned.

"He just looked right for the picture, with his banjo. I told you, he was a prop."

"Did Vee know him?"

"Ain't my pigs, ain't my barn."

Jane chewed her lip, thinking. "What will you do about P. B.?"

"Keep her. Vee was doing her best. It ain't easy to raise a child."

Noreen's kids sat, playing finger games, humming, day-dreaming. They were poor, didn't eat regularly, were ill-dressed, dirty looking. They had to work, even the littlest of them. But they looked somehow all right, like they might take care of each other, like they were secure. Why were they this way?

Why wasn't Jane sweet and grateful for so little?

"Where's Abraham now?"

"Somebody said he had a gig with a band, some kind of barn thing. Farm-sounding gig, in Frisco."

Jane thought, Don't call it Frisco.

"Name sounded made-up to me. Can't remember."

They all got up and washed dishes and returned them to their shelf, scrubbed the pot, put everything to rights.

Noreen sighed and said, "This sure is nice."

A floor and walls make a difference, Jane thought. And electricity.

Noreen and the kids left the cabin the way they came in, single file, silent, out the gate to the Chevy.

Jane washed her face and hands in the sink, drying them with a dish towel, which she left damp, crumpled on the floor, a message to Momma.

SHE glided the Chevy on dying fumes into a tight space in front of the *Prospect*. The security guard silently admitted her to the building. The night staff moved like ghosts through the usually bustling place, no unneeded chatter, the smell of coffee, smoke. Everybody else at home with family, recovering from turkey and drink.

Jane waved at Sandy at the switchboard.

"You're coming up in the world. Got lots of calls, some for you, one about you."

"What do you mean, about me?"

"Lady wanted to know where you were. I told her Sacramento."

Jane glowered. "You told her?"

"That's it! Nothing else! I didn't know anything to tell!"

"Who was it?"

"She didn't say. Then your roommate called." Sandy read her note. "She said, 'Don't talk to Sweetie.' Didn't say why."

"That it?" Jane spit it out.

"No. You got a message from Wright. Said you should look into the guy in the picture. Said there was something funny about him, that he had another woman, who was jealous."

Was this Grete threatening her, through Momma?

"That it?" she repeated.

"Nope. Somebody left you this." Sandy handed her Daddy's worn pocketknife. "Left at the reception desk."

Jane turned it over in her hand. "Who left it?"

"It was just sitting there with a scrap of paper on it, your name."

"Benny Hopper?"

"Have you got some other name I don't know about?"

Find him before he finds you, before he ruins this.

"Do you know a bar that has something to do with a barn or a farm or farm animals even?"

"Do I know a bar? I know all the bars! Even the ones to do with a barn! Even the baaaaaad ones!" Sandy cackled as she made a list of three.

—————◦—————

CHAPTER EIGHT

BARS

Jane entered the Marina District's Horse Trough Tavern, conspicuously alone and awkward outside her usual places, no one to help her fit in by association, and pushed her way to the crowded bar. A hundred things fought for space in her head. She looked all around and didn't see Daddy or any obvious musicians.

She spotted a burly guy behind the bar, the other servers making space around him without his doing anything obvious to demand it.

"What can I get you?"

"Acme. You the owner?"

He nodded, giving Jane a wary up and down. "Howard." He handed her the beer.

"Nice place you got here, Howard, very nice."

He didn't answer. A damp paper turkey slouched on the bar.

"I'm Benny Hopper. Nice to meet you. Why'd you call it the Horse Trough?"

Howard reached under his counter and brought up a horseshoe, set it on the bar, patted it.

"This was my granddaddy's. I got lucky after football and bought this place."

He looked like an athlete gone to fat, ham-armed, tattooed.

"Who'd you play for?"

"You don't know?"

She had nothing to offer, no quip like any real boy would have. She'd done so much with Daddy, talked a lot of baseball, but not football at all.

He stared at her, waiting, she thought, for her to ask the questions anybody who followed football might ask.

"Bet you get tired of talking about those days, eh?"

He raised his eyebrows. "Ain't that the truth. All that in the papers."

The sports section? Something else? She played it safe. "What's your take?"

"My take?"

"What do you think about it?" She had to get out of this, over to the real line of questions.

He stopped pushing his cloth around the counter and said, "Really?"

What was going on here?

He gripped the bar with both hands, his arms bent, muscles bulging under fat, and leaned forward into her, like they were conspiring.

"Justice isn't everything it's cracked up to be."

"Justice?"

"I was convicted. Did my time."

She prepared to hear he was innocent, it wasn't fair, he'd been framed.

"I shoulda lost it all. Everybody said I would."

"Shoulda lost it all," Jane repeated, her voice dipping.

"Everybody expected me to lose everything, come out of Folsom a loser, living on the street, nowhere to turn."

She looked around at the packed bar, full of men of an athletic shape and the beautiful women who follow them.

"Hell, even the guys who retired from the game heroes, they don't have what I got. I got much more than they do."

Now she really wanted to know. "Why'd this happen to you instead?"

He smiled, revealing regular white teeth, sparkling. "People like a criminal."

She felt her nearness to him.

"I'm not sure . . ."

"It's the American dream—the outlaw life. Be the best, be great, jump over the rules. Rules are for the other guy."

"For the average Joe."

"He hates his job, his boss is a jerk, his wife complains night and day—that guy loves to see somebody come out swinging, win the fight, ring the bell. Gives him hope. My grit, my luck, gives all the schmucks hope."

"So . . . how'd you get the tavern?"

He laughed. "I get out, big guy backs me, I open this place —hit from day one. Everybody wants to rub shoulders, they'll pay to rub shoulders. This is just a piece of it. I got a much bigger pie, much bigger, opening bars all over town."

"In a depression?"

"I ain't depressed. Are you?"

"No, sir. I'm one of the happy guys."

"Good for you, kid." He straightened up, grabbed a clean rag. "Stay happy."

"So everybody knows what you did? It's out in the open?"

"Break the rules big and come clean, air the cut. Leaves a scar, but a scar's interesting."

He adjusted the paper turkey, made it upright again.

"This is very educational."

"Glad to help." Howard started to walk away from Jane's spot at the bar.

"Wait!"

"Yeah?" He turned, annoyed now, free lesson over.

"I'm looking for somebody."

"A body?"

"Somebody. A banjo player . . . Somebody told me he might play here."

"Somebody told you that?"

"A different somebody."

"Well, your somebody's wrong. Nobody plays music here. Just the records."

Sonny Boy Williamson was playing on a phonograph behind the bar next to a propped-up album cover—"Good morning, school girl."

"You wanna open a tab?"

She shook her head and put a bill from the wad she'd stolen from Momma on the counter, rising to go.

Howard rubbed the horseshoe. "Get lucky, son. Luck matters too."

SHE stepped out of a jitney in the Sunset District, Forty-Eighth and Rivera, in front of the block-long Jones-at-the-Beach, its windows turned to the Pacific and its door to the Doelger-built suburbs springing up all over the sand dunes, pretty little boxes, each inches from the next. Where the houses weren't built yet, they would be in minutes.

Up and down the street people poured out of cabs and jitneys, full of liquid charm, to join the newspapermen, musicians, boxers, and racing fans that made Jones their headquarters. There were also Sunset locals, rougher, windblown.

She followed a rowdy group inside. In the center of the dining room was a stone fireplace, four sides open, flames burning. On the right was another, where meals cooked in front of customers, steaks spitting and popping before they were forked onto horse-painted dishes. Most of the crowd was drinking, lined up on the left side of the room at a dark bar carved with racehorses, under a huge painting of a brown horse on the beach, the word "Bullet" painted underneath.

Many were newspaper men, some from the *Prospect*, but also other papers. All seemed to be writers, no copy boys, no secretaries, no accountants. Sandy'd sent her to some kind of secret club.

Again she pushed her way into prime bar space, planning to grease up before asking questions. She saw nobody was drinking beer, and when she said vodka, the bartender asked if she wanted a martini. She didn't know if she did but tipped her hat. He shook vodka and a couple other things together with ice in a silver urn, etched with horse heads, and strained it into a fancy glass, dropping an olive into the bottom.

"Vitamin V," Jane said.

"Another little writer was in here ordering one last night. Who started that?"

"Izzy," she said. "Must have got it from Izzy Gomez." The crowd agreed, smiling at the name of the guy who didn't charge writers. She was learning to answer questions the right way, the way that made people nod and smile. She grinned, feeling happy in this moment. She was good at taking a goal apart, figuring out what it required to get there, deciding if it was graspable or not. She could see she was fitting into this world, and that meant something.

The bartender said, "My grandfather worked at the Occidental Hotel, in Martinez, where people would wait for the ferry. That's were the martini was invented. They called it the Martinez."

"Baloney!" yelled Lambert from the other end of the bar. "It was invented in New York. Like everything." The *Prospect* crowd booed Lambert and toasted the bartender's grandfather.

"I have the evidence," Lambert pushed. "There's an article about it. I read it! From the *Times*. I can prove it."

"Awww, shuddup!" somebody yelled, and the horde laughed.

"It's the accurate fact, I can go back to my 'partment, bring it back!" Lambert slurred his words, swaying as he testified.

"Don't give a sulfur egg for facts!" yelled Beauchamp, the *Examiner's* gossip guy. "I prefer truth to fact any day!"

"The truuuuuth! So that's what they're calling it now!" This came from a blousy lady on Beauchamp's arm.

Lambert fell off his stool but climbed back up, yelling, "No truth without facts!"

"Totally different items," said Beauchamp. "Facts are temporary. Truth is forever."

"That is a ridiculous assertion. If truth is a greater thing— and it is, because it takes us further than facts, makes meaning of facts—still it cannot exist without the facts at its base."

"Facts are dirt," Jane said. "Truth's the crop that grows from it."

Lambert's mouth dropped open. "From the mouth of a nincompoop!"

"Horsefeathers!" yelled the guy next to Jane. "Reporters and your quote, unquote ideas! My horse Bullet's got more truth in his right front hoof than you got in all your big fat brains!"

Bullet was the horse in the painting over the bar. This guy was Jonesie, the bar's owner. Jane jumped on it. "Your horse is pretty smart?"

"My, Professor, can't pull nothing over on you! You must be the last guy on earth who don't know this. But I don't mind telling you." He said it loud so the rest could hear it, too, probably like he did every night. "So, my Bullet means everything to me. Damn horse sat at the head of my Thanksgiving table! Better manners than my sister's family! My sister's husband? Can't hold his liquor! But Bullet can! Drank him under the table!" That caused guffaws and elbowing.

"Anyhow, guy who runs Bay Meadows? Says to me, 'Horses can't swim.' I say my horse Bullet can swim the Golden Gate. So my partner bets a thousand on it. Then the SPCA gets their panties in a twist and talks the Marin city council into stopping us from shoving off there. So we go out on a fishing trawler with a sling and net, and lower Bullet into the water from the side of the boat. I go with him. I love that horse." He stopped to wipe his eyes of real tears. He put the handkerchief away and continued. "I slather myself with grease and put on a life preserver—I can't swim—and I ride Bullet's tail like it's . . ." The crowd whooped so loud, slapping backs and endorsing Jonesie's heroism, that Jane couldn't hear the end of the joke. "Takes us twenty-three minutes and fifteen seconds. SPCA's waiting for us, but they have to admit I look a lot worse than Bullet, so they tear up the ticket and get drunk with the rest of us! Them's the facts *and* the truth!"

The crowd was still laughing when Sweetie entered the bar on Mac's arm.

From the double takes breaking necks all around, this was a new sight for everybody. She was especially well put together, in an expensive-looking dress, pale green silk with puff sleeves, a belted waist, and a large collar. Her knit hat matched the dress and her leather shoes did, too, with no scuffs. Long gold earrings dangled near her jaw, matching a bangle on her tiny wrist. She twinkled, wearing nothing she had apparently made or altered. Fresh as Easter grass.

Mac and Sweetie were each handed a martini, now the official drink of the evening. He raised his glass and twisted his forearm through hers, and they sipped, entwined.

God, Jane thought, sitting alone in a crowd on that stool.

Then he kissed Sweetie, his head so much larger than hers, concealing her face, the rough skin of his hand contrasted against her smooth, white neck.

Something gathered in the base of Jane's throat, ready to sound. She felt like the voice in her head might pop out in the room, say something wrong, so she swallowed it, wanting just to feel this loss for the long seconds of the kiss.

Lambert yelled, "Grub!" and she saw she was starving, so

she joined the throng moving into booths around the edges of the room. They ordered up a midnight meal of chicken loaf, terrapin stew, steak à la cliff, baked potatoes with sour cream and bacon, and more pitchers of martinis. They were noisy, none more than Lambert, and while the group kept it up, Jane listened. She was part of this. Irritating thoughts circled the outer rim of her brain—she had something real to do here, a problem to solve—but she ignored them now, inside this warm social blanket.

As she finished her steak, Lambert scooted next to her, putting his arm around her shoulder. "I wouldn't rely over-much on Mac and this particular paper, Boy."

"Why'd you have to do that?"

"You could write any number of places, you know, it doesn't have to be for Mac."

"He's giving me my break, isn't he?"

"He doesn't give things away. Not like his word is his bond."

"Yours is?"

He was so drunk, acting even more like an ass than usual, she had every reason to ignore him. She hadn't forgotten what he'd done, stealing that moleskin, disrespecting her. Setting her up for a fall. But something kept her in her seat.

He was not the kind of person she'd choose for a friend or advisor, so devious and contrary. But still, he had perceptiveness. She'd seen it every day, his knowing something would happen, what it would mean. He was alert to the big picture, a whole system, when most people saw just the little bit in front of them.

"What have you got against Mac?"

"I got nothing against him! Fine with me he's gonna fuck it all up. Everything's temporary. It's just we could be a great paper, but we won't. Because he wants to do it the way he wants to do it. Trash it. Trash it up. Make it trashy."

Jane thought this was just getting sad, his drunkenness. "Why do you think he'll trash it?"

"He isn't committed. Not the kind of guy who sticks around, grows something. He'll be gone, on to the next shiny opportunity right before we crash."

Everything was waving and yellow. She didn't want this conversation. A guy like Lambert had to ruin everything. Couldn't just let it go, let it be nice. "Good night, Eeyore," she said, and went back to the bar, as too-drunk people will do.

The crowd there was more bitter and sloppy now than before. When Jane asked for another martini, the bartender shook his head no, not like he'd deny her, but like he didn't advise it, though Jane nodded her head yes, full enough of herself to contradict him.

He poured her drink, and she finally asked what she'd come for an hour before—whether a banjo player with a curved scar on his cheek performed there.

"Nah, Jonesie's all the entertainment we need," he said, which she saw was true.

She looked down at the name of the last bar on her list and the letters swirled, so she turned the paper to the bartender.

"Topsy's Roost, over at Playland-at-the-Beach. They got a band."

Coins slipped, tinkling, from her fingers as she overpaid the bill.

SHE raised her brows high to hold her eyes open. What did I say to that guy on the stool? Who was he? She saw herself setting her glass on the edge of the bar and it toppling, spilling, wetting her sleeve. Staring at her wrist, so slim. She remembered bending to pick up the glass, butting heads and laughing, though the other guy looked angry.

She'd fallen into the taxi, saying the name of the third bar
—Topsy's—to the driver, who'd rolled his eyes in the mirror.
She'd slept to the rocking of city streets. The driver shook her
awake, yelling, "Twenty-five cents!"

She nearly fell as she got out, the wind off the Pacific
slapping her hard in the face.

This is it. You're here. Wake up.

Set in an amusement park, Topsy's was a nightclub and
chicken dinner house, built to look like a chicken shack, people seated at human-sized coops in the balcony. Guests could
slip down a massive slide from their tables to the dance floor.
Waiters ran around dressed like they were headed to a square
dance. A band, one level below the entrance, played Gersh-
win—"They can't take that away from me."

A barn of a bar, with a band.

A man in a white cowboy hat said, "Howdy," looking
pained. "May I help you?"

"Sir," Jane said.

"Sir."

"Looking for a member of the band."

He motioned below. "Would you like to take the slide?"

"I'd rather walk," she said, too woozy to slide.

He pointed and Jane followed his finger, walking around
the rim of the second floor toward a set of stairs on the opposite side, past fancy people caged by chicken wire, ladies in
clinging chiffon, silk, crepe de chine, satin, cut on the bias,
metallic lamé, fur, hems flaring all the way out on the floor,
puffs, ruffles, plunging backs, men less spectacular but im-
pressive in black tuxedos, shiny black shoes, cufflinks. Everybody clinking champagne flutes, laughing at the weirdness—
them, in this stage-set farmyard. A waiter rushed by, platter
up, fried chicken, biscuits, okra in the air. Jane pressed up
against a coop so he could pass.

When she got to the other side of the barn and down the

stairs, she looked at the band, about sixteen of them, playing swingy country music, or country swing music, she wasn't sure, the way it blended. She couldn't see them well and couldn't figure a way to get closer to them other than walking right up the empty dance floor, so that's what she did. The music announced her—"Nice work if you can get it."

She was halfway there when—*Whoosh! Whoosh! Ahhh!*— a man and woman in shiny black and white flew down a slide, their arms up, each holding a drink, landing right ahead of her. Someone above yelled "Yee-haw!" and people laughed, and then the slides filled with more couples heading to the dance floor, which grew crowded as the singer crooned.

Jane pushed through the dancers and arrived at the foot of the stage, looked up at the band, all costumed as some confused combination of cowboys and farmers. She saw the pianist, a drummer, a trumpet player, and in front of them, Daddy, on banjo, sitting—he never sat while he played—wearing clean, new overalls, one strap undone, hanging to his waist, its clasp shiny, over a bright, red-checked shirt. His cowboy hat had a narrow brim, tilted up so you could see almost all his forehead. Everything about him looked wrong, a Daddy doll, store-bought, silly version of the man. Inauthentic.

She stood in front of the stage and the musicians played on. Daddy looked but didn't seem to see her. Then his face cracked and his right hand dropped. He turned to another guy and handed him the banjo. The band kept playing. The guy passed the banjo to somebody else backstage, who took over where Daddy left off. Daddy picked up two sticks—canes— using them to cross the stage and walk down its steps to her. Dancers jostled him, left and right, until he reached her.

"Jujee."

She nodded to the back of the room and led him through the crowded floor toward the exit. They went slow and careful. She'd done this, swinging that crowbar at his knees.

She felt him behind her and pictured him swinging a cane at the back of her head. She kept walking, waiting for the hit, but it didn't come, and then they got to the back of the room and she opened the door, and they were on Playland's boardwalk. Fog, piped music, the rumble of a roller coaster, women screaming.

He took off his stupid hat, setting it on a decorative barrel. His hair was cut and clean, more brown than blond now.

"What's wrong with you?" he asked.

She felt the strangeness of her man's clothes, new again with Daddy looking at her.

"What's wrong with *you*?"

"I know," he said. "I thought the camp was a nightmare. *This* is the nightmare. Brought on by myself, but a nightmare still." Even admitting his failure, his voice expressed tragedy— I'm too good for this. But she knew he must have suffered to be here, playing this ridiculous version of himself. Daddy was rough, but he had taste, real taste, style, a kind of honesty. Nothing about this costume or this setting would feel right to him.

"Never thought I'd miss the levee." He lit a cigarette and then another when she reached for it. "So this is how you express yourself."

"This is how I climbed out of the ditch and got work."

He said, "That it?"

"Pretty much."

"Incognito," he said.

"Sort of."

"So are you funny?"

"No," she said. "I'm not funny. But what I am shouldn't matter."

He said, "You're a one-man guy."

"Whatsat?"

"Like me and your momma. Sometimes it looks like you're for another person, but really you're for yourself."

Jane wished she could defend herself against this. But she'd had to be that way.

"I'm sorry," she said, "for hitting you and leaving you."

"You're apologizin' because you want something?"

She felt the red in her cheeks.

"One-man guy," he confirmed.

"I didn't mean for all that to happen."

"What do you mean, you didn't mean to?"

"I didn't plan it."

"So you didn't plan it. But you did it."

"What do you mean, I did it? You did it too! You hit Momma!"

"You don't see me backing out of it, like what I intended matters. It's just what you do that matters. You and your momma have the killer instinct. Hand on the plow. Never release. Don't matter why or how."

She couldn't take that.

"I did what I had to do. So did you! And if that's what you think, then why've you been looking for me?" Her voice cracked. "Are we done?"

He rearranged his shoulders, stood up straighter. "It don't excuse what I done, I know. I was out of my mind that night." He shook his head. "I just want you to know—I know I was wrong. Very, very wrong. For hitting her, for a lot of things. I'm your daddy, and I shouldn'ta done that. Shouldn'ta done anything like that, puttin' you in that position, between the two of us."

"My whole life . . ." She stopped, knowing it would take a while to parse, that she'd have to figure it out in private. She cleared her throat. "Anyway, that it?"

"I hope you can do somethin' with it, climb up over."

She'd already done that. She moved on. "Did you know Vee before the picture?"

"Did you?"

"No," she said. Then she decided to tell him. "I met her once, last week, that's all. The night before she was hurt."

"What do you have to do with that?"

"I've been trying to keep your picture out of the *Prospect*. People are gonna look at you there with her and start asking questions. Did you . . . ?"

"I didn't do that."

"You didn't hit her, choke her."

"No. And seems to me folks are gonna start looking at you, too, now."

She nodded.

He dropped his cigarette, ground it out. "I gotta get back. Can't lose the gig."

She dropped hers and grabbed his wrist. "Tell me what you know."

A cream Chrysler squealed up behind the building, lighting the other end of the parking lot, and she dropped Daddy's wrist.

"People act so unpredictable here," he said, jerking his head at the car.

She said, "Let's just walk for a minute then. Just a minute."

He picked up his canes and followed Jane out of their dark corner of the lot, away from the still-rumbling car, toward a nearly empty roller coaster, two couples and one guy all by himself flying by, screaming.

"We both look like suspects. You there in the picture with her. Me . . ."

"Lookin' like me."

"That, but also, I was supposed to meet her at Breen's the night she was hurt."

"But you didn't?"

"No."

"Don't look good for either of us."

"Why would someone attack her? If we can figure this out . . ."

"Good night, Playland revelers," a voice boomed over loudspeakers. "The Playland party is over tonight. Return tomorrow to relive the thrills! For now, please find your nearest exit and go safely into the night."

The roller coaster screeched into its station, wobbly couples climbing out, laughing. The solo guy stepped out carefully, giving them a look.

Daddy turned and started walking back toward Topsy's, leaning on the canes, Jane behind him.

"It's hard to say why. There's a lot of parts."

She kept her mouth shut. Anything she said might stop his talking.

"I ain't proud of it, but I wanted some of what Uno has."

"Momma?"

He laughed. "Well, maybe her, too, maybe not." He shook his head. "But I mean he has an arrangement with the photographer."

"Uno?"

"He's a kind of arranger for her."

"What's that mean?"

"She lets him know she's coming, he arranges for something interesting to happen when she gets there."

"Interesting?"

"People to take pictures of—desperate, dangerous, sad people—like that."

"He's a scout?"

"More than that. He doesn't just say, 'Hey, there's some people down by the river.' It's more like, 'I'll get some people together by the river for you.' And she pays him for it. He does all right that way."

"That's how you and Noreen and Vee and the baby came to be in that picture."

"You know Noreen?"

She nodded.

184

"That's how. But it isn't just us. It's a lot of them. He does a lot of work for her."

"There's poor people everywhere. Why's she need to fix it up through him?"

"It ain't that she needs help finding people. She needs help finding special people."

She thought about *Family*. It was special. Daddy was special.

Then she thought, Even Uno has an eye for it.

"There's this one," Daddy said, "of a man—Tom Jesson. *Hunger*."

Jane's skin cooled. It was in her pocket. "I've seen it."

"Got a lot of attention, lot of money too."

"From who?"

"Papers pay her more than they pay other photographers, I've heard."

"Why would they?"

"Her pictures sell more papers than other pictures do. She doesn't just photograph a dirty, poor girl. It's a beautiful, dirty, poor girl. Somebody special. Her pictures get in all the papers, across the country."

Jane knew Vee was beautiful but had looked at her and thought, *off*, feared, *off*. But it was her strangeness, her difference that made her stand out.

Jane thought of Mac insisting on getting the *Family* photo back rather than just going with some other picture. It would draw more eyes.

Daddy continued. "She don't give you a picture of a hungry man, she gives you a picture of a dying man, so you can see he's dying. If she calls him hungry, he's gotta be dying-hungry."

"What are you saying?"

"That picture? She took so long in that shoot, propping Jesson up all over the place, promising him money for his family, he died before the shoot was over. Right there on the dirt with the photographer and Uno and their cars right there. They didn't take him to the hospital. They took his picture. That picture? He's dead. Eyes open."

The eerie blankness of his staring eyes.

She thought, That's what makes it good. Nothing between him and you. No pretend. Long as you're alive, you're faking, convincing, persuading. Because he's dead, there's none of that. Just the truth, his hunger.

"Uno got paid. The photographer got paid. Some folks probably got more government food deliveries that week. Can't say if Jesson's family got paid . . ."

"That's terrible." Focused so long on how she'd been cheated, mistreated, now Jane felt deep, righteous hate toward Grete, for what she'd done to other people.

"I don't like to say it, but I wanted part of that. Wanted some of that money too. I done a lot of things I'm not proud of for money. I'm 'shamed about that."

She knew what hunger did, especially when it combined with hope and ambition.

This was the story she'd write. But she couldn't let Daddy be her source. Protect the family. She had to hide him from the news.

"Who else knows? Who'd go on record?"

"Lotta people know, but nobody's gonna talk. Won't risk uncovering stuff they themselves done."

She wouldn't talk if it were her.

"But she writes it all down, all the figures, in a ledger. I put my *X* there, for my five dollars." His cheeks reddened, mentioning the *X*.

All those notebooks he helped her make, when he couldn't read or write himself. She hadn't thought much about that before, but now she saw his humiliation, taking Grete's money, unable to write his name. That understanding expanded, taking up space.

She brought herself back. She'd seen piles of leather books in Grete's darkroom. Some of them had to be the ledgers. There would be pages of names, columns of figures.

Now we're talking.

As bubbles popped in her head, the Chrysler door swung open and a man sprung out in the dark, his arm extended.

Daddy pushed her hard with both hands, slamming her into a wall, her cheek hitting first. As she went down, she heard *crack, tzing, ping*, before darkness.

She woke a few minutes later, maybe, on the threshold of Topsy's back door, music stopped, headlights blinding. She pushed up, her face pounding, onto her hands and knees, gripped the doorway to rise, walked through the parking lot, full of cop cars. The empty roller coaster screamed by. The Chrysler was gone. Daddy was gone, again.

CHAPTER NINE

STORY

S he told them she'd gone out back for a smoke, next to some other guy, a stranger, when shots went off, said she dove and hit the wall, that the other guy took off. Nobody was really hurt, so the cops weren't as interested as they should have been.

An old cop told her she should go home, to bed, but she didn't have a home or a bed—she couldn't go back to Rivka's. She didn't belong anywhere but the paper, so she had him drop her at the corner of Fifth and Mission. When he drove off, she went into the paper, up its spine, her cut-up, swollen face and ripped, dirty clothes shocking everybody into spilling coffee, dropping telephone handsets as she marched past Lambert, Jorge, and the rest, straight into Mac's office.

"I got our story."

Mac didn't answer, just stared, his mouth open.

"Wright has people, a team, who help her fix photos, fake them. She pays everybody. The photos are great, the best, because of this arranging, and the papers—we—pay her more than we pay anybody else because she cheats."

"Hey now . . ."

"That famous one, *Hunger*?"

She pulled it out of her pocket and laid it on his desk, Jesson's blank eyes looking straight at her. She felt and then saw that Lambert and Jorge had entered the office and were standing behind her, looking over her shoulders.

"He's dead. Tom Jesson died, right there, while she was propping him up, trying to get the right shot. She let him die for the picture."

"This is a story," Jorge said, and turned to Jane. "What's your evidence?"

"Quotes," she lied, patting the pocket where her moleskin was. "Plus our records of how much her pictures earn compared to everybody else."

Mac shook his head. He didn't like that part.

She wasn't going to wait to do the rest of the research. She knew what the story was. She was going to get it out now.

"Somebody's dead! It's not just Vee's coma. Tom Jesson's dead. I was shot at tonight, and I'm not waiting. I'm writing the story. Either you take it, or somebody else will."

"Who killed Vesta? They do it for Grete?" Jorge asked.

"She's not dead yet, right?"

"Whatever."

"I don't have that all the way yet."

"Who's your source for what you've got?"

"I can't say. But Vee was hit and choked because she was coming to us to tell the story. She met me the night before. I'm 'BH.' I never showed up." Of everything she'd said, this last bit slowed her.

She felt Lambert's hand on her shoulder.

Mac said, "Jorge, set 'em up, the parameters. Let's go, goddammit!"

She knew he didn't want this story. It made the *Prospect* look bad. But he knew they had to do it. It was the story.

Jorge divided up the bits between her and Lambert, and they got to work at side-by-side desks in the big writing room, at the center of the action together.

She read through her moleskin, notes that came close to what she needed but not enough to get her all the way. She knew much more than she could report. She had to jump that gap.

Her notes from Noreen said she'd been posed, that Grete had chosen what to include in the frame and what not to, but that wasn't enough, and Noreen wasn't reachable by telephone for more information. She had to do something she didn't relish.

She got a switchboard girl to call Tumbleweed. She waited, the telephone at her ear, hearing a high-pitched squeal. She looked around. Nobody else seemed to hear it. The newsroom looked yellow to her, fuzzy. How could she ask for Momma's help without getting into everything else, without letting her know where she was, what she was doing? She'd have to trust her.

It clicked on the fourth ring. "Joe Jeffers."

She froze at the sound of his voice, at what she knew he'd done, the photograph pimping she was reporting on. It was crazy to call this number. She hung up. What would stop him from calling the cops on her for the things she'd done, leaving Daddy for dead, taking the car, taking money from their drawer? Momma was wrapped up in it too. They were tangled together, Momma, Daddy, Uno. The new baby.

She told the girl to re-call it. This time he picked up on the first ring. "Sweetie?"

She hung up again.

She'd thought Sweetie hated him. She never said anything about him. Had they been talking all along? If Sweetie did talk to him, what did she tell him about Jane? What did Uno and Momma know?

"Woo-hoo!" Lambert slammed his desk, rattling hers. "Coming together, Hopper! How about you? Getting what we need?"

She wasn't.

"Haven't got all day!" His face was red. He pushed his

telephone back and pulled his typewriter closer to the edge of his desk. "One slip at a time. I do grafs on what I got. You do 'em on what you got. Fill a half slip, put it in the pile. Don't worry—do they go together or in what order or even if we need them. The other guys'll paste 'em together, and we'll see what we got!"

He was off and typing again.

A pile of empty half slips sat on the crack between their two desks, accusing in their blankness. She wasn't ready, didn't have the quotes. But she saw him racing ahead and thought about how she had to make things right, had to beat Grete, who must have arranged to have Daddy shot.

That song Daddy mentioned ticked at the back of her mind—"Can't plow straight and keep a-lookin' back."

That's how, like she'd learned from Momma. Keep your hand on the plow. Your horse pulls your plow, you hold on behind. Don't need to push. But lift your hand, relax it? Plow lifts up out of its rut, and you fail to do the work. If your hand holds on? Plow turns the soil. Just loop the reins around your neck. If you look left, your horse veers left. If you look right, your horse veers right. You have to look ahead, to the end of the row, to lay that track down straight. Take your hand off the plow, look the wrong way, the field is ruined. You're ruined.

She started typing, her notebook open.

First a graf describing *Family* as it appeared in the other papers. She set it on the desk, yelling, "Boy!" and somebody swooped in to grab it.

Then a graf on a different version of the photograph's setting, as she imagined it from Noreen's description, dirty diapers, piles of clothes to bucket-wash, broken machines to re-make, bottles, imagined memory.

She described the black-haired, buzz-cut boy, who looked Cherokee or Mexican—she just decided Cherokee, flinching at the fact that she was bad at seeing who people were. But she kept going, straight ahead, in spite of that, speed beating doubt.

She described how Grete bullied Noreen into better pictures, better poses. She wrote about Noreen, Vee, and Daddy—"the unknown male"—having no real family relation.

She wrote that Grete burned out things she hadn't physically moved out of the picture that made it to the paper. She wrote a paragraph describing the FSA rules on altering and staging photographs, the rules Grete was supposed to follow. Then a graf explaining why they had that policy. Then a graf describing how dodging and burning work.

Then a half sheet about money.

Then the hungry man, the dying man.

The words came as fast as she could make sense of them. Typing these grafs, shot through with fiction, felt as fine to her as anything ever had.

With Lambert typing right next to her, about the big picture, the federal money, where it came from and where it went —those papers that published *Family*—she felt like she did that night typing with Rivka, connected to someone else who also wanted to do good work, or something like that, ambitious work. She saw that about Lambert. Though she hated him, she respected him too. He worked hard. He knew how things were done.

She needed quotes, so she found what she'd handwritten from memory out of Grete's blue leather notebooks and used it to make a quote from Noreen: "We make just enough for cornbread, and when we gotta buy gas it comes out of that. We had to do what the lady photographer said. We had no choice. She said she was going to help us. But she didn't give us nothing."

She read it under her breath a few times, thinking, It's the kind of fiction that's true.

But it wasn't enough, so she added more to come out of

Noreen's mouth. "That great, fancy lady told me to move my kids out of the picture because some people wouldn't want to help a lady with so many kids from so many different daddies. She only wanted a little blond baby because that would sell a lot of papers. She cleaned up bottles 'round the camp because people don't want to give money to poor folk who have enough to buy something to drink. If folks are merciful, they shouldn't care about the quality of the ones they give to." Noreen never said that right out, but she meant it. It was true.

It took a while to get it done.

She'd upheld Noreen's dignity and taken Grete down. Everything was close enough to right that she felt almost complete about it.

Jorge talked to two editors, looking at the copy, his sleeves rolled, tie gone, suspenders dangling. He poured vodka into a glass for himself and offered some to Jane.

"I'm a bourbon guy," she said, deciding in the moment, and slumped into her chair, feeling old, like fifty.

Right away, a new brunette receptionist clicked over to her desk, her eyes popped wide when she saw Jane, maybe expecting someone older, more distinguished, more masculine.

"Here you go, Mr. Hopper," she said, handing her a glass of bourbon, while Jorge read the last of the half slips aloud.

Then he boomed, "Run it, dammit!"

"Boy!" Lambert yelled, and Wally ran over to grab the remaining copy, glaring at Jane.

"You're a surprise," Jorge said, slapping her back.

Lambert stood, stretching. "You look like shit. But not too shitty to celebrate."

She felt so high now; just one bourbon was gas on fire.

"Somebody get him a coat and hat!"

The pretty receptionist came back with some other slob's clothes in her hands.

Jane slipped the coat on and it fit. Patting the pockets, buttoning the jacket, her eyes watered. She fit.

"Meet you out front," she said as the others dispersed.

She took Lambert's keys from her pocket and set them on his desk.

Then she slumped back into his chair and twirled, so that her vision was a blur of desks and typewriters and walls and windows.

SHE put her key in the lock, surprised the knob turned. Rivka hadn't changed it.

She'd had one drink in celebration of the story at Breen's, but she couldn't stay. It had been so long since she slept. She needed to take everything in, and there was nowhere else to go.

"It's me, Jane!" she called, going upstairs. No answer.

The front parlor was different. It had never been really clean, but now it was much messier, full ashtrays on the piano, side table, arm of the velvet sofa. Music books strewn not just on the piano but on the floor all around it. A plate with bread crusts and a piece of bacon balanced on a pillow on the floor against bookshelves. A bottle of rye and two glasses sat on the mantel, where the painting of a tractor no longer hung. All the costume drawings were down now too. The always-closed sliding doors to the interior parlor were open, and that space was a disaster of wooden crates, some open.

Two glasses on the mantel—Jane couldn't imagine who Rivka would invite in for a drink. Maybe Sweetie had come to collect her things and sat for a bit before leaving.

She walked down the hall to the kitchen. Dishes in the sink, on the counters. Sheet music on the table. At least she's got privacy for practice, she thought, wondering if that was a good thing.

Feeling bad for Rivka, so alone, she collected dishes in the parlor and kitchen and began to clean, filling the sink with hot, soapy water, laying out a towel on the counter to drain them on. While she worked, she sang, "Hand on the plow, hold on."

"Kind of elevates the work, I imagine."

She turned to see Oppie standing in the doorway in his slacks and undershirt, no socks.

"Something in this room is out of place," she said.

"Don't you belong on the stoop, dusty doorman?"

"Explain yourself," she said.

"Let us begin with you." Rivka passed Oppie, coming around to the table, wearing a slip—a slip! She'd never gone around in a slip before. She was always dressed in street clothes or pajamas. She sat at the table and lit a cigarette. "What are you doing?"

"Cleaning up. Somebody's got to."

"Tidiness has suffered without Sweetie."

Jane said, "Looks like there've been gains."

"Did you return to insult me?" Rivka blew smoke.

Jane dried her hands on a towel and turned back to Rivka. "I'm sorry. I've wrecked things here, I know. I took what you offered and then just messed it up for you. I'm sorry."

Rivka left a silence there for a moment, squinting at Jane, and then said, "It was not your fault. Sweetie had reason to move on. She needs someone to help, someone to help her. If anyone gets between her and that, all is disrupted. Besides, it was time for somebody higher up. Mac will be good, until she bores him or she finds someone higher, publisher maybe."

"Which she certainly will," Oppie added, taking the chair next to Rivka. "Bore him, I mean. Her charms are ephemeral."

"What's that?" Jane asked.

"They don't last."

Jane thought about it for a minute, disagreeing. Oppie was wrong. Sweetie lingered. "Didn't know you were such a relationship expert."

"Just sharing the fruits of my research."

Rivka said, "From your decades of successful social inter-actions."

"I read a lot. The fact I maintain antisocial boundaries merely hides my basic sensitivity."

Rivka put her hand over Oppie's, surprising Jane. He looked awkward, his spine stiff, struggling to maintain a comfortable posture with his shirt off, his hand held.

"Bashful dogs get no scraps," Jane said. Oppie rolled his eyes.

Then he said, "Are you going to say what's happened to you?"

Jane touched the cut on her cheek from the wall at Playland. "How about a drink?"

He went down the hall and she yelled after him, "No vodka!" and he came back with a bottle of bourbon, dried off three clean glasses, poured two inches of the golden stuff into each, and pushed one in front of each girl. Rivka cut up sharp cheese and apple to go with the drinks, a reviving combination, food and drink. Nourishment.

A couple weeks before Momma, Daddy, and Jane had left for California, right before Granny died, she stood with her in the garden. The dust had destroyed everything for them there, but Granny took her out to the patch right behind her tar shack home.

"I got you a surprise."

In one corner of the ruined garden, she pulled a tomato off a spindly volunteer stalk. She reached into her apron pocket for a knife and sliced it in half. She returned the knife to her pocket, pulled out a saltshaker, dusted each tomato half. She handed one half to Jane and took the other for herself. They ate them like peaches, salty and red. Jane could taste it now.

"Simple is good," Granny said. It was.

SHE felt better with the apple and cheese in her.

"Why don't you introduce me to Jane," Oppie said.

She emptied her glass in one take. "Being Benny got me the job."

"Benny still in business?"

"Looks like."

She turned to Rivka. "I was with my daddy tonight. We were shot at." Then she laid her head on her arms, exhausted, and Rivka rubbed her shoulders. When she lifted her head up, Rivka's eyes were warm and Oppie had poured her another glass, which she sipped this time, tasting dark, orange, caramel, fire, lifting the top off her skull, opening things up, so much better than vodka or beer. "I wrote a story for the paper."

Rivka and Oppie exchanged looks.

"Daddy knew all about Vee. Somebody shot at him for it. It'll be in the paper tomorrow. He told me Grete faked her photos, posed them, paid people, all kinds of things like that. She made a lot of money because her pictures are more . . ."

"Arresting," Rivka said. "And gorgeous. But do you really think she makes much money?"

"Yeah! Her pictures are all miles past real," she said, ignoring her own fictions.

"You never really know who a person is," Oppie said.

"You think you got it," Jane agreed, "but you don't. It's right there, but you don't see it. Maybe other people do . . ."

"Expectations influence behavior, causing expected results."

She shook her head, confused.

"We collect the evidence that supports what we already believe. We ignore what supports a different conclusion."

"Can't we ever just think something, right away, fast, just come to the right idea?"

Rivka said, "That is what practice is for. You practice for long time, until you can do your thinking without as much thinking. It will not always be so hard."

"You don't think it's too late for me? You don't think if you're just really behind, really late, and have a lot of bad things . . ."

"It is not too late for you," Rivka said. "Not too late at all. Where I come from . . ."

"Where's that?" asked Oppie.

"Prague," she said, and he nodded. "From there, some people in family, bad things happened, they fell down and never got up. Other people got up, climbed over, got strong. Recovered. Better than recover."

"Like you," Jane said.

"And you."

"I want to believe it, but . . ."

"Believe it," Oppie said, raising his glass. "Huzzah."

"Huzzah," Jane and Rivka echoed, clinking glasses.

"Where did you get your grit, Miss Jane?"

She thought of the field, the camp, the ditch.

"Good genes."

Then she told them her story, as much as she could before the bottle was empty.

ONE block from the *Prospect*, Jane picked the morning edition up off the sidewalk—"Picture worth a thousand dollars, by Derek Lambert, reporting by *Prospect* staff."

No Benny Hopper. He'd stolen her byline.

She looked up from the story to see Lambert pulling away from the curb ahead.

She ran to the car, wrenched open the passenger door as he was beginning to glide into traffic, scrambling, the door hanging open, unsure what to do when she got in there.

"What the hell!"

She reached over to pull the shift, stop the car, managing to get it to neutral with a great grinding. She hated him, had to stop him from ruining her chance—if it wasn't too late already—had to get him to tell Mac to give her back her story somehow. She was the writer! He was a thief!

Lambert shoved her right shoulder.

Her back to the open door, her legs facing Lambert, she kicked the side of his body with her stiff wingtips as hard as she could.

"What the fuck is wrong with you?" he yelled, hunching away from her, his broad shoulders curving to protect his ribs and organs.

But she kept kicking, so he pulled up his knees. Then he rounded up and punched her over her knees, hitting her hard so that she fell backward, her head out the car door.

"What's wrong with you? Idiot!"

She wrenched herself upright. "You stole my byline!" She kicked him again.

They were so close in the front seat that neither could get up the momentum to do much damage, but they both had bloody faces and knuckles by the time Lambert backed up into his own door and held Jane off with his feet.

Her face stung, head throbbed, ribs ached. Lambert's eyeglass lenses were cracked, the frames bent. She was breathing hard. She wiped blood and snot off her face with her arm.

"Liar!" she yelled.

"What about you, Benny? Oh, no, wait, isn't it Benjamina or something? Who's the liar?"

He'd known all this time. Still. "It was my story! I'm telling Mac . . ."

"Do you have to act like such a fucking baby? I needed that article to get out of here. You'll get other chances. This is how it works. There's a hierarchy, get it?"

She kicked at him again, with less vigor.

"I left you a bone, it's gonna get you further here. Do something with it!"

"Great, oh, thanks a lot! 'With reporting by *Prospect* staff.' Yeah, that'll get me there!"

Lambert yelled, "You are what your name's on, hayseed! You're not anything until your name's on what you need it on!"

"I know that! What do you think? I didn't know that?"

"I gave you what you need to do well here! Fuck you if you don't get it!"

Lambert shifted the Chevy back into drive and began to jerk it forward into a stream of honking traffic. Jane kicked at him once more, the momentum throwing her backward, out the open car door, where she landed in the gutter as Lambert crunched into a Ford, people yelling all around them in the street.

Disaster. She should never have trusted him. He was a liar. More than she was.

She got up, stared at by passing accountants, dockworkers, and factory men on the sidewalk, pressed down her hair, and turned to enter the building, yelling at a hobo next to the door: "Get out of my way! I work here!"

SHE didn't race up the spine—her head was pounding from the fight and the bourbon and the wall. She chose the elevator instead.

"Second floor," she said to the old guy manning the controls. He closed the gate, pushed a button, and pulled a lever. "It's not too late," he said.

"For what?"

"This thing can go right back down."

"Right," she said, not paying attention.

The elevator doors closed and then opened, and she

stepped out, intending to march straight to Mac's office, talk over next steps, but she stopped just outside the elevator. The room was full of people but quiet. No typing. Writers, copy boys, editors, switchboard operators silent. There were good suits among them, men whose clothes didn't look so ratty as the writers', their hair slicker, more like roosters, less like dogs.

"Hopper!" Mac called from his doorway. Everyone looked.

She shuddered and then walked to him.

"Shut the door," he said, his face white.

She did it.

"I was going to say you've made a colossal mistake, but it seems you've made a truckload of 'em." He looked her up and down with disgust. "You can't talk this kind of thing into something else." His jaw muscles clenched and unclenched, his nostrils flaring. Otherwise his body was still.

"Mac, you wanted . . ."

"I have lawyers representing three newspapers, the federal government, and a photographer outside, lawyers who claim their clients have been libeled. They say you falsified information about Wright and her photographs and all the newspapers that ran them."

"Well, Lambert . . ."

"He's no longer with this newspaper."

His fist came down on a copy of the paper, open to the city section, an unfamiliar column under a line drawing of a reporter—visor, armband, pointer finger touching the rim of his glasses, thumb under his chin. "Barbary Coast Lines, by Benny Hopper." Her byline.

She picked it up and skimmed the *Prospect's* first ever gossip column, about Dr. R. J. Oppenheimer, theoretical physicist at UC Berkeley—

Oh, the money we spend. Piles of federal research
dollars flow to UC Berkeley's physics department,

*including Dr. Oppenheimer, called Oppie by his
communist and free-love friends, in spite of his
betraying every possible morality clause in the
university's contract. In particular, he parades an
extramarital relationship with Rivka Tomás, radio
pianist and commie wife of Old Europe. . . .*

He'd written this garbage, given it to her, taken the real
story, the big story, for himself.

Mac barked, "Get out there and talk to the fact-checkers in
the story room. Then the lawyers. Then you're finished. Go
home, wherever the hell that is. You're a disappointment, Boy.
A stupendous failure."

Don't let him do this!

But she had nothing to say, no voice to say it with.

She walked out of Mac's office, closing that door, all the
faces in the room looking up at her, none bleaker than Jorge's,
and headed toward the story room, where three men sat working telephones behind glass, typewriters, notepads, and newspapers all over the conference table. But when she touched the
doorknob, she couldn't turn it because when she'd finished in
that room, she would have revealed her lies, or some of them,
and everything she wanted would be over. There was nothing
for her but what she had in this place.

Keep going.

She walked past the room, toward the spine, which would
take her down, out the back door, to the alley.

"The fact-checkers!" someone yelled.

"Hopper!" Jorge boomed from the end of the room. "Fix it!"

She stopped, looked at all the faces.

Fix what?

Pictures first.

She headed up the spine, not down, to the third floor, past
the linotype room, all the way back to the darkroom, went in,

locked the door, turned on the amber light. She got on her hands and knees under the counter, pushing the first two boxes away, pulling the third toward her. It was sealed shut, the wrong box. Things had been moved. They'd been opening boxes. She grabbed the first one, close to the table front—Kodak Film. Nothing but smaller sealed boxes. No loose photos or film.

Had someone opened her box, found the negatives? She sat under the desk and dragged the second box to her, also a film box, its top open. She reached in and felt the loose pile of negatives. She grabbed the pile, all of them from Grete's collection of bodies.

She stood and fanned them out on the light box: two toddlers digging a hole in the sand with tiny shovels; a chubby hand, dimpled, holding a daisy in its fist; a boy standing on a stool at the sink, his bubble-covered hands holding a dish; a close-up baby's ear, whirled like a seashell; the back of a girl's head, close, her hair braided, French style; Grete's small foot, held in the air, turned in upon itself, artistic. All beautiful and somewhat strange.

She looked at the *Family* negative. If she'd known nothing about these people, just saw the picture, she would have thought they were connected, Daddy married to Noreen, Vee their daughter, P. B. their granddaughter, like Momma and she had been stand-ins, like Daddy had a shadow family, like Vee was Jane's sister in a way. Or like Jane was Daddy now.

The door shook in its jamb.

She had the negative on the table before her. Other papers had run the picture a year before. Only she had this negative, though. Not Roy Stryker at the FSA, not Grete, not the other papers. The original proof that Daddy was connected to Grete and Vee. And that she was connected to Daddy. That either or both of them might be connected to Vee's attempted murder. Proof she'd broken into Grete's darkroom and stolen her work, which by itself was maybe enough for those lawyers and fact-checkers to throw her in jail.

Burn it.

That wasn't her. She wouldn't think that. She wondered if she should let the idea float past her, un-acted on. Did she always have to do what that voice said?

The static was louder now, so that it hurt her forehead. How long had it been since her mind was quiet?

Do it.

To stop the noise, she took a match from her pocket, lit it, and held it to the edge of the *Family* negative.

There was pounding against the door.

Family lit up, cellulose nitrate sparking, toxic smoke popping in tiny explosions out of the square between her thumb and middle finger.

The door unlocked, opened, lighting the room. Flame burned her fingers, and she dropped the picture.

"What are you doing?" Fleming screamed.

The other negatives on the desk in front of her ignited. Fleming rushed out and back in with two mugs of coffee and poured them on the negatives, causing more smoke, but without stopping the flames. Somebody else ran in—"Water won't stop it! It makes its own oxygen!"

Fleming took off his coat and threw it on top of the smoking counter, patting it down with his hands and arms, his torso, trying and failing to save the pictures, jumping back, singed, flames licking up around him.

The cellulose nitrate had aged, forming nitrogen monoxide, nitrogen dioxide, nitric acid, and oxygen. Fleming found it impossible now to fight the film on fire. Smothering wouldn't work, nor would water, the picture generating enough oxidant to keep itself burning until the film was consumed, as it burned the releasing explosive gases. Combustible magic. Poor Fleming couldn't stop it.

She ran out of the fiery darkroom, past all the people, downstairs, into the street where sirens wailed, heroes on their way to save what Jane was burning.

CHAPTER TEN

ACCOUNTS

T he doors were locked.
The windows, dummy.
"Shut up! Don't call me *dummy.*"

She did it though, crawling around the house, behind big-leafed, flowering shrubs, checking first-floor and basement windows—all latched. She sprinted back to the edge of the lawn for a better view, hiding in the shadow of redwoods, to investigate second-floor windows. One was cranked open. Near it stood a cottonwood tree, sturdy, thick-branched, its canopy sloughing white mounds of fluff.

There you go. I told you.

She grunted, then jogged back to the cottonwood, curling her hands around a low limb, testing her grip, and walked herself up the tree, wrapping one leg over the branch and then kicking her other foot hard on the trunk, bringing the second leg up next to the first, breathing hard.

At second-story level, pressing her cheek into the bark, she looked down at grass and fluffy white debris, squeezing her thighs tighter around the branch.

She thought, What would happen if I just let go? Would I break? Land?

Go on, chicken. Get in there.

"I'm not chicken. Let me think."

She held her breath for a second and then whispered, "That's you, Ben, isn't it?"

He didn't answer.

It didn't matter. It was him. She was used to him now, after so much time alone before.

She whispered, "I was gonna do it anyway. Not because you said."

And she scooted along, closer to the window. She stood, holding onto an overhead branch. Then she let go, taking the long step from tree to roof. She walked forward and up, one, two, three, four, five steps, on clay tiles. The last one cracked under her heel, dropping in chunks down the roof, onto the lawn. She lost her balance, began to slip, and grabbed the window's edge to catch herself. Something fluttered in her throat.

She heard none of his criticism in her head, no reaction at all inside the window.

She spread the curtain, looked and saw no one. She climbed her way into a private library. Books not just on the shelves but on every surface, an explosion of books. A room she should live in. She should sit at such a desk, with this view —all the bay laid before her. Everything laid out.

Not now. Probably never. Never mind.

She scanned the shelves for ledgers, not finding them.

Get a move on. They're in the darkroom. They were never going to be up here.

She left the library where she longed to stay, went to the top of the landing, and listened, but heard nothing, nobody.

She crept downstairs to the entry, her fingertips light on the wide oak banister. Then to the kitchen, where the smell of last night's dinner—something strange, spicy—made her queasy. She slipped her hand into the leather bag on a hook—a tissue, pencils, scraps of paper. No keys. She checked all its pockets. Nothing. She tried other bags on other hooks lined up on the wainscoting. Still no keys.

Find a crowbar in the basement. Jimmy the darkroom locks.

She frowned. She didn't want to break in that way, like a criminal.

But she opened the kitchen door to the basement and enough light came through the casement windows below that she went down without pulling the string.

At the bottom of the stairs, from across the basement, she saw the keychain hanging in the lock of the darkroom door. She waited, no sound. Waited longer. Still nothing, no one.

They'll be on the counter, she told herself.

Hands on the plow, girl.

She crossed the basement, passing the boxed rooms of photographs, the chalked words—"sidewalks," "fields," "machines," "architecture," "portraits," the word "bodies."

The door swung silently open to her touch. Inside, no heat of another person.

She pulled the string that hung before her and her eyes ran around the gold-lit room. The books weren't on the counter where they'd been. She opened file drawers. Not there. Then she saw the black curtain with the quote—"The contemplation of things as they are, without substitution or imposture. . . ."

She pulled the curtain to the side, revealing the ledgers lined up on the hidden windowsill. She brought them down, five of them, one at a time, flipping through them.

The first was Grete's journal. She read a couple pages of the tight, careful penmanship—

"We see through the scrim of culture."

"Pictures ask questions. It's the viewer who must answer."

"The camera steals nothing. It only bestows."

She put it down, picking up the next, the record of quotes she'd seen before, the familiar wrong-dictioned poetry of field people—

"You die, you dead, that's it."

"Ditched and done, that's us."

"I'd rather be a son of a bitch than a punching bag."

She put that book down, picking up another. More quotes.

The last two books had what she was looking for, dates, locations, names, payments.

The earliest entries, years ago, included mostly receipts. Grete had made good money then—Jane knew she'd started as a society photographer. Then the numbers changed. Receipts were smaller, from the government, not newspapers. The newspaper money must have gone to the FSA. No big checks like she expected, not what Daddy said. Maybe to him these were big amounts, or maybe he'd just assumed.

Then there were small expenses, paid to unfamiliar names. Bribes? Payments? Gifts?

In the last book she saw Uno's name—$23, $31, $15, $12. Entries for him were all over. She went backward, through November, October, September. He'd been earning at pimping pictures for Grete all of 1936, was earning it still, through 1937. She pictured Momma's drawer, the new slips and underwear, the rubber-banded wad of money, which was in her pocket.

Go on.

She pulled her negative of Jesson out of the pocket, checking the writing on the margin—"Hunger, Marysville, 3/15/36"—and flipped through the ledger's pages, back to March fifteenth. There it was. Uno Jeffers, over and over, from February 7 through June 20. No other entries. No Tom Jesson, no Mrs. Jesson. Nothing made to the starving man's family.

Is Daddy in here?

Flipping through, she found him. Abraham Lincoln Hopper, five dollars. An *X*.

Something in her throat again.

What's it mean to help somebody? Money, food, shelter?

Dignity, respect, equality? Did Grete help any of them get any of this? Did it matter how she helped?

Don't matter. Take 'em and get out of here.

Okay. No matter, the accounts were proof of motive, at least. Grete let Jesson die for her picture, paid Uno for that, never gave a thing to Jesson's family. Vee was gonna tell Jane. Grete had reason to kill Vee, or have her killed.

"Well, well."

It sounded so soft she thought at first it was her brother in her head, but then the hair rose on her arms. She wheeled around, knocking ledgers from the counter to the floor.

Grete reached out and gently, easily, took the book from her hand. She read the open page and looked back at Jane, tilting her head. "You are a surprising person." She set the book on the counter.

She stepped closer.

"You find it hard to stay away from this darkroom."

Warm breath filled the space between them.

Grete reached up to Jane's throat.

Jane squawked, "Don't!"

Two fingers traced the spot where an Adam's apple should be. Jane stepped backward, onto the edge of a ledger on the floor, losing her balance, then catching herself. Grete stepped forward, maintaining the space between them. Her hand moved into the shirt's collar, to Jane's clavicle, tracing its sharp edge. Then her other hand reached up to squeeze the muscle of Jane's upper arm.

Watch out!

She felt too late what Grete aimed to do. She moved her hand to Jane's right breast, squeezed its new roundness, pinched.

"No!"

Grete dropped her hands. "As I thought."

"Get away!" Jane said, too late, much too late.

Grete stood perfectly still, as if not to spook a skittish animal. "Please don't worry, not with me. I know how hard it is to be who one is."

Don't let her work you.

"Especially for a woman. It's one of the things that draws me to you, that you're not just one thing, that you don't pretend to be. You're a smart girl—you see the use of risk."

"Stop talking to me. Don't talk!"

Grete laughed, even her eyes—compassionate—like this was some nice conversation they were having, like they were friends or something, still standing too close.

"I'll tell you a secret. When I first began to take pictures for a living, I used the male pronoun for myself, in the third person—I said, 'He uses this sort of film,' or, 'He prefers the Graflex,' to talk about myself. Some people thought it strange. But it helped me believe I could do the things I intended to do."

She's trying to sucker you.

"My husband suggested I stop that. My previous husband. So I did. What do you think, Benny, was I right to stop calling myself *he?*"

Okay, buy yourself time.

Jane said, "You are what you decide to be."

"That's all? Just a decision?"

"It's the doing it after the decision."

Grete nodded. "Then you and I are quite compatible. I agree—one should become whom she aims to be, whom she's meant to be, regardless of anything else."

"I didn't say that."

"You would modify it?"

Take charge.

"I wouldn't say *regardless.*"

"You're young. You don't know. Prune your aims, stunt your tree."

What was clear outside was murky down here.

"What did they send you for, Benny?"

She knows why you're here.

Grete knew she was fired, knew about the fact-checkers and lawyers. All of it. Why would she be talking like this, after the article?

"Doesn't matter," Grete continued. "I see something in you. You have an outsider's eye, not like the others. Everything's too familiar to them. They don't have your gift."

Outsider, always.

"Of course that gift's not enough. Perception is mostly about memory, and you do have more unique memories than so many in our field—that's what gives you the outsider view. But a meaningful part of perception, maybe the most important part, is acute sensory sensitivity, detail awareness, and that takes training. I could teach you. A mentor is useful. It was for me."

Jane thought, I've worked so hard. My whole life, by myself . . . a mentor . . .

Then—She doesn't know I wrote the article.

She wants to use you.

"You could work for me. I do need help here, in the darkroom, it's true, but also with the people I photograph. You understand them. That's your strength."

It's a strength, not a weakness, to be from that dirt.

"But it's mainly the narratives. I need your help with those. The pictures need the words to put them in context. The words move the viewers' eyes where you want them."

Jane thought, Me, writing notebooks in the field—I have my whole life! But now with a real purpose. I could prove myself. I could do good, like Grete has. God, she has done good. The press. The government food. The political changes. I could use her to do good things.

"You would have to change your name, I mean, after what you've been through."

Jane thought, A real bound book with a new name—what

I've always counted on, making myself, becoming someone, doing something.

You're already your new self—Benny! This ain't why you're here.

You can't say who I am. How do you know why I'm here?

Don't let her change us.

Jane was confused. Vee, more needy than her—with a baby—didn't buckle to Greta. But she was probably dead now, in the morgue! What did that get her? And Jesson—that wasn't right, but what did that have to do with her? And Momma! Why couldn't Jane put this down? Why did she have to hump it all through every row, every field? Vee was not her sister! Jesson was not her daddy! And Momma . . .

Keep your hand on the plow.

What about me?

Hold on, Benjamin urged.

Shut up!

You owe me.

She saw he wanted her to be Benny forever. He wanted his chance too. Jane was his chance. She thought, all right, then. All right.

She looked at Grete, her eyes squinting. "I know what you've done. I can ruin you."

The golden air sparked between them.

Grete nodded. "And I know who you are. I could ruin you. That's the symmetry of it. We need each other. You don't imagine that significant people make no mistakes, do you? We make them, get over them, go on. That's why we're significant. May as well put this bad business behind us, do great things?"

Jane knew people did this every day—in offices, fields, classrooms, jail—every day.

Grab the books. Run.

You want me to ruin this? Jane asked him.

Ruin this. Save us.

This was how it would be.

Her muscles clenched to grab the ledgers and Grete had to have seen that tensing, must have known what it meant, because she swung her arm around, with a jug in her hand, throwing its liquid into Jane's face and eyes.

Her eyes burning, Jane tripped on the ledgers, falling hard to the ground.

She saw the blurry shape of Grete's boots by her head and grabbed one with both hands. But Grete stayed upright, holding onto the desk. Her other boot rose, its silver brace glinting. Jane rolled, but the boot hit her shoulder, pinning her to the floor, next to the jug.

Jane grabbed the jug and swung it at Grete's hip, knocking her to the ground, where she cradled her knee, hollering.

Jane got up, breathing hard, and looked at Grete on the floor, in pain. She'd done that to this tiny, injured woman. She hadn't meant to, hadn't wanted to.

"Stupid! Stupid, stupid girl!"

Get 'em and get out.

She grabbed the ledgers and ran them out of the darkroom, locking the door, trapping Grete inside, leaving the keys hanging in the lock, ran upstairs to the kitchen, wrote a note on a pad on the table and then used the telephone to call the operator—"Wrights' house, top of the hill, Virginia Street, Berkeley"—ran outside and vomited on the lawn.

A wrinkled, whiskey-colored man puffed a great volume of smoke, his foot on the fender of a mattress-loaded clunker. One cabin down, two guys played banjo and mouth harp on the stoop, near babies squirming on the knees of unsmiling wives. Right in Jane's path, mud-caked kids played catch with a rag, balled up by twine—"You're out!" An old woman moved back and forth past a bare window, wiping, sweeping, putting things away.

They all stopped to stare as Jane passed on her way to the manager's cabin.

There was no car out front. Uno was gone. She'd get in and out, no messing around.

Her temple throbbed.

Come on, leave 'er, let's go. There's no reason, he whined.

But she disobeyed, knocking on the door, and it opened.

Momma stood there in a crisp, bright housedress belted over her slim-again waist, her hair combed, tucked behind her ears, neat, respectable.

Jane heard that popping static in her head.

She managed to say, "It's me . . ."

Momma looked confused. "Who . . . what are you?"

She looked left and right at the people on their porches before pulling Jane out of their sight, into the kitchen, which smelled of ham, onions, biscuits.

"I've come to get you out of here, right now, Momma."

Leave her.

The popping grew louder.

"Quiet."

"What?" Momma looked her up and down. "Whose blood is that?"

"I'm all right."

"You gone weird?"

"I'll explain later, not now. We gotta go."

"You get beat up for going around this way?"

"I'll tell you everything later, but now we gotta go," Jane said.

"I'm not going anywhere."

Momma leaned over behind a chair and picked up a baby with rose-red hair sticking up in straight tufts. Her face was complicated, not simple like some babies'. She had deep dimples in her cheeks and light blue eyes. "Elsie."

She looked more like her other sister, Sweetie, than she

did like Jane, which made sense. Jane looked like her own daddy. Elsie and Sweetie looked like theirs.

"I got work to do."

"Listen, you have to go with me now, before it all comes apart."

It's coming apart now, stupid. Get out.

"Shut up."

"What?"

"There's, there's a newspaper story—gonna be more of 'em —about Uno."

"What paper?"

"My . . . my paper."

"What does that mean?"

"The *San Francisco Prospect*."

"Your . . . Who's writing the story?"

"Me. I'm writing the next one."

Momma's brows raised nearly into her hairline, her eyes shining like she thought this was funny. "Then don't put him in the story."

"He's in. There's no taking him out! He's part of the story."

"Then don't write it."

"I have to! It's the right thing!"

"That's a hoot. You wanna do right? Do right by me."

Do right by me!

"That's what I'm trying . . ."

"I did not get all this by acting stupid." That word. "You can't walk in here and . . ."

"Can't you see what I'm struggling to do?"

"What do you know about struggle?" Momma asked.

"I'm making something of myself. I'm a reporter. I'm good. I'm trying to . . ."

"That why you dress like a boy? You think that's gonna last?"

It'll last.

"You think they ain't gonna fire you, they find out what you're up to, faking, lying? City people ain't gonna let you get away with this—tricking 'em. They can't let you get away with that. You can't trust 'em!"

Tell her who we are.

"It got me work, everything I've done. It's just a costume." Jane hated the clothes, the short hair, now. She was humiliated in front of Momma.

It ain't a costume.

"Everything *you* done? I fought us out of Texas—evil people, uncles, bosses, bank people! You have no idea what I done. I fought since I was a child, just to survive, when other people shoulda done that for me. Then I fought for you—keeping you fed, all those library books. I left you Sweetie's address! Gave you somewhere to go! I've always fought for you!"

Fought for you. You!

She'd always sensed power in her corner, a loaned ferociousness.

"I know, but listen! More reporters'll . . . from other papers . . . they'll be coming to interview Uno, cops too. You gotta get out of here before it happens. I'm trying to help you!"

"You think I need you—you!—to tell me what to do?"

She looked five-five, five-six, five-eight, when she said this, up above her actual body.

"You don't know the whole story," Jane said. "There's some things I know, you don't know yet!"

There are things she knows too.

"You talking down to me, Jane?"

"Listen. Uno's made money he shouldn't have. He's connected with someone." Her voice cracked. "Someone bad"—was Grete bad?—"He's acted bad."

"You trying to ruin things for Elsie now? You wanna take down her daddy too?"

Just get out.

217

Jane looked at her sister, a bossy-looking thing, her hand all bunched up in Momma's hair. There was something complaining, questioning, in that baby's eyes. Still.

"Uno's dangerous."

"Bless your heart."

"Can't you just accept I might be right about this? That I can help you?"

"I see you're trying to make yourself into your brother. Make up for what you did."

Now Elsie was wailing, wanting something she didn't have.

"Make up for what? What'd I ever do?"

Okay then, you asked for it.

"You . . . selfish! You know what you did! You pushed out first, took your time—you made him weak."

"I didn't choose that! That's not something a baby . . ."

I wasn't so weak.

"What was I gonna do?" Momma asked. "Was I gonna save the weak one? No!"

"You made me big! I didn't make myself big. You . . ." Then she heard it, a beat late. "What do you mean, save?"

"I saved you. I let him go because you claimed me! You showed me you were the one!"

Hear that? Hear that!

A mallet dropped on Jane's head, cracking her skull. Her fingers flew there. She thought they'd come away bloody, but they didn't. The injury was inside, not a clean break into halves, but a seismic fracturing, through all her body's bones and plates, shattering her into a million pieces. Her eyes squeezed shut and she listened to the crackling sound move through her. When it stopped, she opened her eyes, ruined.

"You let him go? You said he died before he was born!"

"You wanna know? You think you're grown enough to know?"

"Tell me!"

"All right then—it's time. I chose you, not him. I laid him down. Side of the field. Left him in a cotton sack." A sob broke out but Momma swallowed it, hunching her spine up, taking a new shape. "I was all by myself, no Daddy, no Granny—your precious Granny!—all by myself—always with nothing. I made a choice. I fed you and not him, held you and not him. It didn't take long. I made the choice. Choices have to be made! You're here because I did that. You were bigger, stronger—come out like a colt, ready to run. You made me choose you!"

"I didn't! You're crazy!"

"I was fifteen!"

Time did that thing it almost never does. It stopped, leaving her mother frozen, hunched up, her mouth open, her breath a solid mass in the air, the worst possible thing solid in the air. No sound.

You don't remember before.

The noise dissipated, just a muffled, watery sound, lapping.

She remembered rocking in that saltiness. Bumping up against each other, kicking, struggling for space, but the fluid padding those bumps so it wasn't bad.

She remembered knowing he could have gone on like that forever, that he had everything he needed there.

But not her. She wanted out. Too confining, no room to grow. She wanted to make noise.

Then his kicking and jostling became more bothersome. They were squeezed from every side, especially the top, at Jane's feet and Benjamin's head.

She remembered the sense of threat he vibrated.

But the pushing invigorated her, a wave at her feet, like she was a swimmer heading for shore. With each new wave, her fingers grabbed the walls of her exit.

His weak hands clasped her feet. "Stay!"

"Let go," she answered. "Let me go."

That's what she saw, memory or vision, it didn't matter.

She chose you. She thought I wasn't good enough, before she even knew me.

It was unbearable.

She thought, Everything's over. There's nothing I can do.

You're here, ain't you?

You're the lucky one. Dead's better than this.

Load of crap. Dead's not better. You think you're tragic— you ain't dead.

Time began to melt again, everything coming back to movement, noise, Momma's yelling, Elsie's wailing.

A hoarse scraping came up through Jane's body, out her mouth. "How long did he cry?"

"I don't remember."

"You do."

A long time.

"Watch yourself," Momma said.

"This ain't my fault!"

"You turning against me now? After I chose you? You turning against your sister?"

Elsie's screaming reached a new register.

"You've been lying my whole life. This whole life . . . one big lie. You could have saved him! You could have saved both of us!"

Could have kept us both.

"There was something wrong with him! He was damaged."

She could have saved me.

Momma went on, "You listen to me, there is only, ever, so much to go around. Everybody chooses. That is what it takes!"

"I didn't ask for that. Never . . . not . . . my . . . fault."

She heard wheels on gravel.

Momma bounced Elsie hard on her hip so Elsie's head bobbled and she quieted.

"Get out," Momma said, looking over Jane's shoulder at the car. "Out the back window."

Jane turned and saw the Chrysler from Topsy's parking lot. She turned back. Momma was holding Elsie too tight, her pink flesh marked with white handprints from squeezing.

It's him. Get out.

"Momma, Uno tried to kill a girl, get Daddy blamed for it! Then he tried to kill Daddy! He shot at him while we were talking."

Elsie threw her head back, kicking her feet, pushing against Momma's shoulder.

"Shot at Abraham? Talking to you?"

The door opened and Elsie stopped screaming to look, her lips quivering.

Uno stepped in, a pistol tucked in the left side of his pant waist, his good-hand side. He took off his hat, setting it on the table. Jane noticed how long his arms were for a short man. She saw his fingers shaking.

"Well, well. Beauty queen's home. 'Cept now he's the beauty prince, I guess."

He kissed Momma's cheek, pushing a curl behind her ear, and then nuzzled Elsie, hiding his face in her neck.

Momma walked away from him, took a bottle from the icebox and gave it to Elsie. She latched onto the bottle, and Momma carried her into the bedroom. Then she came back.

"Jane needs that cabin the Smiths left, Uno. She's back."

"I didn't think . . ." Uno's eyelid twitched, his mouth turned down.

"I said she's back."

Elsie squawked from the bedroom.

"I ain't back," Jane said. "I'm not coming back. I'm somewhere else."

Uno nodded, up and down, fast.

"You don't appear to understand," Momma said. "The

city's mean, meaner'n here. When they find out who you are, it's over, whatever you got yourself for this bit of time. Over."

It ain't over.

"I have a boss. I have to . . ." Though this wasn't true. She didn't have a job.

"This is who you are, here. Who you'll always be."

This ain't everything.

"Baby doll," Uno interrupted. "It's best she go back. We got . . ."

Elsie hollered from the next room, then was quiet, the bottle back in her mouth.

"Uno, hush."

"I'm just sayin' . . ."

"Uno!"

The skin under his eyes puffed up, injured by her tone. His eyes rounded, his pupils so big. He loved her, God help him. He did love her, a love that led him to do stupid, horrible things.

Momma changed her face, put on forgiving, wrapped her arms around his waist, laid her head against his shoulder so he relaxed, placed his arms around her shoulders.

"I know you try hard," Momma said. "I ain't saying you don't try. And I know you mean well, but you keep messing up." She lifted her head and looked him in the eye, his pistol in her right hand, up against his temple.

His lips disappeared into the skin around his mouth.

"Momma, no."

"Did you shoot at Abraham? Or were you shooting at Jane?"

"What'd she tell you? She's . . ." His eyes flashed at Jane, furious, scared. "It warn't my fault, Kate, I didn't know she was . . ."

"Were you trying to kill my girl?"

"Baby, come on. I tried to give you papers. I want to give you my name."

Elsie screamed through the open door.

"I got a name, Uno. And I got Jane back too."

Even in that moment, what Jane heard was, "I got Jane," and it meant something to her. It made her weak, she knew, this desire, but she couldn't help it.

But still, she said, "Wait."

Momma looked back at her, the pistol at Uno's head.

"Did the photographer make you do what you did to Vee and Daddy?"

His eyes flitted back and forth between them. He didn't know the right answer.

"Honey, I done everything for you . . ." He giggled—giggled—afraid of his wife.

He'd done it for Momma, not Grete.

Jane had blamed Grete.

"You chose to do it. To keep the lights on. To keep me and Daddy away."

Jane had attacked Grete, physically, and in the paper, thinking she was the root of it all, which was partly true, but not the absolute root.

The crowbar Uno used on Vee—it was a message, a warning to Daddy and her, too.

Chaotic new information, all out of order. He did it, not Grete, out of love and fear. He was a coward, a vile coward, which makes a person dangerous.

Momma didn't wait for the rest of his story.

She lowered her arm and pulled the trigger, firing one shot into his thigh as he was standing right there next to her, spraying bone and blood all over herself, the kitchen, and Jane.

He cried out and fell. Momma pulled up the skirt of her apron to wipe her hands.

Both Jane's hands covered her mouth, muffling her own voice.

Momma stepped up close to Jane.

"I'll say this so you understand. You take one step, then another, and another, until you don't worry about the next. Until you're done deciding whether you'll fight. That's how you do it."

Uno's moaning and crying nearly drowned out her lesson.

"So, Jane, you in charge? Where you taking us now you ruined this?"

Cain't trust her! Leave her!

"I'm not taking you now!"

She'll ruin everything.

"You deserting your sister?" Momma asked.

Jane felt a sinking—God, will I never. . .

She couldn't cut this cord, couldn't escape. The connection was real, permanent.

Don't let her . . .

I have to, Jane thought. I got no choice. I'll keep 'em close. It's safer.

What about me?

I'm sorry. Really, I am.

She wiped her eyes, went to the bedroom and picked up Elsie, who dropped her bottle and grabbed Jane's nose with wet fingers, surprisingly strong fingers.

Jane carried her past Elsie's crying father on the floor, and the three of them walked out the manager's cabin door, past all the empty porches, tenants hiding inside.

One stringy old lady came out of her cabin, stepping into the mud in front of them, holding a broom like a rifle.

Jane stood there for a beat, her sister in her arms.

"He hit her and I shot him. He ain't dead. You can go on in there and call the cops. They're coming anyway."

The old lady looked like she recognized something in Jane, the same kind of thing that pulled her out of the cabin herself, alone, the only one in the camp, with a broom for a weapon. She lowered it and stepped aside.

BEFORE Jane had steered the car onto Tower Bridge, Momma was asleep. Not fifteen minutes after firing a bullet into the thigh of her pathetic second common-law husband and leaving him crying on the porch and she was snoring like a puppy in the back seat with Elsie in her lap.

"No conscience at all," Jane said.

No response from Ben.

Come on, she thought.

Still nothing.

He was always talking, telling her what to do, creating all that noise in her head. Now she wanted to talk, and where was he?

Listen, if you're gonna live in there, we're gonna need a system, she thought.

No answer. Just the sound of the road and car engine.

You can't always be in charge. I get to make decisions.

Silence.

Really?

Then she thought, Maybe that's it. He's gone. Maybe I get to be alone in here, make the choices. It's just my voice in here now.

She imagined the sound of emptiness.

This is best, she thought. I can think what I want.

I'm still here.

"Dammit, Ben, go to hell!" she yelled.

"What's that?" Momma roused to ask.

"Nothing," Jane answered.

Momma rolled over, pressing her forehead against the window, Elsie snuggled into her strong body.

MOMMA squinted suspiciously at the floors and surfaces of their flat, fancy but dirty, unkempt.

Rivka's bedroom door was closed.

Jane put her finger to her lips and pointed to the bathroom. She took Elsie from Momma.

"Wash up here."

She rubbed Elsie's back, listening to the sink water run. Elsie wasn't so disagreeable sleepy. Her little body warmed Jane's chest. The weight of her felt reassuring, draped on her shoulders. Brother in her head, sister in her arms, Momma in her bathroom. Where was Daddy?

Momma came out, damp, Uno's blood rinsed off her skin. She took Elsie back and washed her up, dropping her wet diaper on the floor on top of the soiled towel, wrapping a clean one around her bottom, pinning it, nice and fresh.

Jane led them down the hall, past the kitchen, to the sunporch room, and gave Momma the nightgown from the hope chest. Momma dropped her ruined housedress and slipped into the nightgown, which fit just right. Jane turned down the covers and Momma got into bed with Elsie, sweet as you please.

Jane didn't bother washing up—she just couldn't. She lay down on the parlor sofa, where she'd first sat, wounded, three months before, running away from home, when Sweetie and Rivka saved her. She closed her eyes and fell to sleep.

"SOME column," Rivka said, yesterday's paper spread out before them.

"I didn't . . ."

"I saw Lambert sneaking around. I know . . ."

"Long story."

"And them?"

"My mother and my sister."

"*Affrettando.*"

"What?"

"In music—everything pressing forward," Rivka explained.

"I guess so."

"What happens next?"

"I'm going into the paper, get my job back, then to the police."

Jane told her all about it, every angle, from what had happened to what she planned to do, as Rivka made her an egg and coffee.

Jane got up her nerve. "Little surprising about Oppie."

"We are many things. You are. I am too. Neither of us is finished."

Jane showered and tended her face, all her injuries.

When she came out, Rivka opened her closet. "My dresses won't fit you."

"The pants are fine."

They're perfect. No dresses.

"Not really."

Rivka spot-scrubbed Jane's suit pants. They were dark, which hid the bloody spots, so that helped. She pulled a silk blouse out of the closet, a pretty, expensive version of the man's shirt Jane had been wearing all this time.

Not that.

But when Jane put it on, it felt so light and fine, its fabric against her skin gave her goose bumps, so she ignored Benjamin's dread. Rivka added a cream sweater, pushing up the sleeves, which were too short. She finished it off with clunky-heeled black shoes, with leather bows on top.

"Use my toiletries. I am no expert there, but I have best goods."

In the bathroom, she felt her face, careful around the gash. She opened the cabinet, where she found a toiletry box, full of unused products in shiny pearl and tortoiseshell cases. She dug around and pulled out one lipstick after another, twisting them up, holding them close to her skin. She chose a raspberry color and pressed it against her lips. It looked like her mouth had taken over her face. She found a shimmery green cream the color of her eyes and rubbed just a little along the lid, above her eyelashes. Her brows were too thick, but she wasn't getting into that now. She tried to draw a line around her eyes with a dark pencil but couldn't do it right so she wiped it off and redid the green eye shadow. She was all eyes, lips, and gash, spiky, dark hair. She looked like a different kind of girl. She pulled her bangs down over her gash but that didn't work, so she pushed her hair back all the way, letting it show. Rivka came in with a black beret and arranged it on her head, smoothing her hair behind her ears where it was poking out. She clipped pearl earrings from Sweetie's left-behind jewelry box to her earlobes.

"Look at you."

Benjamin's desolation rose like nausea in her throat, but she found a way to reduce it to vapor. She studied herself.

"I put it on. I take it off."

SHE walked into the *Prospect* like a woman, not a man. Long strides, yes, but different, her hips swaying slightly under the slacks, as if her center of gravity had shifted to her gut, every movement coming from her middle, not her extremities, her brother silent, moody.

"Benny?" the receptionist asked. That name as a question repeated as she moved up the spine, through the reporters' room, past all the desks, to Mac's office, from which Jane heard a wailing.

She opened the door to see Sweetie sobbing into Mac's chest, his arms around her, uneasy, a guy who doesn't know how to comfort a girl. Jane understood.

"Get out, freak," Mac said when Jane stepped in front of them in her new form. He took impressively little time to recognize her. Sweetie had talked.

"This is the real . . ."

"You heard me."

"I'm a girl. I was lying before."

"Well, no kidding. When have you ever not been lying?"

"I had no choice."

"Everything's a choice!" Sweetie screamed, her face wet. "Every minute's a choice!"

"I had to work, Mac. Would you have hired me as a girl?"

"Girls work here."

"Would you have hired me as a copy boy if I were a girl?"

"Don't be idiotic."

"I did what I had to do."

"Well, let's call Darwin, let him know his theory's working."

"This is me. I'm not Benny."

You are.

"Whoever you are, go. Again. Before I call the cops. Do you smell the smoke from the darkroom you destroyed? Burning up this place."

"I have the evidence."

"Get out."

"This is different."

Sweetie swung all the way around and screamed in Jane's face. "You shot my papa! You and your trash mother!"

"What do you think you know, Sweetie? You were talking to Uno all this time, weren't you? We've never had a secret."

"You lied to me. I heard you telling it to Rivka. My papa didn't kill your daddy."

"Tried to. Or maybe me. You were talking to Uno all along, weren't you? Weren't you?"

Mac interrupted. "Stop it, Hopper."

Sweetie glowered. "We're calling the cops. Telling them we've got you."

Mac wrapped her up in his arms. "Sweetie, honey, stop. Quiet."

"Quiet? Are you quieting me?" Her round lips stretched out, thin, taut, her nostrils flaring, her teeth bared. "After all the tending . . . I have shown you all the tenderness . . . all the love . . . left everything . . . and now you quiet . . . my . . . feelings?"

"Give, give, give," Jane interrupted. "Ain't there some taking going on there too?"

"What?" Sweetie looked shocked, as if she hadn't considered she ever got anything herself in one of those transactions. "No! You listen to me, Mac! That is not it!"

Mac enclosed her in his arms, like you do with a baby in a tantrum, the smart thing to do, but his face was miserable. Jane saw he didn't want to be bound by her. Oppie said Mac would tire of her, and this was what he meant. He might commit to a woman, but it wasn't going to be Sweetie. She wasn't so wonderful when you got used to her. A small part of Jane even felt hurt for her, disappointed in Mac. Sweetie was a kind of sister to her now. The sister to her sister. But that was just a small part of what she felt.

"Lovie," Mac said, rubbing Sweetie's back while Jane stood outside their orbit. "Sit, let me work this out." And he settled her into the couch before yelling, "Jorge!"

The door opened instantly—he must have been just outside listening.

"Bring her something." Though Jorge was not the sort of person who fetched things, this was not the job for a copy boy.

He returned and handed a hot cup to Sweetie, the smell of whiskey and coffee filling the room. She took the cup and set it down to blow her nose and wipe her face, before beginning to drink between sobs.

Jane poured the ledgers out of her bag and onto Mac's desktop, knocking off a jar of pencils.

Mac shoved them all off the desk onto the floor to join the pencils.

"Just let me . . ."

"Just let you what? Humiliate me again? Put the paper further at risk? I got teams of lawyers working on your last extravaganza. I got construction guys recreating operations, just so we can put out a paper. Mr. Mercer—I don't know what he's going to do." Even his forearms and hands looked hot.

"Listen, this story—all of this—is complicated."

"No kidding?"

"She tried to bribe me when I was getting these account books. I hurt her."

"What the hell!"

"Self-defense. And Sweetie's right. Her papa's hurt." She'd already decided but still had to do it. "I shot him, getting my mother and sister out of there. Uno was Wright's photo pimp, helped her cheat, steal . . . all that. He's the one who attacked Vee."

"No!" Sweetie yelled.

Mac said, "Slow down."

"You haven't any heart at all, Jane!"

"I have all the evidence now. This scheme of theirs, to make special pictures, sensational pictures, so much more moving than everybody else's because they were faked. He got paid well because she got the applause, we got pictures that sell papers."

"Of course they do! But we didn't know . . ." Mac said.

"I'm not saying we knew. I'm saying this is part of the story. Uno did it for the money. But not Wright. I think she just wanted to make the best pictures. Have the biggest impact. Be the best."

She took the negative of the dying man out of her pocket again and laid it on Mac's desk, and he pulled it toward him, looking down.

"How'd you get it?"

"When I went to get the *Family* picture, I . . . I went into the darkroom looking for it, and I found this."

"And you took it?" Jorge said. "Took it?"

"I did take it. Yes, I did. Because that's what I had to do."

"This just gets better."

He held the picture close up to his eyes and then stretched his arm out, looking at it from a distance and then close up again.

"Stole it. Broke into Wright's darkroom and stole it," Jorge repeated.

Mac held his hand up, stopping Jorge.

"Come on, this should have been called *Death*, not *Hunger*. Should have called it *Murder*! They let him die, left him there. They didn't pay his family. We ran that picture. Paid her for it. Now we have evidence."

"Everybody ran it," Mac said. "It wasn't exclusive."

"Right. It's the story Vee wanted to give us—the story of the man they let die for his picture. That's why Uno attacked her, put her in a coma. He couldn't let her stop the gravy train. He made it look like my daddy did it . . . I can't explain it all . . . need to write it . . . but then he tried to kill Daddy, or me, I don't know. Because Daddy was talking about Jesson now too. Uno's small-time, nothing, but he's the one who swung the pipe, choked her."

Sweetie yelled, "Liar!"

"She fed him information, told him where to find us."

"Liar! I didn't tell him to attack anybody! I just told him where Abraham was working."

Jane felt weak in every part of her body.

"And those pictures," Sweetie yelled, "got food, housing, for people all over Sacramento! People we know!"

"They didn't save Tom Jesson. They could have driven him to a hospital, but they didn't."

That picture might have killed Daddy and her. What did it really give Noreen or her kids? P. B.? But still, Sweetie was at least partly right.

Mac walked around his desk, punching one fist into the palm of the other hand.

"You shot my papa!" Sweetie's snot was flowing.

Jorge got up, opened the door, and yelled to the newsroom, "Out! Everybody!"

The four of them waited for the floor to clear. Finally it was silent. Just them.

Jane straightened up to lie. "Your father attacked my mother. It was a terrible fight . . ."

"No!"

"I tried to help but failed."

Then, "Defending her, I shot him."

Sweetie sobbed into her hands.

"It was a fight between man and wife, brought on by the stress they were under."

Mac nodded. "The stress they were under." He sat down on the couch next to Sweetie. "Your papa was under tremendous stress." Several lines dropped out of his face.

Sweetie whimpered.

"Wright's a hard woman, very hard. She made impossible demands on him. It was not his fault, Sweetie."

Sweetie kept nodding.

"Nobody will know he's your father. We won't put his name in the paper. It doesn't have to be part of the story."

"No!" Jane started.

Mac looked at her sharply. "His name won't be part of the story."

Sweetie turned into his shoulder, burying her face.

"It's the heart of the story!" Jane insisted. It couldn't all fall on Grete. It needed his name.

"Sweetie, we've got to get you safe, out of here."

"What?"

"We won't let some gossip guy follow this up to you."

"I was just helping him, helping Papa. I had no idea . . ."

"I know, I know," Mac said. "But I've got to get you safe. I'm not going to keep you here, selfishly. For myself. I've got to protect you, Sweetie."

"Protect me . . ."

"I have friends in New York, the fashion district."

"Fashion?"

Jane thought she saw a prick of light in the palest blue part of Sweetie's right eye. Then she thought, She's like me, hopeful.

"Ruby will get you a cab back to my place. Get yourself cleaned up, packed, right away. I'll be there tonight, and we'll get you on a train." He knelt in front of her, put his hands on her cheeks. "You did the right thing by your papa."

"Thank you, Mac, thank you!"

She hugged him hard once more and got up, left, without looking at Jane.

Mac was a good idea man. And a bit of a coward.

When Jane heard the elevator doors close, she said, "That was a display."

"What's this alleged evidence?"

She picked up the ledgers, setting them back on his desk. "Records of the people, the picture subjects, she paid to pose in her documentary pictures. Their names, amounts paid, the list of photos they appeared in, newspapers that ran them."

Mac interrupted. "So it's a government and corruption *and* murder story?"

"Murder?"

"Not yet," he answered.

"This time with evidence," Jane said.

Mac asked, "What did you have against Wright in the beginning, before you knew?"

She thought of Grete's pictures, beautiful pictures, and how they were lies, a whole harvest of invention, lies that made the people she knew look hapless and weak, not like they were. Or not entirely. She thought of Noreen, who hated the way she was photographed, for pity. But Jane also understood something about them was true. She didn't answer.

Jorge said, "This could get us out of the piss-storm we're in because of her first story."

Mac mumbled curses.

"Let me write it," Jane said.

Mac set down the ledger. "I can't trust you."

"I'm the one for this," she said.

Mac kept flipping through the book.

"Please. I have to do it," she begged.

Let me prove myself, re-prove myself. Do it right this time.

"You're a disaster," he said.

She looked out the glass at the writers trickling back in. "I'll fit in."

"They'll eat your lunch."

"Let me deal with them."

"Who are you, anyway?" he asked.

Jane could feel his shift.

"Who are you?" he repeated.

"Jane Benjamin," she said.

Jorge laughed at her new name, her third name.

"It's not a joke," she said. "Don't make fun of me, Jorge. I mean it."

Mac said, "Okay. Get every damn thing right. Jorge, you sit right next to her. Check every word. Make sure she backs up everything, double, triple. But Jane, I'm putting Jorge's name on it. Not yours, for Chrissakes!"

"That's fine." She understood.

"But you'll do the work," Jorge added. "All of it."

This was good. But she had to twist the screwdriver one more time to make sure.

"So you want me then?"

"Oh, Jesus," said Mac. "Now you *are* a girl. Get to work."

"Mac?"

"What!"

"Lambert?"

"Heading to New York, whoop-de-doo."

She tucked a stray piece of hair behind her ear and knelt to pick the remaining ledgers and pencils up off the floor. She did feel bad about Lambert, somewhat. She wasn't sure what she felt.

"Jane."

She looked up from her knees.

"You look fine."

She stood up but dropped her head, hiding the red in her cheeks. That capillary rush made her angry at herself. This man seemed smaller to her now. The Mac she'd pined for wasn't real. She'd made him up, a suit of her own crafting. She'd longed for the suit and not this man, which was a good thing to see. She didn't need to calculate the effect of his loss as a potential lover. He was still her boss, for now, and he wasn't going to fire her, for now. So that was blush-worthy.

Yes, she still wore a costume, but this one got closer to the skin. She wondered, Does anyone ever present a pure naked self to the world?

Even in this rush of relief, underneath she sensed Benjamin's shrinking, his fear of disintegration. He needed her as his shell. Without her being Benny, would he dissipate completely, his particles spread over the landscape, ungathered?

The writers were mostly all back in, at Jorge's command, silent, staring. Books in her arms, she left Mac's office and went out to the newsroom, all eyes on her, and set the books on Lambert's old desk.

"Okay!" she yelled, looking around. "I was faking it. I needed the job. This is me. I'm not Benny. I'm Jane Benjamin. Got it?"

From the back of the room, somebody said, "Sheesh. That time of the month?"

"Okay, okay."

Hank Ikeda stood before her, his mouth open. "How do you do this?"

"Choose it and do it," she answered, knowing it was more than that.

She rubbed her hands over the sticky top of Lambert's desk, took a handkerchief out of her bag, wiped off his cigar smudges, laid out a ledger, pencil in hand, and got to work.

EPILOGUE

This was the hour when *she* became *I*, when I first began to speak with my own voice, the one I'd use in the *Prospect* for the next eight decades. They kept me, even with all the trouble I'd caused, all the trouble I'd cause in the years to come.

I said before, "You think you're a body, but you're not." You're the power inside it. But you get that power from your voice. It was complicated. It still is. I haven't worked it all out. I never became the person I intended to be. But I did become *someone*. And in a way, partly, it began that afternoon, rewriting that story, the right way, fixing my mistakes, learning how to do it right, defining myself for myself, understanding that I would move from point to point on an infinite continuum.

BY the time I got back to Rivka's that night, Elsie was asleep on the sunporch and Momma and Rivka were cleaning house —a strange sight, Rivka wielding a washcloth. Better that than to sit at the table and be hectored by Momma, I guess.

The front parlor was gleaming—the connecting one still full of dusty crates—but Momma didn't appear to be tapering off.

Rivka jerked her head toward the kitchen and I followed.

"Your plan?"

"I'll find her a place."

"Where?"

"I don't know, exactly. I mean, she's connected to trouble."

Rivka rolled her eyes. "Your mother? Connected to trouble?"

"She needs some kind of work, work she can do, needs to be someplace safe she can afford. Where she won't be looked at too close."

"You want her among relatively safe outlaws."

"That's it."

"Outside Lands."

"Pardon?"

"Sunset District."

The neighborhood of Topsy's and Jones-at-the-Beach.

GRIT stung the skin on my face and arms as we trudged from Jonesie's wind-stripped Victorian to the abandoned railcar.

"Almost there," he hollered, against the wind.

I followed close on his heels, my arm shielding my eyes. Momma was just behind me, one hand under Elsie's bottom, the other holding her baby's head to her chest. It wasn't really that far between the two structures, but in a sandstorm, it seemed like miles. The Outside Lands, all right.

"There's the outhouse!"

She was going to hate this. It'd be worse than the government camp, worse than a tent by the river. Away from everything, out here in the blowing grit, just to be a cleaning lady. It'd be like what she'd originally run away from—dust piling up past windowsills, looking like snow, blocking the door. Having to climb out the window to go anywhere, hang wet sheets on doors, stuff windows with rags. Still, the dust would get in. Outside Lands looked like Dustbowl Texas.

Finally I could see it. Closer to the surf sat a railcar, its blue paint chipped away to a pale, watery color, some kind of washed-up carcass. Curtains in the window. A fire pit, made of busted-up concrete with a grill on top, sat just to the side.

Jonesie waved his arm for us to follow.

We walked up the steps to an entry slider on a metal track.

Through the rectangle of glass on the top half of the door, it was dark. He turned the handle and the door clanged open. Inside, a cat jumped off a table, out the door, yowling. We entered and Momma shut the door behind her.

"They used to call this Carville, out here, so many people lived in these. Mayor got rid of most of 'em. We saved ours. History," Jonesie bragged.

The space was tiny but neat—the last maid had tidied up before she'd run off with Jonesie's silver. At the end of the car was a narrow bed with a white pillow and sheets and a rough blue wool blanket on top, laid out smooth. On the left was a kitchen table for one. On the right was a makeshift kitchen, with a hose coming in through a hole drilled in the side of the car, wound up in an old ceramic basin set on a board on a trestle. Just above the sink was a driftwood shelf bearing a coffee pot, cast iron pan, bag of cornmeal, can of beans, can of Folgers, coffee mug, and plate. Like I said, less than what she'd come from.

A low roar rose, different from the wind or the waves beating the coast. It grew louder.

"Feeding time at the zoo," Jonesie said. "Them lions get noisy."

For crying out loud, I thought. Back to the starting line.

Momma looked out the window in the direction of Jonesie's Victorian, though it was invisible with all that sand.

"I'll take it," she said. "When do I start?"

"Are you sure, Momma?"

"Did you hear me?"

Jonesie said, "Start tonight. Go get your stuff, settle in first."

"I don't have stuff. I'm ready."

That's all it took to set her up in a railcar at the back of Jonesie's property, behind a gray, weathered mansion at the edge of the sandy world.

But then she was accustomed to grit, and this would be her own space, not some man's. It probably felt right, too, that it was a railcar. She'd always been heading away from something, to something else. Maybe that's what she liked about it.

Or maybe she just wanted to get out of Rivka's, fast. Two queen bees wouldn't work.

Jonesie went back into his house and returned with a big dresser drawer with a pillow in the bottom. Momma looked down at her baby girl, too big already to fit in a drawer as a bed.

"You can carry this from room to room in the big house while you clean during daytime and then put it in the back seat when I drive you to the roadhouse to clean there at night!" His voice was cheerful, resourceful.

Momma bit her lip and looked around the railcar and at Elsie.

Elsie chuckled, dimpling high on her cheeks under her eyes, looking right at me, like she was thinking, Well, are you gonna?

Okay then, I thought.

"Why doesn't she stay with me and Rivka for a while? Until you're settled. We can work it out, get some help."

You could see Momma's wheels turning. Her face flushed, angry.

Then she rubbed some milk off Elsie's cheek and cleared her throat. "Just for a time then. Just until I'm settled."

I waited for her to hand Elsie to me. I didn't reach for her myself. It was better that way.

I'M not trying to say this was the *something* I was going to do. But it was one of the somethings. I was choosing not to be a one-man guy like Daddy said I was. I was going to give up some things I wanted, for my half-sister. I didn't know then, of course, how much I'd give up.

AT first, things did work the way Jonesie said—Momma cleaning the house by day, the roadhouse by night. Then, as her personality began to assert itself, she took on more responsibility. She started serving food at the roadhouse, then ordering supplies, then doing the books. She did this for just a year before she made herself into the new Mrs. Jones—Queen of the Outside Lands—lording it over the customers, the writers and boxers and singers and swindlers, reigning from that old Victorian, glowing with electricity, basement to attic, all the power she wanted. Good thing she never got those papers from Uno or Daddy. She liked Jonesie's papers better.

But Elsie stayed with me.

The arrangement worked all right. We could get out there when we needed to—Momma didn't come to us—but I didn't have to see her all the time. Our relationship was something we'd tend or avoid, as we chose.

Even when we said or did despicable, unforgivable things, and didn't see each other for months afterward, we were still tied by a rope I couldn't unknot. Momma and I always came back together, grudgingly, permanently.

Rivka hired a housekeeper who watched Elsie when we were at work. She arranged for those crates from the old country to be carted away, stored somewhere else, and we turned that interior parlor into Elsie's room, right there in the center of the flat. And when I started making more money, I paid the housekeeper extra for taking care of Elsie.

She thrived on Clay Street.

She was impossible to resist, those plump dimples, knees, fingers. Everything about her said, "Love me. Keep me." And I did. But her wailing pink lungs—"I'm healthy, a person to invest in"—made me feel bad about Benjamin.

I studied it, interviewed experts about it, the connection

between family members, pretending the questions weren't personal. I understood that kin must save kin, but biologically, historically, that's only true when benefit outweighs cost, as I learned from my own parents. Then it was also complicated by genetic distance. She was half my mother's genes, half Uno's, who was my enemy, not my kin. What does that make her? I wondered. Half me? Quarter me? Does it make her Benjamin? No, she was just herself.

She wanted everything she could get from me—food, touch, time, attention, validation, loyalty. Even when I wanted something else, something for myself, designed as I was to spread my attention over a great landscape—her, of course, always her first, but also men and women I loved, my work, secret stories into which I would throw myself, another child who came out of me, P. B., who sometimes made Elsie jealous.

I thought a lot about how I was like Momma and how I was different.

Evolution requires you to save enough of yourself from a child so you can care for the others, the rest of it, yourself. Propagation of the species. Survival.

Women like Momma often leave more surviving young than the others. They know how to work the system—when to pretend to be subordinate, when ambition will pay off. Like Momma, I couldn't help doing the math, and the sums didn't always work out. I had to make choices that made Elsie unhappy, both of us unhappy.

But then those wailing pink lungs—a person to invest in, one of my *somethings*.

I had a therapist once. I married him. I told him what happened on the day I was born, or what I'd been told about what happened. I even told him about Benjamin's voice in my head, which was a mistake because that's the kind of thing people want to fix—"It's pathological"—that's how he saw it.

It's not how I see it.

It's been a comfort, these years, to rely on Benjamin's judgment.

He got me out of that ditch. Then he rode along after, lighting me up, adding a vibrancy, a nerve I don't know I would have had otherwise. I believe he's proud of that now.

You might say it's not true, that his voice is really my own self, another part of my own self, chiming in. But I know the difference. It's Benjamin. He's not dead. He's alive, electric with ideas. I give him that credit and he accepts it.

My body has never been the thing. My body is clay. My self is different.

I don't feel too bad anymore about what happened on our birthday. I figured that out. As Uno said, "That warn't my fault!"

I think Benjamin sees it like that too. The way his voice works in me now, seems like he wants the best for me. Seems like that's usually his purpose—usually.

I'm sorry Daddy ran off again. Though maybe it was good, his disappearance. That might have turned out the way it should.

I did get it wrong about Grete. She wasn't a killer. She didn't try to kill Vee. Didn't kill Jesson, just let him die, so obsessed was she with what she was trying to do. She was ambitious. How could I, of all people, hold that against her? But she came out all right. No jail time. Just the right amount of scandal to add another layer to her reputation. If anything, those headlines made her more in demand. She'd always been such a difficult woman that her new criminality made her more appealing. Howard at the Horse Trough Tavern was right about that.

Then there was Vee.

I visited her until the end. I'd hold her hand, spread the paper out on her bed. I'd read it aloud as she slept, getting thinner, whiter, every day. I relied on those visits—that spot of calm in a noisy life. I read her the paper, never my own gossip columns. They didn't seem right for her. She was too good for that. She was good.

I'd tell her stories about P. B., how she was so smart, so pretty.

Then one evening I came by Vee's room and she was gone, no bed, the room just clean, antiseptic. She'd never once woken to accuse me.

Still, I've tried to pay my debts all the way around, raising Elsie, helping with P. B., sending her money.

I know—that wasn't enough.

There was often a Vee at the center of my stories, not the gossip columns but the ones I wrote under another name. She was always the sore spot, more than anybody else, the thing that kept me trying to do better, though I didn't like to touch that.

ON rare days now, I roll through the city, conveyed by the dwindling number of writers still interested in documenting my charm. I try to give them what they want, the eight-decade insider's swing-slang curatorial tour. I craft my stories to support their point—sometimes, that San Francisco still defines "cool," that it always will, and others, more of this now, that it's fallen, too crass to recover. This is what their readers want. Hello, kids, I wrote those scripts, dozens of times over, eighty years of gossip columns behind me. I was the original, the three-dot hipster, inventing the shifting state of this city in limited digits. Telling the truth.

Now my voice is reedy, but I have no choice but to talk. My fingers tremble over keys. I can't control a carriage return. I don't understand the computer they've given me. I speak into a headset to record this now, for myself, really for nobody else. I gave my first Royal typewriter back to the *Prospect* decades ago. The receptionist there must think I'm already dead, the way he describes me in a thick accent to the few who ask. Maybe he's right. I require one two many splashes of bourbon in my coffee to enliven the now-slack face I crafted so long ago.

In a black beret and a too-loose cream wool suit and pumps, I direct the young writers who still come around with their phone cameras and electronic notebooks to wheel me down to the old neighborhood, where the *Prospect* building still stands, now mostly full of digital drones, not writers. I tell them about the switchboard and linotype and the elevator operator and the bottles in every man's bottom drawer and the boys on the bench and the constant haze of cigarette smoke.

Then I have them roll me to Benjamin Way—yes, they did it in 1980. And that's where I describe my pickled old friends, how they'd drink four-ounce martinis and I'd drink bourbon on the rocks, and we'd barter secrets and flick ashes and break promises over the long-gone, seventy-two-foot bar at Breen's, torn down in seventy-nine, the same year Elsie decamped for Prague with my third husband, the publisher.

Then these young writers take a picture of me in my dotage, filter it to look old, and post it on the Internet—me in my wheelchair, a shiny cane in my lap. How ironic, the old-school broad dispersed in the Twitter-verse. Huzzah.

I bring them here to talk, I say, so they'll know that the city used to be different. And that newspapers were. Some of the change is good, I say, some not so much.

But that's a lie. That's not why I do it.

I stop with these witnesses on this stretch of Benjamin Way to press a thumb on my black, bruised heart, to remind myself who and what my ambition killed. And the others it hurt that winter, when I was eighteen years old, about to land the best job in the best city in the world. I go there hoping they'll find me out, report me. But they never do. I never let them.

My ambition has led to this life, which has never been boring, never.

If I really wanted to be seen, I wouldn't hand them eighty years of *Prospect* columns under my chosen name. I'd take them east, through fog and hills and farmland and delta, where we'd stand on a levee, hot and dusty, the bitter sunny smell of tomato leaf in our nostrils, and, longing to confess, I suspect I'd lie about how it all began.

ACKNOWLEDGMENTS

Thank you to Andy, Will, and Henry, for expecting me to be my own protagonist.

Thank you to Kelly, Yvonne, and Tim, who showed me that the grit gets in you.

Thank you to the writer- and editor-friends who read early versions of this manuscript, offering their generous, practical advice—David Corbett, Emma Dryden, Dorothy Rice, and Casey Mickle, who said I should be nicer to Momma.

Thank you to the friends who read this before it was ready, to cheer me on—Beth McClure and Deirdre Wilson.

Thank you to Baobab Press editor Danilo John Thomas, for seeing something in my first chapter and putting it in a beautiful anthology—*This Side of the Divide: Stories of the American West*—alongside writers I urgently admire. And thank you to *Soundings Review* for accepting an even earlier version of that story, a yes that kept me going.

Thank you to Brooke Warner, Julie Metz, Lauren Wise, Shannon Green, Jennifer Caven, Katie Caruana and the entire She Writes Press team, for their passionate, feminist expertise.

Thank you to the workshops that showed me ways to write this story—the Creativity Workshop, the Book Passage Mystery Workshop, the Community of Writers at Squaw Valley, the Napa Valley Writers' Conference, the Bread Loaf Writers' Conference (Helen Schulman squad), the Belize Writers' Conference, the Stories on Stage Sacramento Workshops, Ellen Sussman's Novel in a Year, and the Sonoma County Writers Camp.

Thank you to writers, teachers, and friends who delivered intelligent critiques of excerpts of this book when they were needed—Jodi Angel, Kate Asche, Tom Barbash, Karen Bender, Ruth Blank, Kari Bovee, Mary Camarillo, Valerie Fioravante, Joey Garcia, Dana Killion, Marilyn Lanier, Kathy Les, Charlene Logan-Burnett, Amanda McTigue, Kel Munger, Geoffrey Neill, Bill Pieper, Tigh Rickman, Angela K. Small, Sue Staats, Amy Sedivy, and Maureen Wanket. Thank you to the wonderful workshop readers whose names I have failed to list.

I relied on many works of history to learn about the people and places and period of this novel, especially Linda Gordon's *Dorothea Lange: A Life Beyond Limits* and *San Francisco in the 1930s: The WPA Guide to the City by the Bay*, a Federal Writers' Project of the Works Progress Administration. Also essential were iconic columnist Herb Caen's *Baghdad-By-The-Bay*, Robert Coles's *Doing Documentary Work*, Dorothea Lange's and Paul Taylor's *An American Exodus*, and Paul C. Smith's *Personal File: An Autobiography.*

ABOUT THE AUTHOR

photo credit: Anita Scharf

SHELLEY BLANTON-STROUD grew up in California's Central Valley, the daughter of Dust Bowl immigrants who made good on their ambition to get out of the field. She teaches writing at Sacramento State University and consults with writers in the energy industry. She serves on the advisory board of 916 Ink, an arts-based creative writing nonprofit for children, and co-directs Stories on Stage Sacramento. She has served on the Writers' Advisory Board for the Belize Writers' Conference. She and her husband live in Northern California with an aging beagle and many photos of their out-of-state sons. To learn where you can read her stories and more, go to shelleyblantonstroud.com.

DISCUSSION QUESTIONS

1. Scientists suggest that our experiences and those of our ancestors live on in our DNA, affecting our and our children's health and behavior. Is that true for Jane? Can she escape biology or family history? Can any of us?

2. What influence does Daddy have on Jane? What explains the way she circumscribes her loyalty to him? How do you feel about their reconciliation and his disappearance afterward?

3. What do you think about Momma after learning what happened when she delivered her twins at fifteen years old? Does this sufficiently explain the way she treats Jane? Should Jane continue to tie herself to such a parent? Why or why not?

4. Jane says the voice in her head belongs to her dead brother, Benjamin. What do you think? How else can the voice be explained? How does this voice affect what she does, who she becomes?

5. What do you think about Jane choosing to raise Elsie? What kind of mother would Jane make? Would it have been better to leave Elsie with Momma?

6. Does Jane really have to pretend to be a boy to succeed? Could she have earned the same opportunities as a girl? Why or why not? Does any part of her situation seem familiar today, or does it live in the past?

7. What do you expect a masculine character to do and be? What do you expect a feminine character to do and be? How do the characters in the novel match or diverge from those expectations?

8. Jane becomes a skillful liar about her parents generally, the fight that sends her to San Francisco, and her very identity. These lies lead to her lifelong career success. What do you think about her lying habit and skill? How does it help her, and how might it hurt?

9. Grete Wright crosses boundaries to make the best, most moving, most powerful photographs, arguing that facts are less necessary than truth. Are documentary photographs or stories more powerful and useful with or without artistic framing? What do you think about the relationship between fact and truth?

10. Some characters in the book concern themselves with basic survival in a time of poverty and hunger. Others work for worldly success. How do they get what they want? What are they willing to discard to win? Is it necessary? Is it worthwhile?

11. Vee may be the only character who risks herself solely on behalf of others, trying to report the death of the hungry man. How do you explain what makes one person altruistic, when others focus only on protecting themselves or those in their family?

12. The Okies living along the side of the road are generally despised and blamed for local problems. How might ongoing generations of such families feel about field-working migrants today, and why?

13. Though the active story ends in 1937, we learn that Jane will write for many decades, becoming an iconic San Francisco gossip columnist. In what way is someone like Jane particularly suited to weather the decades in such a field? What do you imagine for the stories she writes under a different name?

14. This novel was inspired by historical incidents, photographers, migrant laborers, and newspapers in 1930s California. How are the lessons of this period relevant today?

SELECTED TITLES FROM SHE WRITES PRESS

She Writes Press is an independent publishing company
founded to serve women writers everywhere.
Visit us at www.shewritespress.com.

Eliza Waite by Ashley Sweeney. $16.95, 978-1-63152-058-7. When
Eliza Waite chooses to leave a stagnant life in rural Washington
State and join the masses traveling north to Alaska in 1898 during
the tumultuous Klondike Gold Rush, she encounters challenges
and successes in both business and love.

Lum by Libby Ware. $16.95, 978-1-63152-003-7. In Depression-era
Appalachia, an intersex woman without a home of her own plays
the role of maiden aunt to her relatives—until an unexpected
series of events gives her the opportunity to change her fate.

Hysterical: Anna Freud's Story by Rebecca Coffey. $18.95,
978-1-938314-42-1. An irreverent, fictionalized exploration of the
seemingly contradictory life of Anna Freud—told from her point
of view.

A Girl Like You: A Henrietta and Inspector Howard Novel by
Michelle Cox. $16.95, 978-1-63152-016-7. When the floor matron at
the dance hall where Henrietta works as a taxi dancer turns up
dead, aloof Inspector Clive Howard appears on the scene—and
convinces Henrietta to go undercover for him, plunging her into
Chicago's gritty underworld.

The Great Bravura by Jill Dearman. $16.95, 978-1-63152-989-4.
Who killed Susie—or did she actually disappear? The Great
Bravura, a dashing lesbian magician living in a fantastical and
noirish 1947 New York City, must solve this mystery—before she
goes to the electric chair.

The Velveteen Daughter by Laurel Davis Huber. $16.95,
978-1-63152-192-8. The first book to reveal the true story of the
woman who wrote *The Velveteen Rabbit* and her daughter, a
world-famous child prodigy artist, *The Velveteen Daughter* ex-
plores the consequences of early fame and the inability of a
mother to save her daughter from herself.